Blossom

ALSO BY QUEEN PEN

Situations

Blossom

a novel

Queen Pen

ATRIA BOOKS

NEW YORK · LONDON · TORONTO · SYDNEY

ATRIA BOOKS

A Division of Simon & Schuster, Inc.
1230 Avenue of the Americas
New York, NY 10020

First Atria Books trade paperback edition May 2007

ATRIA BOOKS and colophon are trademarks of Simon & Schuster, Inc.

For information about special discounts for bulk purchases, please contact Simon & Schuster Special Sales: 1-800-456-6798 or business@simonandschuster.com.

Manufactured in the United States of America

10 9 8 7 6 5 4 3 2 1

The Library of Congress has cataloged the hardcover edition as follows:
Queen Pen.
    Blossom: a novel / Queen Pen.
        p.   cm.
    1. African American women—Fiction.   2. Sisters—Fiction.
3. Female friendships—Fiction.   I. Title.
PS3617.U444B55 2006
813'.6—dc22   2006042718

ISBN-13: 978-0-7432-8449-3
ISBN-10:   0-7432-8449-6
ISBN-13: 978-0-7432-8450-9 (pbk)
ISBN-10:   0-7432-8450-X (pbk)

Acknowledgments

*F*irst, before I thank anyone, I have to thank God for the struggles and pain, for it was those times that have made me the strong, well-grounded, real person I am. I have to thank you, God, for always having my back and making me wise enough to see what my true purpose is in this life. I thank you for making me strong enough to complete this book at a time in my life when living was extremely hard for me. I thank you for my four beautiful children, 'cause without them I would not have had natural survival tactics. I thank you for all the wrong relationships you put in my path, 'cause now I know when I share my story with others I can talk from experience. Moreover, I can help heal from those same experiences. My God, thank you for creating me the way you have. No matter how hard I have had it, I would not change anything about my past. Because that would mean I would not be who I am and where I am at in life. I thank you for never giving up on me even when only you knew I was ready to give up on myself! I must say, you are the best person to have in someone's corner.

I want to give my appreciation and thanks to my mother. You have always had my back even when I did not realize it or accept it. Thanks for raising me with values, morals, strength, the wisdom of knowledge of self, and survival tactics. I have carried all of that with me throughout life. Thank you for being the grandmother you are to my children. Who would think I would have come this far from writing that letter to the president (smile)? And all of those songs and stories I used to write at six years old. There are really no words to explain how I feel, Ma. All I can say is thank you!

To my little sister, Charnice . . . . Man, what happened? You were just a little baby in your crib. Now I know I am getting old! I watched you grow into the young woman you are. I bore witness to your going through that transformation from young teen to young woman. And I must say the transformation has been somewhat rough. But, like always, you pull yourself together and find your way back. Thank you for holding your nieces and nephew down. I know that can be hard when you do not have children of your own.

To my grandmother, A.W.: you are da' bomb diggity! Thank you for being there for my mom when I was younger and she was hustlin' and bustlin' to make life right for us. You helped her hold me down while she did what she had to do, you and Aunt Nita. I love you so much! I wish you would move back to New York—I miss dat' good food on a regular basis! I love you and I always have your back!

To my children, Donlynn, Quintin, Lyric, and Karon: you guys are the reason I continue on striving. I truly live for you all. And though you may be too young to understand or see how Mommy has to struggle and sacrifice for you, just know that I do. And I have no regrets for doing so. It is you, my children, who have made me whole and who have made me humble, because for you I have learned to humble myself to make some situations better for you. I breathe every breath for you, until I cannot breathe anymore. To the Robinson family: thank you for all you have done for Quintin. I do not know what I would have done without you or Buffy.

And to some it may sound awkward or weird, but I could not give thanks and praise to my children without acknowledging the fathers of my seeds. Through everything I have been through with you guys (excluding Buffy), I still have to thank you for blessing me with my children. And I must say to my son's father, K, thank you. Because you were there at the beginning of the creation of *Blossom*. And even when I got discouraged, you read what I had written to that point and pushed me to continue.

I cannot mention my children without mentioning or thanking my ob-gyn, Dr. Paul Kastell. I know I have probably been one of your most difficult patients! I harassed you throughout my pregnancies from prenatal care to the delivery room. Thanks for *always* being there for me.

To my other sisters, Kashan, Khjim, and Kalisha. You know how it goes! We've seen so much and been through a hell of a lot through the years! But we are still standing and that's all that counts! Kashan, do not give up! I told you, girl, the self-publishing thing was very hard, but it gives you insight and strength that you will walk with for the rest of your life. This insight and strength will come in handy when you do a book deal with a major! Khjim, I am going to keep it short and funky: you are stronger den' da' word (private joke)! You have truly bumped into some huge obstacles in life, and you always pulled yourself together and made it happen! Kalisha, you have worked it out since Sterling Place! Oh, I know it's hard being "us," but you also always find a way to pull it together. Rather, God always makes a way. This means you are being looked after, and that is a good thing!

To Auntie Cheryl, Uncle Keith, and my li'l cousins Ashley, Asia, Kia, and Keith Jr. You guys have always been there for me regardless! No matter what is going on or where I am at in life, you have been there for me. Aunt Cheryl (Nonie), you've looked at me like one of ya' daughters and Lyric like she was one of ya' own. I have learned so much from you and I love you! Uncle Keith, you stepped in and took on that father-figure role for me, and you're "Pop Pop" (smile) for Lyric. Ashley and Asia, you guys have grown up to be very special young women. It is a shame that so many people had a chance to bring you girls to the top (where you belong!) and did just the opposite. That says a lot about certain people's characters. I told you from the beginning, this industry is a dirty game! Very few are motivated by morals and heart. But so many are motivated by power, money, and ignorance. In other words, not too many are motivated by God, but a lot are motivated by the devil! Ya'll time will come!

To my aunt Nita and aunt Diane, thanks for being there for me throughout the years. And to my cousins Zahn, Zarea, and Sabrina, even though ya'll gave me a hard time when we were younger (smile), I learned so much from you! I cherish those memories from our younger years. All those talent shows and concerts we used to put on definitely led me to the road I have traveled down. Aunt Sharon and Felicia—thank you for sharing your home with me in the late eighties. Felicia gurl!!! We had some times back in the day! Remember the hotel when I kicked the door down and tried to cut ya' baby daddy up? I love you, kid! To Ouie and Dorien, Aunt Tee Tee, Aunt Colette, Uncle Gerald, my cousin Terence, and Dawn. My cousin Robin Kearse—you need to bring ya' butt back to New York. My godmother Judy. Nicole and Rasheem. Pam and Tony, you always held Donlynn down and I thank you for that. I love you guys! To my cousin Mike (Poppa Mike): you and Paulette looked after me and helped raise me in my younger years, and that has meant something to me until this day. I luv ya'll. To Nelly, another one of my road dogs—thanks for everything, homie. I thank you and Nana for always being there for Lyric and me. Luv ya'll!

To my homies—friends are so important to have, especially in the line of work I'm in. Beverly Ali, you have truly been a good friend to me. You've watched me blossom into the person I am today. We have a bond that is unexplainable. Thank you for everything; thank you for loving Karon the way you do. Monique Joyner, we've had some times, gurl! You know me like a book, inside out! You've dressed me like I would've dressed myself. You are the best! You have so much talent that you need to build on. Follow ya' gut and pursue ya' dreams. To Simone, Tracey, and Ms. Wicker: no matter what, you never treated me differently. Thank you for playing it neutral, and thanks for loving Ron Ron and Lyric, no matter the situation. To my friend Ayesha Dawkins, words cannot even explain your friendship. You have had my back from day one and that is just who you are. Your heart is huge, and friends like you are rare. Like Monique, you are talented in what you do and you need to follow up on it! There were times if it wasn't for you . . . I don't know what I would have done. To Steph Overton, you know you're my partner in crime! Thank you for being there when I needed you and for letting me chew ya' ear off when I need to. Monica, you know you my homie! You are the type of person who never gets what she deserves and you're okay with that. Nothing that anyone does or says about you changes your disposition. You don't change like the weather. You are kindhearted and modest at all times! Doris, you truly know the meaning of loving someone no matter how long you may see that person. It's crazy, because I consider you one of the closest people to my heart, and our friendship stays in turmoil. Nevertheless, as long as you know I love you *back*! Thanks for *always* being there for me and knowing that nothing and nobody else matters, 'cause we know what we got! To my homie Miss Jones: you know the type of friendship we have comes rarely in this industry. But that's what makes "us" different; we're not industry. We are who we are and we know who we are. I cherish our friendship; we definitely have a lot of growing and healing to do, and I do not mind doing it with a friend like you. Luv u! Monifa—now, you of all people know we have come a long way! You are the shit! And I wish you only the best. You know people like us are always the underdogs in this game. And that's all there is to it, 'cause you are one of the most well-grounded and talented artists in this game. But people with their heads stuck up in the clouds do not recognize what needs to be recognized in this game. Luv u, homie. Missy Elliot, we may not talk like we used to, but you still my dog! You were in my corner from day one, back in Virginia when I was working on my first album. You are another rare stone that's rarely seen in this business. Your heart has managed to stay warm and good throughout your travels in this game, and that's so hard to accomplish in this industry. They say the apple doesn't fall far from the tree, and this is true when it comes to you. You are your mother's child, and I cannot thank you without thanking your mom for doing so well with you. I wish you nothing but the best! Pepa (Salt-n-Pepa), you watched me go from point A to point Z! From me throwing down in Q Club—getting kicked out—to becoming a women and mother, you always put the right buzz in my ear, and I love you for that. Treach, all of the same goes to you. But I have to add, you are truly real and you've never changed. You give the true meaning to one of my sayings: "Just because you may physically leave the hood, you don't have to take ya' heart." I see a lot of Pac in you. I love you. Queen Latifa, boy oh boy!!! I hope the world knows how genuine you are. Like Pep, you've seen me transform into who I am. Even if we haven't gotten to kick it like that in a while, you were there when I was a young hothead against the world. And plenty of times, you have snatched me by my collar and brought me to my senses. The littlest things you have said and shared with me in the past have become part of the biggest changes in my life. You may not have known it then, but now you do, and I thank you for that! And just like with Missy, I cannot thank you without thanking your mom, for she has definitely bloomed a unique and rare flower, which could come only from a strong woman like her. I luv ya', Dana! Mary J., thank you for just being you and never being ashamed of who you were and what you have gone though. You have saved the lives of a lot of women, you have saved the self-esteem of so many women, just 'cause you weren't ashamed to share your testimony. And you've made me feel so good about being who I am today, and you are one of the reasons I know it's okay to share my story no matter how painful some of the chapters may be. I love you!

To my heart, my road dog, my other half, Tish (rest in peace). You have missed so many pivotal points in my life. You were supposed to be there when everything first kicked off for me! Yo, we knew each other like nobody did! We've seen a lot and done a lot together. Some of my hardest lessons were learned with you. I miss you so dearly. I know you've looked down on me plenty of times and had a good laugh! I don't know what happened, but I do know God separated our paths. However, I do know that every road traveled is a lesson of its own. And I miss you, homie!!

To my ride or die homies, the ones who were there back in the cashing-in-food-stamps days: Shelia, Tracey, La La, Missy Lu (I'm waiting for you to come back so we can go on the road!), Anna, Black Cathy, Dez, Big Karen, Melinda, Renia, Keisha (rest in peace), Crusin' (rest in peace), Shamore, Myra, Jackie Rowe, Suzette, Mom Duke, and my homie Manny. To Boogie (rest in peace): damn it, man—they took a good person when they took you. But of course you know that, 'cause God takes only the best! I miss you. To Big Man (Clyde): What's up, my homie? You watched me from Sterling Place. Luv ya! My brother Gitty, thank you for always being there for me. Even when you were tired of my hand being held out, you still looked out at the most needed times. Even though we don't get to kick it like we used to, I love you! My homies Jus, Pop, Anthony, Lil' Dolla, Stacey, Blood, Sean Hill, Klein, and Brent (you be home soon, homie!).

To all my homies locked down, it's sad to say, but there's so many of ya'll I can't even begin to name. But I'll make an attempt, hoping I forget no one. To Kendo, Lou, Brent, and Shyne (you a soldier and you got courage, heart, and morals, and that's more than I can say for a lot of cats who are out in the world with freedom!). Lil' Kim, you know, no matter what, you always my homie. Where you at right now, I wouldn't wish on any of my enemies, 'cause I know, kid! I hope you spent ya' time doin' you. Meaning getting one with ya'self and doing a little soul-searching. Luv you, mama! To Mo, you truly a ride or die chick. You being locked down cannot take nothing from your character, 'cause you are who you are and you're a loyal. Hold ya' head—this can only make you stronger and open ya' eyes wider! Cassidy—hold ya' head, homie. Moreover, know that everything happens for a reason: ain't no such thing as coincidence. If you are a man of God, trust there's a purpose and reason why God makes certain moves in our lives. Just try to look at the bigger picture.

My homie Teddy, you kept ya' word years ago, and because of that, I finally got to shine and live my dreams. I honestly can say I don't know where I would have been if you hadn't sent Dave to find me that day. You are and always will be my "big brother." I love you, kid! I love you, Donna, and the kids.

Leland Robinson, I knew we would continue our friendship once we both got away from all dat bullshit at Motown! You my dog, son. Luv ya'! K K, you always looked out for me when I was signed up there and even after—you a good dude! Lakiya Oliver (Motown), Elise Wright (Motown), and Jimmy I. (Interscope Records): I have to thank you, 'cause you were my first experience of being mainstream and it has been the best so far! I have to admit I learned a lot from you and how you run ya' shit. I think those qualities you hold, that the next man doesn't, come from actually being an artist. And never losing focus on the *love of it*. Thank you for trusting Teddy about me. Tone Capone, Mark Pitts, and Wayne Barrows—you guys have been some of the few people who have been able to see who I am and appreciate who I am. Yeah, I have to admit I never was one to have management. And the only time I did, it was the best choice I could've ever made! Still, I don't rock with a manager, and I never will unless it's with you! I love ya'll!

My girl Shaka! You know we're one and the same. You have come so far and have even further to go, and trust that the path will get better. It only can, 'cause deep down inside, you have a good heart. To April (No Amore Clothing), Wendy Williams and Kev, Vinny, Nick (Hipnotiq), James (Azzuré Clothes), Kate, and Sophie (Lover Girl).

Malaika and Krishan, I thank you for thugging it out with me. Thanks for believing in *Blossom* and running with it! Can't wait 'til the next one.

For everyone I might have forgotten, please forgive me, but take into consideration that I have a lot on my mind. Trust and believe that you were not forgotten on purpose. For those who have read this and didn't see their name, and feel they should have,

*_____ write it here and you won't be forgotten (smile and sign).

I dedicate this to my mother,
just because that's how it's supposed to be.
To my children, Donlynn, Quintin, Lyric, and Karon.
To my ancestors, because if it weren't for their sacrifices,
Blossom would not have been possible!
Moreover, to my fans; you all have kept me going
when I thought it did not make sense to.

Blossom

1

When Kim walked into Tamika's crib with two big garbage bags full of clothes, Tamika and the rest of the girls were sitting at the kitchen table drinking Red Alizé and listening to music. Tamika's crib was the hangout spot for her crew, the place they gathered for a birthday celebration, whenever one of the girls got into a beef with her man, and on and on. Tamika's mom broke out about two years ago and moved to North Carolina, leaving the four-bedroom, two-bathroom apartment—in the middle of the hood—to her daughters: Tamika, and her seventeen-year-old sister, Blossom. The apartment was rent controlled and only $550 a month. Her mother's bedroom was now empty—aside from the futon bed Tamika had put in there—so was the bedroom once shared by her brothers. Lamont had been locked down for three and a half years and Lucky passed away years earlier. But their belongings still occupied the room. There was another bedroom in the front of the apartment that belonged to Blossom.

Kim stuck her head in Blossom's room. "Hey, shorty, I got some hot shit for you."

Kim was the hustler of the crew. She was the kind of chick that didn't have time to wait for a man to give her something. She always found a way to get it herself.

Blossom jumped up from her bed. "What you got? Let me see!"

"Damn, shorty! Come in the kitchen!"

Blossom grabbed one of the garbage bags and followed Kim into the kitchen.

"Y'all startin' early, huh?" Kim asked the group of girls.

Tamika replied, pouring another cup of Red Alizé, "And you know it. The sun been down for two hours now! Damn, you had a good day at the stores!"

Tamika is the mother hen of the girls. You could drop all your worries and problems on her, no matter what.

"I hope you got my coat, Kim. I asked you last week to get dat coat," Trina said.

"Calm down, Trina, I got you. Do you got my Ones? 'Cause you still owe me for that Juicy sweatsuit."

Trina was the dream chaser. She's the one of the girls who believes in miracles. Happy-go-lucky is her middle name. She is the "smile" of the group.

Trina stood up and reached for her purse, pulling out a wad of money held together with a rubber band.

"I got ya paper and then some," she said.

"I hear dat hot shit! Let me hold somethin' big-timer!" Tamika shouted.

Now was Shareen's time to say something. She was the mouthpiece of the girls. She always says whatever's on her mind. Defined the word *blunt*. She was not mean; she was real.

"At least one of us hit da jackpot! Shit, I'm still standin' at shore waitin' for my boat ta pull in," Shareen intervened.

"What did I miss?" Kim asked.

"Nothin', except dat dis bitch got lucky wit' dat cat from Jersey," Tamika answered.

"Yeah, and there's more like him where he from. I told ya to come on to dis jump-off tonight. Him and all his friend is gonna be there. He told me to come wit' my crew and everything would be taken care of," Trina explain.

Kim sorted through her stolen goods and gave each girl an outfit in her size. She gave Blossom four outfits; she always looked out for her. Blossom took the clothes and in a dry voice said, "Thanks, Kim."

Kim noticed Blossom's attitude. "Whassa matter wit' you, you don't like them?"

"Naw, it's not that," Blossom replied.

"Den what's up?"

Blossom pulled Kim to the side while the other girls looked through the bags, in deep conversation. "It's just that I never get to go anywhere. What's the use in having all these clothes and nowhere to wear them except school. I wanna hang out, too."

"What ya sister said?" Kim asked.

"Come on, you know how she feels. I'm almost eighteen years old and she treats me like a baby. My grades stay up. I don't hang in the streets or none of that shit . . ."

"Aight, I'll kick it wit' her and see what she says."

A huge smile came across Blossom's face. "Thanks, Kim. Good looking!"

"Wait, I ain't promisin' you nothin'. I jus' said I'm gonna give it a shot."

Blossom went back to her room to try on her clothes as Kim returned to the girls.

Kim spoke out loud. "Tamika, why don't ya let Blossom hang wit' us tonight?"

Tamika looked at Kim like she was out of her rabbit-ass mind. "You sound stupid."

"Why not? She gonna be with us, ain't like nothin' can happen to her. Come on, Mika, she's almost eighteen and she's a good girl."

"Yeah, and I want her ta stay good. Dat's why her ass ain't gon' be doin' no hangin' out."

Shareen interrupted. "Tamika, bitch, please. Me and you both know dat shit don't mean nothin'. You could put a padlock on Blossom's ass, dat don't mean shit. Trust, if she really wanted to do some shit, she would find a way. You gon' have ta let go eventually. She's graduating this year, then what you gon' do?"

Next, Trina added her opinion. "For real, Tamika, Blossom needs to hang wit' us as much as possible so she can learn da ins and outs. So nobody can play her when you do decide to let your clutch off her. Let her live, she got all of us dere to protect her."

Tamika shook her head back and forth.

Kim continued. "I mean, shit, she done heard it all anyway sittin' in dis house wit' us."

Finally, Tamika gave in. "Aight . . . Aight already! Fuck it, she can roll. But, I'm tellin' y'all, y'all betta help me keep an eye on her."

Wasting no time, Kim yelled, "Blossom!"

Blossom was ear hustling from her room and heard everything that the girls had said. So she knew she was in like Flynn.

Blossom ran to the kitchen, already dressed. "Yeah!"

Tamika looked at her little sister, searching for a resemblance. Blossom was a clear, brown-skinned girl with thick eyebrows that complemented big hazel-brown eyes and long curled eyelashes. Her hair, which stopped right in the middle of her back, was one of the many features she and Tamika shared. Blossom had grown up right before Tamika's eyes and Tamika couldn't handle the thought of somebody taking advantage or playing her. "Damn! So you just knew you were hangin', huh?" Tamika spoke.

Blossom ran over and hugged her sister. "Thank you, Mika!"

The girls looked like a million bucks when they left for the party. They blasted Lil' Kim's first album, *Hardcore*, all the way to New Jersey in Tamika's new Navigator that Rob, Tamika's boyfriend, had brought her two months ago. Forty minutes into the ride, they were pulling up to the mansion where the party was being held.

"Which way should I go? I don't even see anywhere to park," Tamika said.

"Look, pull over there where it says 'VIP Parking,' " Trina replied, pointing. "He told me my name should be on the VIP parking list."

Tamika pulled up to a white man in a black suit holding a clipboard.

"Hi, we're on the list."

The man replied, "Yes, what's the name, please?"

"Trina Black," Tamika answered.

"Okay, may I see your ID, Ms. Black?" he said, looking at his clip-board.

This was some other shit! the girls thought. Trina reached into her bag then handed the ID to the man. He checked it and handed it back. He handed five gold rose pendants to Tamika.

"Stick these gold rose pendants onto your clothes to get into the VIP sections, and free drinks all night including champagne. Just so you know, the pins are twenty-four-karat gold, so you might want to hold on to them. Pull ahead and someone will take your car and show you in. Enjoy yourself."

The girls pulled up a long path until they saw some more white men in suits. The girls were hyped!

All eyes seemed to be on them as they entered the mansion. They wandered from one room to another checking out the VIP rooms and looking for Trina's friend. The men stared in thirst, wanting to know who this group of beautiful women was. They finally reached the last VIP room upstairs, heavily guarded by security. They were checked for their gold pins and allowed to enter. In the middle of the room was a huge ice sculpture of a hundred-dollar bill. A long table was filled with bottles of Cristal champagne. Well-dressed people danced around the room and servants were moving about with trays loaded with hors d'oeuvres.

"There he is," Trina said.

Trina walked over to T Mac. He smiled, one of his wide, sexy smiles.

"Baby girl, for a minute I thought you wouldn't show," he said, pulling her into his arms.

Trina turned her head toward her friends. "These are my peoples. Tamika, Kim, Shareen, and Blossom."

T Mac in turn introduced his friends to each girl. Tamika had a good sense for picking out a cat who was handling. She wasted no time in making her move. Trina was all up under T Mac while Kim was talking to T Mac's friend. Shareen hadn't made up her mind yet; she was playing it neutral. Blossom was keeping to herself, enjoying the music, sipping on a flute of champagne. Almost every man in the room noticed her, including T Mac's brother, Dude, who decided right then he wanted her.

He walked up to her and said, "What's the matter, you're not enjoying yourself?"

She turned and looked at him with her big brown eyes. "I'm just chillin'."

"What's your name?" he asked.

"Blossom," she replied.

He looked at her with disbelief. "Is that so? Well, that's different." He reached his hand out to shake hers. "I'm Dude."

"Dude?" She looked at him as if he was crazy. "That's different, too! What's your real name?"

He smiled. She seemed so sweet and pure. Something that he didn't come across often when it came to women.

"That *is* my name!"

She gave him a funny look and he laughed.

"Well, how about this? Let us continue this conversation over dinner."

"Oh, yeah?"

"Yeah," he answered.

"That's something to sleep on," she replied. She knew Tamika wouldn't go for her going out to eat with no grown-ass man. He looked much older than her.

"What's there to sleep on? Either you want to or you don't."

"Aight, where?" she asked before thinking.

"Wherever you want, sweetie."

"Don't say that. We might end up having dinner in another country."

"And? Ain't nothin' but a word. I know what I said, I said wherever you wanted. And that's what I meant."

"Aight. I'm gonna think about it and let you know."

"When and how are you gonna let me know?"

She spotted Tamika coming back into the room. "Give me your number and I'll give you a call."

"An even exchange?" he replied.

"Yeah, aight," she said, walking off.

He grabbed her gently by the arm. "Where you going?"

Tamika walked over just as Blossom was answering.

"What's up?" Tamika asked Blossom.

"Nothing much. I was about to go to the bathroom."

Dude gave his homeboy the eye, to let him know he needed him to keep Tamika occupied. A bit tipsy from the champagne, Tamika was not paying shit too much attention.

"I'm gonna walk her to make sure she's all right," Dude said.

"I'm a big girl. I can go potty by myself," Blossom replied, walking off again.

Dude ignored her and followed behind anyway. Following behind him was a big dark-skinned man.

Blossom noticed the man following them and asked Dude why.

" 'Cause that's his job, baby."

She left that alone. She also noticed outright stares and whispers from the women they passed on their way to the ladies' room and the men were giving Dude his props. There was a long line outside the bathroom. Dude whispered something to a tall black man who walked into the bathroom then came out with the bathroom attendant. The man told the attendant to help him clear everybody out of the bathroom and to direct them to the other ladies' room. Blossom watched, trying to figure out why he wanted everyone out of the bathroom. Then she realized that Dude was making everybody leave the ladies' room so she wouldn't have to wait.

She whispered to Dude: "You didn't have to do that. I didn't mind waiting."

"Well, I mind you waiting. Now go ahead. Take your time. I'll be waiting right here."

Blossom couldn't help but wonder what was up with this Dude guy. She wondered if he was some kind of celebrity. If so, she had never heard of him.

Dude was that guy all the girls want and all the guys respect, just 'cause he was that "nigga." He was sharp; the feds couldn't even pin anything solid on him—more or less didn't know for a fact if he was living dirty.

It was a stop-and-go journey back to the upstairs VIP room because every person Dude passed wanted a word with him. The big black guy was right over his shoulder at all times, blocking people from getting too close. Blossom was again the target of envious stares from the women. If looks could kill, Blossom thought, I'd be dead and buried. She overheard a couple of the girls whispering.

"I don't know. I never saw that one before."

Now, Blossom was young and semisheltered, but a punk she wasn't. She turned to the girls and said with a smile, "Yeah, well, I never saw y'all before either."

Dude peeped it and laughed. When they got to the entrance of the VIP room, there was some sort of commotion going on inside. There was a crowd in the corner where their people were. As they approached, Blossom saw Trina holding an empty champagne glass like a weapon. T Mac was standing in between Trina and his kids' mother, Darlene. Tamika, Shareen, and Kim were standing by waiting for the girl's friends to make a move or say something.

"Oh, you wanna play stupid, huh!" yelled Darlene.

T Mac responded, with a serious face, "Darlene, you betta go ahead, girl. Before you get ya dumb ass hurt."

"What, nigga! Hurt? . . . By who? Muthafucka, you betta not play ya'self!" she yelled.

"Come on, Darlene, da nigga ain't worth it," one of her friends said, pulling her by the arm.

She could tell that it was the alcohol in Darlene doing the talking.

Darlene pulled away from her friend and, raising her voice, said, "NO! Fuck dat! I'm tired of this crab-ass, punk-ass, bitch-ass nigga! Fuckin' pussy-ass nigga!"

T Mac gabbed Darlene by the neck and pushed her away from the crowd.

"Yo, bitch! I told ya strung-out ass I wasn't up for ya shit if you came here tonight! And I told ya ass I wasn't fuckin' wit' you no more. I told you I'm gon' take care of my kids and dat's dat!"

She swung, not at him, but at Trina, hitting her in the cheek. Trina instantly punched Darlene back in the face. The rumble was on! Darlene's friends pretended to be breaking it up while at the same time getting their hits in. Tamika and the rest of the girls joined in and went buck wild. Even Blossom was thumpin'. Trina and her crew turned out to be too wild for T Mac and his boys to handle. Trina and the girls got the best of Darlene and her crew. They definitely were on some real Brooklyn shit. T Mac and the guys let the girls go blow for blow for about ten minutes before they broke it up. Then T Mac had security throw Darlene and her friends out. Baby mother or not, he was tired of the bullshit and felt totally disrespected that she had pulled a stunt like that at his and his brother's party. Trina and her people were contemplating whether to leave or not.

T Mac copped a plea to Trina. "Yo, I'm sorry 'bout dat. Dat's my baby's mother. She be trippin'."

Trina just looked at him. "Man . . . Whateva. You shouldn't have invited me if you knew ya girl was gonna be here."

"She not my girl. She just da motha of my kids. Come on, baby girl, don't be like dat. I promise, if you stay, I'll make it up to you."

Trina still paused before answering. "Yeah, and how is dat?"

"Don't worry. I got you. It a be somethin' nice. Just say you staying to party and ya leavin' wit' me." He smiled.

Returning his smile, she said, "Aight, I'll stay. But I don't know nothin' about leavin' wit' you."

They both laughed and continued to party. It was five-fifteen when the girls said their good-byes to the guys. Dude slid Blossom his number on the low. Tamika, Kim, and Shareen, on the other hand, openly exchanged numbers with the guys they had stuck with the whole night. And Trina, let's just say she took T Mac up on both of his offers. And the girls had an empty seat in the truck on the way home.

•   •   •

Tamika was standing at the stove when the phone rang.

"Hello."

"What's up, girl! How you be?" Trina yelled on the other end.

"Bitch, where you at?!" Tamika snapped.

Blossom walked into the kitchen, correcting her sister's grammar. "It's 'Where are you and where have you been?' "

Tamika rolled her eyes at her little sister, knowing she was right.

Tamika continued. "Bitch, where you at? We been callin' ya crib and ya machine keeps pickin' up. Callin' ya cell, you ain't pickin' up."

Trina laughed. "Y'all was worried about me?"

"Ain't shit funny! Yeah, we was worried. We ain't seen you in two days. Since you left wit' dat nigga."

"My bad, I'm in Aruba! Girl, dis shit is like a fuckin' fairy tale!"

Tamika's mouth dropped open. "Say word! Bitch, you lyin'. Stop da game playin'! Fo' real, where you at?!"

"I told you, in Aruba!" Trina laughed again. "I waited for him to run downstairs before I called. I ain't wanna look like a crab all hype and shit. But, girl, remember when he said he would make it up? Well, this is how he's makin' it up. The day afta the mansion party, he took me to the city. We had breakfast and he took me shoppin'. We went back to Jersey, straight to the airport. And the rest is history."

"You can't be fo' real!"

"Realer den real, kid! You ain't speak to his friend yet?"

"Oh, him. Naw, I didn't give his friend my number, he gave me his. But I didn't call yet. Rob has been on my back since the party."

Trina sucked her teeth. "You need ta get rid of his tired ass! I'm tellin' you, he got it, too! All of dem cats got it. And the cat, Dude, he's da ringleader. He doin' it more den any of dem."

"Who dat?" Tamika asked.

"Da one who Blossom was talking to. The dark-skin cat who had the bodyguard nigga followin' him," Trina answered.

"You ain't neva lie! So when you comin' back?" Tamika asked.

"I don't know . . . Look, I gotta go; he back. Tell da girls I'm aight. And call his friend, girl, trust me. I'm gonna call you later."

2 *A week later*

Blossom was sitting in the lab when the teacher came over and whispered to her.

"You're wanted at the office. A family member is here to get you. Something about a family emergency. You're excused for the rest of the day, Blossom."

Blossom rushed from the classroom and down to the office. She had no idea what her teacher could have been talking about. All types of things ran through her head. She hoped that her mother was okay . . . or could something be wrong with Tamika? She was out of breath by the time she reached the office. What she saw—rather *who* she saw standing at the counter—blew her mind. Before she could say anything, Mrs. Wilson, the office aide, approached her.

"Hi, Blossom. Your uncle is here to get you. He's already signed you out."

Blossom didn't want to make a scene, so she just went along with it. "Thank you, Mrs. Wilson. See you Monday."

"Thank you, Mrs. Wilson," Dude said, with a wide smile.

Blossom wasn't sure if she was doing the right thing. Walking from the school building with Dude. This man could take her somewhere, rape and kill her, she thought. She didn't know him. Once they were away from the view of the office window, she began to speak her mind.

"Yo, what the hell you doing here? I mean how'd you know . . . wait a minute, did you really just bogart your way into my school and . . . look, I hope you don't think I'm going anywhere with you."

"Yes, I do expect you to come with me." Duke spoke calmly. "But if

11

you chose not, I'll understand. And to answer your question about how I knew where to find you . . . Let's just say I got my connects. So, are you coming or not? I don't care for Brooklyn too much, don't want to be out here too long." He pointed to a tinted-out 600 Benz.

The same big bodyguard from the mansion party was in the driver's seat.

"No, I'm not going. But thanks for getting me out of school early. No offense, but I don't know you good enough to be driving away with you and another man." She turned and walked away toward the bus stop. He jumped into the backseat of the car and pulled off. Five minutes later, the same Benz pulled up again. The back window rolled down.

"You sure you don't want to come?" Dude said.

She got in the car this time. They drove off, heading toward Manhattan.

The first stop was at a Gucci store, where he picked up a suit to wear to a friend's wedding. Pointing to a pocketbook, he asked, "You like that bag?"

"Yes. I have that same one, as a matter of fact."

"Excuse me, Miss Lady, so do you see anything else you like, that you don't already have?"

She looked around and then pointed to a pair of fancy shoes and pocketbook combo.

"That. I like that setup."

Good taste, he thought to himself.

"And where might you be wearing something dressy like that to?"

"With you to your friend's wedding," she said, walking away.

Dude paid for the shoes and they left the store.

"I have one more stop to make, right across the bridge. Black, go to Birham," he instructed his man.

Looking at her watch, Blossom noticed it was already five o'clock. She knew Tamika would be looking for her, wondering why she hadn't reached home yet. Noticing she'd checked her watch, Dude said, "You got somewhere you gotta be?"

"Not really. Let me see your cell, please."

He gave her the phone. She called.

"Mika, it's me. I'm going out with a few of my friends. I went straight to the library after school."

"Aight. I'm goin' out, so I might not be here. I'll be home late."

"You going out with Rob?" Blossom asked.

"I am not tryin' to see his dumb ass now. Dat nigga got mad and came and got the truck a little while ago."

"Get outta here! Why?"

" 'Cause he is stupid! Dat's why I'm out! I got me a date."

"With who?"

"Excuse me? None of ya biz. Call me on my cell if you need me. Oh, yeah, Lil' Richie came by twice for you."

"For what? What he said he wanted?"

"He didn't say. You better stop treating that boy like dat. He's a good guy. I'm out. See you later." She hung up.

"You're not in trouble, are you?" Dude asked.

"No. My sister's going out anyway."

"I could have told you that."

"How's that?" She was confused.

"Like I said before, I got connections."

She left it at that. He didn't have to say it in so many words. She knew it must have been his homeboy from the party. Just as soon as she handed him his phone, it rang; something that it had been doing since she'd gotten in the car.

"What up, playboy! You missing in action, huh?" There was a pause. "Yeah? Well, that must be some good shit; you just up and bounced with Shorty." Another pause as he listened. Laughing, he said, "Nigga, you crazy! Everything is straight out here, though. I went and saw Shorty on that shit we was talking about. So I got that straight. Oh, yeah, ya BM is on some stupid shit again. You need to call her dumb ass! . . . Okay, hit me when you're on your way back in and bring me some of that sunshine."

"So, how's your brother enjoying Aruba? . . . Must be nice," Blossom said when he was done.

He looked at her with a blank expression. "What you talking about?"

"Come on, you know what I'm talking about. Your brother—isn't he in Aruba?"

"How you know that?"

"You're not the only one with connections, you know."

He just smiled and pulled her into his arms.

They pulled into the parking lot of a huge jewelry store. They all got out. They walked through the store down a row of jewelry counters. The clerks acknowledged Dude like they knew him.

They were all smiles as he approached the counter.

"Dude, my man!" a short foreign man said, reaching his hand out to Dude.

Dude shook his hand. "What's up, Birham? How's everything?"

"It's always good to see you, my friend."

Dude introduced Blossom. "Birham, this is my future wife. Blossom, this is my man Birham."

Blossom shook his hand and smiled. They entered a room where Birham went over to a small refrigerator and brought out a bottle of Cristal.

"I knew you were coming, so I got you a little something." Birham passed the bottle to Dude.

"You did, did you?" Dude replied with a smile.

Birham answered, "Come on, man, you know it isn't like that with you and me. We a little better than that."

"I know. I'm just fucking with you. So, is everything ready?"

"Yeah, and I think you gonna be real happy with the pieces."

He went over to a safe and pulled out three big jewelry cases. He returned and allowed Dude to inspect them. Dude's face showed his satisfaction. He closed the boxes and instructed Black to go to the car and get the money.

"What you got nice for my young lady here?" he asked Birham.

"What you looking for? Nice necklace, ring, earrings?"

Dude walked over to a display case and checked out the merchandise, pointing to a platinum chain with a medium-size, diamond-flooded key pendant.

"Let me see this right here."

Birham reached into the display case and handed the chain and pendant to Dude. Dude put it around Blossom's neck.

"You like it?" he asked.

"Yes . . . But I can't take this."

"Why?"

She couldn't answer him. She felt like he was going to want something in return. She didn't want to have to tell him why she didn't want to accept such an expensive gift.

"I just can't."

Dude ignored her and instead asked Birham, "How much?"

"You know I'll hook you up." Birham looked at a little white tag hanging from the necklace.

Dude looked at the tag. "Damn!"

Birham laughed. "Come on, you know I got you. And you gotta look at the diamonds. Very clear, my man!"

Moments later, Dude was looking at the pendant through a jeweler's loupe.

"Aight. That's what's up. I can't front, that's a good look. So, what can you do for me?"

"Um . . ." Birham began pressing on the buttons of a calculator. Then he said, "Give me ten."

"Good lookin'." Dude smiled.

"Ten what?" Blossom turned to him and spoke under her breath.

"Don't worry about it."

At that moment, Black walked back in with a medium-size Gucci bag. And handed it to Dude. Dude bent down and unzipped the bag. He pulled out about twenty large stacks of money in rubber bands. He handed the bundles of money to Birham.

"You want to count it?" Dude asked Birham.

"Come on now. Do I ever?"

Dude reached back in the bag, pulled out two more stacks of money, and handed them to him.

"Here, this is for my baby's chain."

"You don't have to give it to me now," Birham offered, like he usually did.

"Naw, I don't like to have debts." Dude rejected his suggestion, like he always did also.

Birham took the money and thanked Dude. Black picked up the jewelry cases and put them into the Gucci bag. Birham gave Dude the bottle of champagne and they all said their good-byes.

On the bridge going back toward the city, Dude reached over and kissed Blossom on her cheek. "You going to be my wife. You watch and see."

"Is that so?"

"That's so. Are you hungry?" he asked.

"Sure am!"

"Black, you up for some Mr. Chow?"

"Always, my man. That's where we're heading?"

"Yeah. I'm going to call now and make reservations."

When they arrived at Mr. Chow's, Dude was greeted with open arms by the manager. "Hello, stranger. I was wondering what happened to you. We haven't seen you in a long time."

Dude smiled his smile and shook the man's hand.

"You know, I'm always on the go. I came by, though, about a month ago, but you wasn't here," he said.

"Oh, yes, I was out sick."

Dude introduced Blossom. "Adam, this is my future wife." Adam shook Blossom's hand and escorted them to the bar.

Black was sitting at the far end of the bar, facing the entrance, Blossom noticed. As quiet as he was, he had a strong presence. His well-built frame and clean bald head stood out. You could see the muscle cuts through his shirt as he sat up straight observing the room. Dude and Blossom sat a few seats down, to have some privacy.

"Let me get a Rémy XO straight." Dude turned to Blossom and asked, "What you want, baby?"

Blossom didn't know what to say. She remembered trying an apple martini a couple of times.

So she said, "Apple martini, with Grey Goose."

He ordered their drinks and continued their conversation.

"So, since when you drink?" he asked.

"I don't really drink."

He rubbed her cheek. "Look, you don't have to ever fake the funk with me, baby. Just be you; I won't pass judgment. I want you to be real with me and I will be real with you."

She looked at him, smiling, and said, "Okay."

The warmth in his voice made her think he was sincere and put her at ease.

"So if you don't want to drink, you don't have to."

"Shit! Like hell I won't. Trust me, I want to drink that drink."

He laughed. He hadn't felt like this in a long time. Yeah, he'd had many women, but nothing serious since Kandi. They had broken up a little over a year ago. Since then, he'd just been dating chicks, but nothing serious. He felt like Blossom was the one. He hadn't known her for any time at all, but he knew. She was pure. He didn't have to worry about bumping into no nigga in the street that had already had his girl. She was sweet, but still had common sense.

They got up from the bar and were seated at a table for dinner.

"You like lobster?" he asked her.

"Yeah."

"What about chicken?"

"Yes."

"Okay." Dude waved the waiter down and he came hurrying to the table.

Of course the waiter knew him by name also. "Hey, Dude. What will you and your lovely young lady be having this evening?"

"How've you been, Rico?"

"I'm living."

Dude smiled. "That's your motto. We'll have ten pieces of chicken satay, Beijing chicken, ginger lobster . . . Oh, and let me get the scallion pancakes with the chicken satay."

"No problem. You want rice also, right?"

"Yes, thank you. Let me get another apple martini with Grey Goose and a Rémy XO. And, Rico, take care of my man Black also."

Rico took Black's order and disappeared for a few minutes.

"It seems like you're well known here," Blossom observed. "As a matter a fact, that seems true everywhere we've been."

"Well, I'm a nice guy."

"Aight, so where's your girl? Or should I say your wife. 'Cause at your age, you're probably married, right?"

He looked at her and laughed. It seemed to him that she'd gotten a little loose with the alcohol in her system.

"And what age might that be?" he asked.

"I don't know. Thirty-eight, forty?"

He busted out laughing. "Oh, really. Is that what you think?"

"Just a wild guess," she answered.

"Wow! Let me guess; you're seventeen years old . . . Right?"

"On the nose! Now back to you. How old *are* you?"

"Twenty-five—"

She interrupted him with a laugh of her own. "The devil is a liar!"

He just smiled. "What's the problem?"

"Oh, there isn't a problem. You just sound crazy."

"Why is that?"

" 'Cause you know you're not anywhere near twenty-five years old."

He pulled out an ID that was stashed way in the back of his Gucci leather wallet. "What does that say?" he asked, holding up the ID and covering the part that displayed his real name.

"You could've bought that. They do sell fake IDs, you know," she replied with a slight smile.

He was liking this side of her. He moved closer to her.

"Look, baby, I don't have to lie to you about anything. I told you you were going to be my wife. What, you thought I was joking?"

"It's not that I thought you was joking. I just didn't take you serious." She leaned over and gave him a soft kiss on his lips that seemed like they were sealing some sort of deal.

Dude and Blossom stood near the front door waiting for Black to bring the car from the lot. Blossom had drunk one and a half apple martinis and was feeling nice. Dude had a little buzz on as well.

"Hey, Dude."

He turned around. "Hey, what's up?"

"I saw Black outside," a woman said. "I figured you wasn't too far."

He grabbed Blossom's hand and pulled her closer to him. "This is Blossom, my future wife," he told the woman.

"That's nice. How's Kandi?" she asked, brushing him off.

"Shit, I don't know. And really don't give a fuck. We gotta go. Good night."

He held Blossom's hand tight as they walked out and climbed into the car.

"That was my ex's homegirl," he stated.

"Yeah. I kind of figured that," she nonchalantly answered. "You know she probably on her cell right now giving your ex the four-one-one."

"Yeah, knowing her, she is. Black, head back to Brooklyn to Blossom's crib."

"How you know where I live?"

"I keep telling you I have connections."

Blossom reached over and gave him another kiss. But this time she used her tongue.

"Who said I didn't want to go with you instead of home?" she whispered in his ear.

"Who said I didn't want you to go with me . . . ? But me and you both know that you have to go home."

She slid back to her side of the car. He wished he could take her home with him. Even if she didn't have to go home, he couldn't bring her with him, not to his house, not yet.

She sat thinking about everything he had said to her in the restaurant. She felt relaxed and comfortable with him.

"I'm a virgin."

He gave her a puzzled look. "Huh?"

"Just thought I'd let you know. You said that I should keep it real with you, right? Well, I'm letting you know for future reference . . . You know, before we get in a certain predicament . . . So I guess it really wouldn't make sense to have went home with you anyway . . . Huh?"

"Look, I wouldn't have wanted anything from you if you spent the night with me anyway. And just for the record, I already knew you were a virgin. Plus, I wouldn't want to sleep with you right away anyway . . . It's a man thing, you wouldn't understand."

"So . . . You don't think differently about me?"

"Like what, in a bad way?" he asked.

"Yeah."

"Why would I feel like that?"

"Because I know you're used to women that are way more experienced than I am. And me being a virgin could be a turnoff for you."

"Not at all, baby." He pulled her close to him, kissing her on the forehead.

They rode silently for a few minutes.

"And there's this guy, I wouldn't say he's my boyfriend or nothing. I mean we're not a couple, but we may do things that couples do—you know, spend time together and stuff, but we're definitely not a couple."

"Well, I have to take your word for that. Just let him know you have somebody now. That way he won't expect to be doing things that couples do with you anymore."

She started to laugh until she realized that he wasn't laughing. He was dead-ass serious. So she just left it at that.

Soon as they pulled on her block, the guys on the corner seemed to stop what they were doing to stare at the Benz. When they got in front of her building, she noticed Lil' Richie sitting on her stoop.

"Damn, we must've talked him up."

"Who's that, your friend?" he asked.

"Yeah, that's him."

"He's waiting for you?"

"I don't know. He could be waiting for his homeboy to come downstairs. But anyway, when will I see you again?"

"Whenever you want to."

She smiled. "Okay. Thank you for a nice day. And thank you for my chain."

"It's nothing, baby. Just call me when you ready to hook up again. Don't forget about your shoes and pocketbook in the trunk, sweetie."

She got her things from the trunk and walked back to the back window of the car. She leaned into the car and gave Dude another long tongue kiss. Lil' Richie was watching her every move. He had been sitting on the stoop for hours waiting for her. They were supposed to have gone to the movies and to BBQ's to eat. And now here she was hours later, getting out of a Mercedes-Benz, holding a big Gucci shopping bag, tongue-kissing some man he had never seen before.

Blossom stood at the curb until the car drove off. She walked over to her building as if it was any other day.

"Hey, what's up, Richie?"

He looked at her like she was out of her mind. "What's up? You tell me what's up, Blossom. Who was that and where have you been?"

"Excuse me?" she snapped.

"You know what, Blossom . . . you something else! You have me waiting for you for mad hours, then you come asking me what's up like shit ain't happen."

It was just then she remembered about their plans that had been made a week ago.

She toned down her attitude. "Damn, Richie, I forgot about this evening. My bad, boo."

He stood up in disgust. "No, it's *my* bad! I shouldn't have been out here this long waiting for you, Miss Baller!"

He walked off without even looking back. Blossom felt bad. She stood on the steps for a few minutes, stuck, before walking into the building.

When she got to her bedroom, she stood in front of the mirror behind her door staring at her chain, Gucci shoes, and pocketbook. She suddenly felt sad. She started thinking about Tiff, her best friend. She wished Tiff could've been there to share all of this excitement with her. Tears came to her eyes. She crawled under her comforter and cried until she fell asleep.

Dude was steaming because of the phone call he'd just received and had Black race back to New Jersey so he could change cars. He didn't want to go over to her crib in the Benz. He knew Kandi had a habit of attacking his cars when she was in a rage. He had a million and one things to do and now this shit was added to the list. He took out one of his pre-paid cell phones; he switched them up every two weeks.

"Yo, where are you?" He spoke into the phone. "Aight. Come meet me at the office right now."

His other cell phone rang. He looked at the number and pressed a button to send it straight to voice mail. It rang again. He finally answered.

"Yo, what the fuck you want!" he shouted.

"Fuck you, nigga! You wanna play me?! I'm gonna show you some shit! You hear that?!" He heard a loud crash through the phone. He could tell Kandi was breaking shit up.

"Guess what that was!" she yelled on the other end.

"You stupid bitch, I don't give a fuck about none of that shit! That's why I'm not with your dumb ass now, you stupid little cunt! It's really a wrap for you, shorty! I know one thing, though, you better be out of my shit by the time I get there, bitch!"

Dude switched cars and met up with T Mac to go over to the crib with him. Kandi was gone by the time they had reached the house. She had destroyed every television, cut up his clothes, and stabbed his furniture as well as trashing the house in general, down to the dishwasher. He stood in the middle of the living room shaking his head. This bitch has overdone it this time, he thought. T Mac and Dude's cells started ringing back-to-back. T Mac ignored Darlene's number when he saw it on the caller ID. But the phone just wouldn't stop ringing. The screen said ten missed calls before he decided to answer.

"Yo, what you want? I'm not up for your shit right now."

Darlene whispered on the other end: "You need to get over here now! Right now!"

T Mac couldn't understand her. "What you sayin'?"

She tried to talk louder. "I said you need to get over to my crib, nigga. Right now!"

He sucked his teeth. "Darlene, dis not the time for ya bullshit."

"Look, Kandi is over here wit' a gun talkin' 'bout she gonna kill herself!"

"What?!"

Just then, Dude, who'd stepped out for a minute, returned to the room. "Yo, man, that bitch took my hitters! My Glock and my Smith and Wesson!"

T Mac hurried and hung up. "Yo, man, dat was Darlene. We need to get over to her crib. She said Kandi over dere flippin' out. She got a hitter, talkin' 'bout she gon' kill herself!"

"What?"

They rushed out of the house and headed to Englewood, where T Mac had bought Darlene a four-bedroom house three years ago. He knew he was not going to be with her, but he felt he had to set her up right on the strength of his kids. They hadn't seen each other since the big fight at the mansion party. T Mac, Dude, and Black pulled up in the circle-shaped driveway, behind Kandi's BMW. T Mac stuck his key into the front door, but it wouldn't fit. He looked at the set of keys and tried again.

"This bitch changed the locks," he yelled.

T Mac fiercely rang the bell. Darlene came to the door in her house-coat. From her red eyes, he could tell that she'd been crying. T Mac was tempted to kick her ass about the locks but refrained. This wasn't the right time. Darlene put her pointer finger over her mouth, imploring them to be quiet, then led them downstairs to the basement. Kandi was sitting in the middle of the floor with a Glock cocked back and pointed to her head. She was sobbing hysterically and mumbling. She looked up and saw Dude.

"What are you doing here?!" She pointed the gun at Dude.

He started walking toward her and she jumped up.

"Don't you come near me! You devil muthafucka . . . After all I been through with you! What happen to all of our plans? You tell me what I'm supposed to do with my life now that you're gone!" she yelled at him.

Dude and the rest of them stood speechless. Kandi started walking closer to Dude, never taking her eyes off of him to acknowledge anyone else in the room.

"How come it's so easy for you to move on and I'm still stuck!" she demanded.

Bang! She fired a shot off. Everyone ducked. The bullet went into the wall behind Dude. "Look, just give me the gun, Kandi. Let's just talk about this, baby."

"Baby! Now I'm your baby!"

He moved closer. "Look, me and you both know why we're not to-gether. But that doesn't mean I don't have love for you. Please just give me the gat, Kandi. Your godchildren are upstairs. Think about them."

She started to cry again. She put the gun down and ran into Darlene's arms. Darlene held her tight and cried with her.

"I'm sorry . . . I'm so sorry," she whispered to Darlene, her head buried in her chest.

"It's okay, boo . . . It's okay," Darlene said.

Dude picked up the gun and handed it to Black. He then walked over and took Kandi out of Darlene's arms and began to hold her.

"Could you all excuse us for a minute?"

Darlene, Black, and T Mac walked back upstairs.

"What's going on with you, Kandi?" He sat her on the couch. "I mean, what's really going on? You and I know this is not the first time you pulled some crazy shit like this. You know we both agreed to split. Why do you keep pulling stunts like this?"

"I love you! Why can't you see that?" She began crying hard again.

He took a deep breath, burying his face in his hands, then looked up and into her eyes. "Have you been going to your therapy sessions?"

"Not in the past month."

"Why? So, I'm just wasting my time paying her? I thought we had an agreement, Kandi."

"Look, I'm not crazy. Yes, I might have some issues, but I'm not crazy. Only thing wrong with me is I'm still in love with you, while you're not in love with me. And I'm having a hard time dealing with being alone."

"You . . . Kandi, you know you don't have to be alone. I told you it probably would take some getting used to, but you gotta move on. You could find someone that will make you happy. Look, the bond we have can never be broken, sweetie. I think we can do good being friends. Nobody can never break our friendship."

She looked at him with tears rolling down her face. She shook her head from side to side.

"I remember when you couldn't even stand to see another man look at me. And now here you are pushing me off on another man."

She stood up, walked upstairs, and went straight out of the house. Dude followed and watched out of the foyer window. Kandi got into her car and sped off. Darlene and T Mac came out of the kitchen.

"Where's Kandi?" Darlene asked.

"She left," Dude replied.

"Where did she go?"

"She didn't say. T, go get Black. Let's roll out."

"Wait a minute. What do you mean, she didn't say? You just let her leave like that!" Darlene yelled.

"Look, she's grown and it's much more to this shit than you know about! So stay off my fucking back!" he snapped.

One of T Mac's phones started ringing. It was Trina.

"Hey, what's up?" he answered. "I know, some shit came up, but I'm gonna be on my way in a minute, though . . . So don't eat nothin'." He laughed. "Yeah, that sounds like a plan. See you in a few."

Darlene lost it.

"You disrespectful nigga! You standin' in my home chitchattin' wit' ya bitch! Dat's why I changed the locks on my door, nigga!"

She went to swing at him, but he caught her hand.

"Yeah, you changed the locks and I changed my bitch. I think my change is more beneficial than yours." He picked up his cell from the floor. Trina was still on the line. "Hello . . . Sorry 'bout dat, baby. Be there in a minute."

He walked out and slammed the door. Darlene ran to the door, snatched it open, and started yelling, "Fuck you, Terry! And don't come back here! You can forget about ya kids, too!"

T Mac looked at her and laughed. "You a sick bitch! It's the kids you hurtin', not me. Call me when you see the wizard and get a brain. You dumb bitch!"

3   *A month later*

A month later, T Mac moved Trina into a house, but he insisted that she either go to school or work. She decided to do both. Not much changed with Darlene: she was still on a rampage, cracking codes to motherfuckers' voice mails, cursing T Mac out. She just did not know how to give up. Kandi was just as bad. Those two being friends was a deadly thing. Kandi began to stalk Dude and soon realized that he was really into Blossom. One evening she followed him when he went to pick up Blossom. She noticed that he drove around the corner to wait for her even though there was a space right in front of her building. Why was that? she asked herself. Because of the harassing phone calls from Kandi, Blossom had had to change her telephone number three times in the last month.

Dude wanted to plan a surprise trip to Hawaii for Blossom's graduation and birthday. But Kandi was cool with his travel agent. Dude hid the plan from Kandi because he still had a certain kind of love for her. He thought about going through T Mac's people but then remembered Darlene. She was like Inspector Gadget. So he just decided to go to a different travel agent. The last hurdle was to get Blossom away for a week without her hounding-ass sister losing her mind. His patience was getting low with Tamika anyway. He understood her being protective of her little sister, but he needed to go to the next level with Baby Girl. He could wait for the sex. He was more focused on his business, street and legit. He purchased two more rigs, which made eight in all. Within two years, Dude had purchased eight trucks. And over the last two years, he'd built a trucking company, which was the first thing he purchased years ago when he received his lawsuit money. He had been hit by a city bus when he was young. The bus driver was pissy drunk! The bus accident left him with both legs and one of his arms broken. He was cast up for almost a year, had pins in his legs and arm, and had to go through three operations. He was not eligible to receive the $1.1 million settlement until he was twenty-one years old. But the city was responsible for picking up the cost of private education from junior high through college. He'd attended real estate school for the past year and was preparing for the test to get his real estate license.

He wasn't dumb. He might have been young, but he had more sense than some older cats in the streets. He didn't know how he was going to get Blossom out of the house and off to Hawaii, but he had three weeks to figure it out.

Meanwhile, not too much had changed with Tamika. She'd given in and let Rob have another chance. Which meant she pushed Dude and T Mac's homeboy away. Rob wasn't shit. He was a control freak and it seemed like Tamika liked him that way. As for Kim, she was still in the stores. She was going hard! She was trying to save money for a tummy tuck and lipo. She had gone out with a friend of T Mac and Dude's about six times since the mansion party. This was good for her. She usually didn't keep a guy too long. She had what you call zero tolerance. And as for Shareen, she was just Shareen. She just wanted to drink and smoke weed. But one thing about her, she always held a little job.

Tamika was standing in the kitchen with her mouth dropped open. She had just hung up on Dude. He'd caught her off guard; he was the last person she'd expected to be on the other end of her phone. Blossom had never spoken about Dude to her. A feeling of betrayal and disrespect filled Tamika's heart. She started pacing the living room back and forth, and kept on pacing for a solid hour. You could almost see the steam coming out her ears. Her conversation, rather the screaming match, with Dude had been a heated one. He had been very polite, but

Tamika hadn't been able to return the courtesy. She couldn't wait for Blossom to walk through the door. The phone rang and she rushed to answer, thinking it was Blossom.

"Hello!"

"Damn, girl. What's wrong with you?" It was Trina on the other end.

"Oh, I thought you was Blossom. I'm gon' wring her neck!"

Trina paused before answering. "Why, what's up?"

"Do you know dat little sneaky bitch been fuckin' around wit' dat nigga Dude! Ya nigga brother from Jersey."

Trina played it off. "How you know?"

Tamika began to explain. " 'Cause the nigga called here a little while ago. I'm not gonna front. He was polite, but fuck dat shit! He talking 'bout he really likes my sister. She's a good girl and how he's calling outta respect. And how he's got nothing but respect for her. Basically, he wants to take my lil' sister to Hawaii for her birthday and as an early graduation gift . . ."

Trina's mouth dropped open. "Get out! So what's the problem?"

"What! You bumped ya head, bitch! What you mean, what's the problem?"

"Tamika, he's a good guy. Yo, you gonna have to let go of her sooner or later. At least he's not a slouch."

"You really lost ya mind! How you sound? You sound like you just tellin' me to give my sister away ta some drug-dealer nigga I don't know! Have you forgotten she's going on eighteen years old!"

Trina tried reasoning. "Yeah, and all you gonna do is push her to break out like a wild animal when she turns eighteen. At least he called and didn't try to be sneaky about it. If she was my sister, I would let her go."

"Look, what you do is your business. But my sister is not going out wit' no grown-ass man! You old enough to do as you please, but Blossom ain't old enough yet."

"You a mess. Trust me, he's a good guy." Trina sucked her teeth.

At that moment Tamika heard Blossom's key in the door. "Yeah? Trust me, I don't give a fuck! I gotta go. Here she comes."

Tamika hung up the phone quickly. She heard Blossom's room door close. She stormed straight to the back of the apartment. She turned the knob to open the door, but it was locked. She banged on the door.

"Blossom, open the door."

Blossom took a few seconds before doing so. "What's up?" she asked Tamika.

Tamika walked in and noticed the shopping bags on Blossom's bed. "What's dat?" she asked.

"What's what?"

"Those bags on ya bed."

"Clothes. I went shopping after school."

"Shopping? Wit' what money? . . . Oh, let me guess. From ya boyfriend?"

Blossom just stood looking at her. She didn't know what to say. She had already come up with a lie to tell her sister. But that was out the window.

Blossom replied with a confused look on her face. "Huh?"

"Huh, my ass. You fuckin' heard me! Ya boyfriend, Dude!" she yelled.

Blossom felt chumped. It sounded like Tamika already knew something. So it didn't make sense to lie.

"Yeah."

"Yeah what?" Tamika looked at her like she was crazy.

"Yeah, he gave me the money to go shopping."

"What da fuck is goin' on wit' you?! I mean how . . . When did all of this shit wit' dis nigga happen?! What, you think you grown now!"

"NO, I don't think I'm grown, but I'm not a child either. I do what I'm suppose to do, my grades is up to par. Why you sweating me like I'm some inmate or something!"

Tamika grabbed her by her neck and Blossom quickly grabbed Tamika by her neck. The two were tussling, holding each other's neck.

Tamika shouted. "Blossom, get the fuck off of me!"

"No, you get the fuck off of me. You grabbed me first!" Blossom shouted back.

Tamika punched her in the side of her face. And that was it: the two started throwing down! They thumped for about ten minutes straight. And at the end, they both were too tired to continued.

"I want you out of dis house. You sneaky bitch!" Tamika said, huffing and puffing.

"What?! You can't put me out of here. I got just as much right to be here as you! And If I'm sneaky, you're a hatin'-ass bitch! Don't get mad at me 'cause I have somebody that's into me and your nigga treat you like shit!"

"You can't be for real! Hatin'! If dat's what you think, then you really are a bigger jackass than I thought! And you right, I can't put you out of this apartment. But you wanna act like you grown, I'll treat you like you grown. You can start coverin' some of these bills in dis muthafucka!"

How dare she tell her about the bills! Blossom knew that their mother sent money for her every month. She reached inside of her pocketbook and took out eight one-hundred-dollar bills and threw it at Tamika.

"Here, you crab ass. This should cover shit for a little minute! Being that the rent is only five and change! Spend it on the utilities or the rent. So now that I am a paying tenant, I would appreciate it if you would step out of my room!"

Blossom pushed her sister out of her room, slammed her door, and locked it. Tamika stood on the other side of the door, furious. But what could she do? So she just walked away.

Dude sat in his office chair looking at his watch. T Mac was supposed to be there over a hour ago. He was praying that nothing had gone wrong. Pickups were usually his thing to do, but he knew T Mac needed the practice. He jumped up when he heard the eighteen-wheeler. About time, he thought. He ran out of the office and down to the warehouse.

When he got there he instructed Black to lock down the gate and turn the motion alarms on outside in the parking lot and in the office.

T Mac was driving the huge tractor trailer while Teddy rode behind with Black.

"So, is it all good?" Dude asked T Mac.

"And you know it." T Mac smiled. "You was startin' ta get worried when we took too long, huh?"

"Nigga, you know I was."

"Shit, you know ya man Fernando be puttin' a nigga through some otha shit!" Teddy added.

"Wouldn't you if you had twenty kilos of heroin?" Dude laughed. "What you thought you was dealing with, peanuts?"

"Shit, I ain't know what we was workin' wit'," Teddy replied.

This was Teddy's first time rolling on a run with T Mac and Black. Dude hadn't wanted to let him know the full details. He didn't want him to get nervous. Nor did he want to run the risk of him trying some dumb shit. He had no reason to mistrust Teddy, but he could never be too careful.

"Let's get to work. Whatever boxes have serial numbers that end in five six, those are the ones we're looking for. Let's take out the product and test it," he instructed the men. "T, you told Fernando that I'll have his money this weekend?"

"Yeah. He said don't worry about one of the bricks. He said it's on him."

A big smile came over Dude's face. "Now that's what I'm talking about! The bonus envelope's gonna be looking real good for you guys."

That put a smile across everybody else's face as well.

Blossom raced home from school. Dude had called her on the Nextel phone he had bought her three days ago. He told her he needed to talk to her and she was to come straight home from school; he would wait in his car by her building. The buses were running crazy, so it was already taking her an extra twenty minutes to reach home. Dude was still waiting, so he decided to call her cell again.

"Baby, I'm on my way. The buses are running crazy," she told him.

"Bus? Why are you on the bus? You have a pocketful of money. Why didn't you take a cab?"

She paused for a moment. She hadn't even thought of that. "I don't know. I'll be there in ten minutes."

He felt a set of eyes staring at him. "Oh boy, there goes your warden."

"Who, Tamika?" she laughed.

"Yeah. What the fuck she standing there staring for?"

" 'Cause she a hater! I'll be there in a minute." She hung up.

"May I help you?" he asked Tamika as he rolled down his window.

She replied not with words, but simply rolled her eyes and stuck her middle finger up. He just laughed at her and rolled his window back up. His phone rang.

"What up, boy?" he asked.

T Mac replied on the other end, "Ain't shit. I just got your message."

"Yeah, I need a favor. Can you stay at my crib Saturday? They're delivering my new bedroom and living-room furniture and I'm gonna be in Hawaii."

"What time they comin'?" T Mac asked.

"Like nine in the morning."

"Damnnn!" he shouted.

"Come on, son. You know if I didn't need you to I wouldn't ask."

"I know, man. I'm just fuckin' wit' you. I promised Trina we would chill for the weekend, though. She gon' wig out when I tell her it's a wrap."

"So why don't you just take her wit' you. Y'all could go out there on Friday evening and go to dinner and a movie on that side. And Saturday, after they deliver the shit, y'all could finish doing y'all for the rest of the weekend."

T Mac agreed. "Aight, son. You know I got you. Did you tell Blossom about the trip yet?"

"Naw, and I still don't know how I'm gonna get her to the airport without her finding out. How I'm suppose to get her to pack bags without knowing she's going on a trip?"

T Mac laughed. "Nigga, you know how we do! Why you actin' like you new to this!"

Dude's other line beeped in.

"Yo, son, that's Kandi on the other line. Let me see what her crazy ass wants. I'll hit you back." He clicked over.

"Yeah," he answered.

"Yeah what?" she replied with an attitude.

He took a deep breath. "What's up, Kandi?"

"I need to see you."

"About what?"

"What you mean, about what? All of a sudden it's 'about what'? I just think we should talk. I thought we were friends. Can't friends meet, have dinner, and talk?"

"How'd you get from talking to dinner?"

"Look, can we meet?" she asked in a sweeter tone.

"I'm busy today," he replied.

"Not today. I'm busy, too. Like on Thursday or Friday."

"I can't. I'm going away on Saturday and I got a lot of shit to do before I go away."

He knew he was leaving on Friday morning. He just didn't want her to know all his business.

"Goin' away where! Wit' who, ya fuckin' whore bitch! You don't have time to take me out to dinner, but you can take dat bitch away! You a foul-ass nigga, Dude! I hate ya black ass!"

"Look, Kandi, this is what I'm talking about. You flippin' on the phone, I could imagine the bullshit you'll pull if we get together. Naw, I'm not meeting you! Like I told you, I'm gonna take care of you, make sure your mortgage, car note is paid, and make sure you got money in your pocket every month. And that's only gonna be happening for six months; after that, you on your own! I would never see you fucked up, but you gotta get a job and start holding ya own! I'm telling you I'm cutting my life line loose! You making me play the hard way, Kandi! I'm not fucking with you! And stop calling me with your shit! You keep playing like you're fucking crazy, ain't shit crazy about your ass! You're just stuck!"

Kandi got even more angry. "Fuck you, Dude! I'm gonna kill ya ass! You and your bitch!" She hung up.

Blossom heard a commotion coming from the kitchen when she walked in the crib. Kim, Trina, and Shareen was drinking at the kitchen table. Tamika was on the phone with watery eyes.

"I'll be at court in the morning, boo. I love you, too."

She hung up and started crying. Trina got up and hugged her.

"It's gon' be aight. We gon' see tomorrow what the judge say. I'll give you some dough toward the bail," Trina said.

"What's going on?" Blossom asked.

Tamika looked at her and rolled her eyes.

Kim answered. "Rob got knocked. His punk-ass friend snitched on him."

"Who, Sean?" Blossom asked.

"Yeah. He got caught wit' a brick and twenty thousand in the car," Tamika replied.

"Shit! When he go to court?" Blossom asked.

"Hopefully in the morning. I'm gonna go down there at nine and just sit and wait," Tamika said.

"Wait, I'll be back," Blossom said, and disappeared into her room.

When she returned a minute later, she handed a roll of money to Tamika. "Here."

"What's this?" Tamika asked.

"It's ten thousand toward his bail," she answered.

Tamika took a deep breath. Her heart dropped; she was shocked at Blossom's gesture. She hugged Blossom tight. "Where you get dis kinda money from?"

"Every time Dude gives me money, I just stash it," she replied.

Blossom's cell phone rang. "What's up?"

"What? What you mean, what?" Dude jokingly asked.

Blossom smiled and all the girls, including Tamika, smiled, too.

"I'm sorry," she replied. "What's up, baby? . . . Why, what's up? . . . No, it's not a problem. I'm just wondering what's up . . . Aight, I'll be ready."

She hung up. "He up to something," she said.

"Why you say that?" Trina asked.

" 'Cause he want me to stay with him and go to school from his house. He never asks me to stay with him on a school night. He doesn't even like to have me out late on school nights."

Tamika already knew what he was up to.

"You still a virgin, right?" Shareen asked out of nowhere.

It got silent. Everybody wanted to know the answer to that.

Blossom looked at all of them like they were crazy. "Yeah!"

"You know you could tell us anything, right?" Kim said in a caring tone.

"I know that," Blossom replied.

Tamika interrupted. "Chile, please, this girl is still tight as a baby's asshole. Trust me, she ain't fuckin' yet."

Shareen pushed the issue. "So you mean to tell me dat a nigga like Dude be lookin' out for you crazy, spendin' mad time wit' you, and he don't wanna fuck?"

"I didn't say nothing about what he want and don't want to do. I told y'all what I haven't done. And I have not broken my virginity. My mother told me pussy is worth more when it hasn't been touched."

Blossom had never been in a rush to have sex. Her mother had taught her to take her virginity seriously. She actually felt like her virginity was her ace card. Unlike most of the girls her age, she was untouched and pure.

The girls all laughed and joked.

"So, Trina, when ya man gon' let you have company in dat new place of yours?" Shareen asked.

"Don't start ya shit, Shareen. You know da deal. Dat paranoid muthafucka. But he startin ta feel bad. He told me it a be okay after the people come and put the security system in Monday."

"Yeah, I believe it when I see it!" Shareen told her.

"So what's up for the weekend, girls?" Kim asked, pouring another drink.

"I'm up for whateva. I'm off the whole weekend," Shareen answered.

"Shit, I'm gon' be wit' Terry the whole weekend," Trina said.

"Well, I guess it's just us three this weekend," Kim said.

"I guess," Tamika said.

"I know you're up to something, Dude," Blossom said, rubbing the back of his neck.

He laughed. "Why I got to be up to something? Why can't I just want you to be with me tonight? Maybe I just don't wanna sleep alone."

"OOOH, is the lil' baby scared of the dark?" she mocked.

"Yeah, I am."

She got serious. "For real, is everything okay?"

"Yes, baby. Just want to be with you. I been so busy lately, we haven't spent a lot of time together."

"It's okay, baby. I know you've been busy getting ready for your test. And you just got another rig. I don't feel no away."

That's why he dug her. Never beefing, easygoing, and pleasant. He really was convinced now that it hadn't been a waste making a trip back to Birham earlier. She was worth it, he felt.

After thirty minutes of driving, she noticed they were nowhere near his crib.

"Where you going?" she asked.

"Surprise," he answered.

"I knew you were up to something," she said.

Ten minutes later, they pulled into a gated community. He pulled out a magnet card and put it up to a box outside the gate. A voice came from the box.

"Good evening, Mr. Knoxx. You may enter."

They pulled up to a brick town house. The door had big brass numbers on it: 355.

He turned off the car and got out. Blossom sat in the car. He walked around and opened the door for her.

"Well, what you waiting for?"

"Well, I didn't know you wanted me to get out. I don't know where we at."

She got out the car. He opened the door to the town house with the keys in his hands, and once they had walked in, he handed the keys to her.

"What?" she asked.

"It's yours. This is your place. Paid in full."

She looked around, astonished. The place was fully furnished. The way she would have done it herself if she had to. Every room was furnished in her style. A huge crystal chandelier hung from the foyer's tall ceiling. A plush wine-colored suede living-room set sat in the middle of the room. The furniture was complemented by shiny hardwood floors and a large center rug. A plasma TV sat on the wall, over the brick fireplace. It was a three-bedroom, two-and-a-half bath. Two floors with a finished basement. It was beautiful! From the dishes in the cabinets to the food in the fridge. Even the closets and draws in the master bedroom had clothes, underwear, and shoes in them. She couldn't believe it. She didn't know what to say.

"Thank you" was all she managed.

He hugged her. "You welcome, baby. You deserve it, sweetie." He hugged her again.

"I'm so happy you came into my life. You've shown me so much." Tears came to her eyes.

She had been surprised before; she was in shock now. He walked her through the house. When they reached a bedroom, he said, "Wait here for one minute." He ran to the car. When he got back up to the room with a beautifully wrapped box, she was lying on the bed, butt-ass naked.

"Well, what's the problem?" she asked.

"Nothing."

"So why are you looking at me like I'm crazy?"

He went over to her and handed her the box.

"Believe me, if I thought you were crazy, I wouldn't be handing you this," he replied with a smile.

"What's this?"

"Just open it!" he said, excited.

She ripped it open. Her bottom lip dropped to the floor.

"Oh, my God!"

"You like?" he asked.

She hugged him so tight he could feel her heart beating up against his chest. He slid the ring on her finger.

"It's just a little somethin'. You know, a friendship ring. This should hold you over until it's time for an engagement ring."

"Shit, I can't imagine how that ring will look. How many carats is this?"

"Six and a half," he replied.

"Damn. This is deep. I mean, I'm not trying to sound possessive or nothing, but this means it's about us."

"I'm glad you know it," he said.

"Don't get me wrong. I love this place and everything, but how am I gonna get to school from all the way out here? And am I gonna have to stay here every night by myself?"

"Well, first of all, you need to hurry up and get you license and you can drive yourself to school and anywhere else you choose. Second of all, of course I will make sure you get to school until you get your license. And no, I'm not gonna make you sleep here by yourself every night. But you're gonna have to get use to being here by yourself sometimes."

She plopped down on the bed and held her head down.

"What's wrong?" he asked.

"Nothing . . . Just that." She paused before continuing. "I don't want to sound ungrateful or nothing. But I'm not use to being on my own, by myself. And I just don't want to be lonely. Like Trina; she's got this real nice place, but she can't have no company, so she's always complaining 'bout being bored or lonely there. And I know there will be times when you're not gonna be able to be here. What am I suppose to do then? Ain't like around the way. Where I could just go outside and chill for a while."

He kissed her on her forehead before he spoke. "Look, nobody said you had to be here by yourself all the time. But that doesn't mean I want mad traffic running through here either. Look, baby, one thing I don't never want to do is hold you down. Smother you and shit. I want you to be able to be you and still love me. I want you to have a life outside of me and you. And at the same time have it be all about me and you. See, that's where I fucked up with Kandi. That girl knows nobody and nothing else but me. And I help create that monster she's turned into. This is your place; I trust that you'll have good judgment on what does and does not go on in here. You know who to allow to come here and who not. You know the deal. I trust you."

She kissed him passionately. She was wet and he knew it. But he wasn't ready to go there with her yet. He wanted to wait until they got to Hawaii. This was a perfect time to start putting his plan of getting her on the plane into play.

"Look, I want you to do me one favor."

"What's that?" she asked.

"Skip school tomorrow."

She looked at him like he was crazy. He knew she didn't fuck around when it came to school.

He continued. "I know I know. But tomorrow is Friday anyway. I want us to do a little shopping in the morning. Come on, please. I never ask you for nothing."

She thought about it. He was right: he never asked her for shit! And tomorrow was Friday and it was the end of the school year. She already knew she was passing all of her classes. "Okay, we can do that."

They fell asleep in each other's arms. She fell asleep feeling like she was the luckiest girl in the world. And he fell asleep knowing that he had hit the jackpot.

"Why every time we plan some shit, you always come wit' the okeydoke! Now all of a sudden you gotta fuckin' house-sit for Dude!" Trina shouted as she filled a gator overnight bag with clothes.

"What the fuck you beefin' for? We still gonna do us, Trina. Ain't no big deal! I just gotta wait for the people to come early in the morning and we can be out. I figure we go out there Friday and hang out on dat side, and in the morning when the people come, we can break out."

She sucked her teeth. "Why the fuck you got to wait for the fuckin' shit anyway?" she asked.

He contemplated answering. He didn't want to blow up Dude's spot. Trina could easily call Blossom and put her hip to the surprise. Fuck it, he thought to himself.

" 'Cause Dude is taking Blossom to Hawaii tomorrow for her birthday and graduation. It's a surprise. And he asked me to do him a little favor. Dat all! And where the fuck you think you goin'? What you packin' a bag fo'?"

Trina wondered if Tamika knew about this trip. She just continued to get her overnight bag together. She didn't know what to say. She felt kind of stupid. She should have found out the whole story before reacting. But fuck that! she thought, She was sticking to her guns. Niggas don't admit to being wrong. So she was going to keep playing her shit out.

"I'm staying at Tamika's tonight," she finally replied.

"Didn't you just come from dere?" he asked.

"Yeah, but I needed some clothes for tomorrow and I thought maybe I could get a quickie. But you actin' crazy," she replied, trying the reverse-psychology move.

"*Me* actin' funny!" He laughed in a shady way.

"*You* actin' funny. Anyway, her man got locked up and she wants me to go to court with her in the morning."

He liked that she was a ride-or-die chick. They had that in common. He respected her bond with her friends.

"Oh, that's cool," he told her. "See I don't have a problem with you doin' ya' peoples a favor. Why should you have a problem with me doin' mines?"

She kissed him. There was no need for any more conversation as far as he was concerned. He lifted her shirt off in one motion. Within a minute, they both were naked and making passionate love. That was another thing he liked about her; she had the best pussy and head he'd ever had! And he'd had his share.

4

Kandi paced like a lunatic in her living room. She felt like she should have just taken her life that night in Darlene's house. She tried calling Dude's cell phone, but his voice mail kept picking up. She mumbled to herself.

"I know you see my number, you fucker! Why are you doing dis to me? Don't you see I love you? Do you think I'm gonna let it go jus' like dat?"

Kelly was the one who'd put Kandi up on Dude and Blossom being at Mr. Chow. It was just Dude's luck that he had run into Kelly not only at Mr. Chow but at Birham's when he and T Mac were picking up the rings they had made for Blossom and Trina. No matter how hard Dude and T Mac had tried to be discreet about their business with Birham, Kelly's nosy ass still managed to see what was going on. Kelly could not wait to share her info with Kandi. They bumped into each other at the Short Hills Mall. Kelly ran her mouth on and on about seeing Dude and T Mac buying these big dooky diamond rings. And how they must have been worth sixty thousand dollars! But Birham gave it to them for fifty thousand. She even went as far as telling Kandi how pretty the boxes were. She told her story as if it was nothing, but she knew the deal. She knew she was pushing Kandi's buttons. Kandi had brushed it off like it was nothing, but she was on fire! And now, as she continued to dial Dude's cell, she was still on fire.

• • •

Dude and Blossom were shopping in the Louis Vuitton store when she got suspicious because he went straight to the luggage.

"What are you buying luggage for? You have mad sets of luggage already."

"Yeah, but you don't, baby."

They had only two and a half hours left and he still wanted to take her to Bergdorf Goodman and then grab something to eat. When the couple reached the car, Blossom noticed Dude packing everything that was in the bags into the new luggage they had just purchased.

"I'm making more space. Shit just looks sloppy back here," he said to her before she could ask. She left it at that. He hit Black on his Nextel walkie-talkie to let him know where to meet him. When Black pulled up, Dude could tell something was wrong. Black got out and joined Dude on the sidewalk.

"What's up?"

"Yo, Kandi buggin', son. No disrespect, Dude, but the bitch just ran up on me wit' a gat!"

"What!"

"Yeah! I'm over by the office and she comes rollin' up on the whip talkin' 'bout 'Where dat' nigga Dude at? Is he in the office?' "

"What you said?"

"Man, listen! I told her she betta get the fuck outta my face. And I pulled off on her crazy ass."

Dude handed Black all of his cell phones.

"Answer the Nextel only. I'll call you tomorrow and see what's up. If Kandi call, just hang up on her and don't answer blocked numbers. T Mac's going to meet you at the office; give him the keys to the Benz truck. He's driving it for the weekend. Him and Trina are staying at my other crib to wait for the furniture people to deliver. The alarm people are coming, too, to fix that."

Dude drove to Newark Airport while Blossom slept. When they arrived, he stared at her for a few minutes before waking her up. He kissed her on the lips softly and she opened her eyes and smiled.

"I think I love you," he said.

She looked around in confusion.

"Where are we?" she asked, realizing they were at the airport.

"Come on, baby. We are going to miss our flight."

"Stop playing, Dude!"

He just smiled and started pulling the luggage out of the jeep. "Trust me," he said.

So she did just that. She was down for whatever when it came to him anyway. She remembered she had to call Tamika.

"Hey, Mika, what's up?" she said.

"Nothin'. Waitin' for Rob to come out. We dropped the paper to Rikers Island a few hours ago. The Man said it would take 'bout six to nine hours to release him. You ain't leave yet to go to Hawaii? I thought y'all was breakin' out today."

Blossom was taken aback that Tamika knew about the trip. "We're about to. I'm at the airport now. I was calling to let you know." She played it off.

"Well, girl, bring some sun back for me and make sure you call when you get there . . . And thanks again for the money for Rob."

"No problem. Love you."

"Love you, too."

Blossom was happy. She had the best man in the world, and her relationship with Tamika had gotten back to normal. This was the best birthday yet. She was ready.

T Mac was racing down the highway, trying to make the dinner reservations at this elite Italian restaurant that Dude had put him onto. Before he left for Hawaii, Dude made a phone call to the manager to ask her to make T Mac extra comfortable, as it was a special night for him and Trina. And the fact that Dude laid that good black dick on the manager of the restaurant every now and then helped the situation, too. You know, whenever he was in that "white trophy" mode.

Trina had an attitude the whole ride there, but loosened up once they pulled up to the restaurant. She could not front; she was very impressed. Now she understood why he'd insisted on her dressing up.

The tall, slim, olive-skinned manager saw to it that T Mac and Trina were seated at a table that was secluded. T Mac knew about Dude's on-and-off fling with the beautiful manager, and being the man that he was, he briefly imagined how it must have been to have her in bed.

"So what's up with all dis?" Trina asked.

"What you talkin' 'bout?" T Mac answered. "Can't I just wanna do somethin' nice wit' you?"

"Oh, please, nigga. I know you too good."

Unlike Dude, T Mac was more of the hard rock. He wasn't usually the romantic type toward women. Darlene was the last female he'd given his heart to. And unlike Dude, he still had a couple of his fuck partners on hold. Even though Trina was more than satisfying, he felt like a man had to be a man. But the fifty-thousand-dollar ring he had bought from Birham said a lot. Trina was different from the rest of the chicks he fucked with. She was real, there was no fronting with her. It was something about her personality that he never saw in any of the girls he'd been with.

After dinner, T Mac instructed the waiter to bring a bottle of champagne. Trina was already tipsy, but she didn't mind being fucked up. She wanted to get busy tonight. He had fucked her the way she wanted to be fucked. She was used to him and he was used to her.

When the champagne was opened and poured, T Mac raised his flute to Trina. "This is to you, my woman who once was just my shorty. You been the one thing I been missin'. I know I can be a fuckin' headache at times and you still put up wit' me. I told you when we first hooked up that I would change your life, and it's crazy how you ended up doing just dat for me. You real and I love it. As a matter of fact, I love you, Trina."

Her heart fluttered. She never had a man tell her that or treat her the way T Mac did. And her throat felt like she had swallowed an apple. She tried to hold back her tears. He put his glass down and pulled out a perfectly wrapped box. Trina opened the box, saw the blinding rock, and practically leaped across the table and hugged him. He removed the huge diamond from the box and placed it on her left-hand ring finger.

"This is your official friendship ring, baby," he said.

"Shit, I'm scared to see the engagement ring, let alone the wedding jump-off!" she replied.

T Mac smiled. "Trina, you have proven to me in many ways dat you are the one for me. Besides my baby's mother, I haven't been tight wit' a chick like dis. I hope dat you don't make me feel like a fool."

Tears ran down her face. Trina knew what he was about—he was a street cat, a thug. For him to open up this much meant something to her. As far as she was concerned, this was good enough for her. He had her heart and it was all about him.

"Girl, please," Darlene was saying into the phone. "I doubt that very much. You know T like I do. And you know dat tight-ass nigga ain't spendin' no fifty thousand dollars on no bitch just like dat! And plus you know dat bitch Kelly just be talkin' to be talkin' straight up just 'cause she got a set of jaws and a pair of lips!"

Kandi interrupted her tirade. "I'm tellin' you, Darlene, he did and so did dat muthafucka Dude. They both was at Birham and they both brought diamond rings. And some serious shit at dat. They didn't buy no bullshit rings either! This I know for a fact!"

Darlene paused before answering. "I'll kill dat nigga! He just fucked me last week, dat bastard!"

"Well, I been tryin' to call Dude, but it keeps going to his voice mail. He said he was goin' away tomorrow. Probably takin' dat bitch away!" Kandi said.

"Like I said, I'll kill dat nigga!" Darlene replied, and slammed down the phone.

• • •

Soon as T Mac and Trina walked into Dude's house, Trina's cell started ringing.

She looked at the caller ID before answering. "What it be like, shorty!"

"Ain't shit, shorty," Tamika replied. "What's up wit' you?"

"Well, besides me staring at dis six-carat rock sitting on my finger—"

"Bitch, you lyin'! Dat's what da fuck is up!"

Trina heard a voice in the background at Tamika's end. "Who dat?"

"Rob ass. All hyped about takin' a shower," she answered.

"Oh, dat's what's up, bitch! Ya man is home. You 'bout to get dicked down, huh?"

Tamika laughed. "Yeah, somethin' like dat. Yo, he wanted me to tell you thank you for the money you put toward his bail. He said he gon' give it back soon as he get his grind back on."

Trina replied, "Dat's what friends are for. Let's go for lunch and drinks tomorrow."

"Dat sounds like a plan. Have fun tonight."

After hanging up, Trina took her overnight bag up into the guest bedroom and ran a bath. She took candles out of her bag and began setting them up around the sink, tub, and floor. She pulled out a long, backless, sexy, soft white silk nightgown. She had picked it up in Vegas a couple of weeks ago when she and T Mac were out there. When she was finished setting up, she called for him to join her. He walked in and got the surprise of his life. This was why he was digging her so much, he thought. She did the type of things that took him away from his crazy life.

He set the champagne and glasses down on the edge of the Jacuzzi and joined her in the tub.

The woman was sitting in the car, dressed in black. Her mind had drifted off to a place far away. Her palms were sweaty. In her hand, she held at least fourteen keys that were a possible match for the lock to his door. She put her hood to her head and got out of the car. She tiptoed to the door and began trying the keys. The fourth key turned the bottom lock. She entered the house and walked around the downstairs for a minute. She walked to the kitchen and saw a picture of the man who had once loved her. And in that very same picture, she saw him hugging the female she didn't know but hated! There was a picture of the new couple with friends. Two new women in the place where she and her friend used to be. She broke out of her daydream and stormed upstairs. She walked from room to room. When she got to one of the guest bedrooms, she saw a shine of light from the bathroom where the door was cracked open. She could see the outline of two bodies hugged up in the bed. They were asleep. She walked over to the couple and stood over them for a minute or two. Tears were running down her face. She pulled the 9mm Glock from her waist and pulled the trigger. The bullets riddled their bodies. T Mac with two bullets in his chest and one in the head. Trina with two in the head and one in the stomach. T Mac actually opened his eyes for a moment before losing consciousness. She calmly picked up the cordless phone off the charger and dialed 911.

"I just shot my ex-boyfriend and his girlfriend," she whispered into the phone. She pulled the six-carat diamond ring off the bloody finger and put it in her jacket pocket. Leaving the couple for dead, she then turned around and walked out. She noticed some neighbors who must have heard the shots running out of their home. She jumped into her car and sped off.

T Mac and Trina lay in each other's arms. Trina's brain mass was splattered on the walls and pillow.

Tamika's phone rang at about nine-forty in the morning. "Yeah," she answered with a sleepy voice.

Blossom was on the other end, excited. "What's up, sista girl! Oh, let me tell you how beautiful this place is, Mika! What you doing, sleep?"

Tamika cleared her throat. "Rob came home last night. You know he wore my ass out. So, you havin' fun?"

"Girl, you have to see this place! Anyway, I'm calling to let you know that we got here safe and to give you the number to where I'm at."

"Girl, I'm beat. Call me back and give me the number."

"Naw, take it now," Blossom insisted. "Just in case you need me."

Tamika sucked her teeth and got up to look for a pen. She wrote the number down and hung up after promising Blossom she would call her. Just as she hung up the phone rang again.

"Mika, have you spoken to Trina?" Blossom asked. "Dude's been trying to call T Mac since we got here and he can't reach him."

"I spoke to her last night. T Mac hit her off wit' a six-carat, so you know she probably still fuckin' down! But we suppose to see each otha dis afternoon for lunch. I'll tell her to tell T Mac to call Dude."

Tamika hung up then climbed on top of Rob while he slept. She kissed him on the mouth, trying to get seconds. Just when she got him where she wanted him, the phone rang again.

"I know dis better not be you again, Blossom!"

"Hello, may I ask whom I'm speaking with?" a man's voice asked.

"You called *my* house. Who's dis?"

There was a pause. "I'm sorry. This is Detective Ross, in Englewood, New Jersey. Do you know a young woman by the name of Trina Black?"

"Yes . . . I do. Wha's dis about?"

He replied, "I can't discuss it over the phone. Could you please come to the precinct as soon as possible?"

She wrote down the information the detective gave her. Her body went cold when he mentioned that she should ask for Detective Ross in Homicide.

Tamika jumped up and woke Rob up.

"Baby, get up! Rob, get up!"

She started throwing on the first thing she could get her hands on. Rob was still asleep. She started shaking him harder.

He rolled over with an attitude. "Yo, what the fuck—"

She cut him off. "Look, get up! Da police call . . . Homicide said my number was the last number dialed from Trina phone and I need to come down . . . He couldn't tell me nothin' over the phone." She started crying. "I don't understand why. I just spoke to her last night. I hope her crazy ass ain't go and do no dumb shit! I bet it's dat stupid-ass baby motha of T Mac! Damn Trina!"

Rob jumped up and threw his clothes on. Neither of them bothered to wash the sex off themselves. Tamika left messages for Kim and Shareen. The whole ride to Jersey her stomach was in knots. She kept dialing Kim and Shareen on her cell, without luck. She didn't want to bother Blossom and Dude until she found out all the details.

Thirty minutes later, they pulled into the parking lot of the police station.

They walked in and asked for Detective Ross in Homicide. The young officer at the front desk directed them to Ross's office. Tamika held on to Rob's arm, but he was just as nervous as she was. She looked around the floor when they got off the elevator. She noticed a huge cagelike space that was obviously a holding area for people in custody. She looked at the few faces in it, thinking she would see Trina. But there was no sign of her. Then a tall, brown-skinned, handsome man tapped Tamika on the shoulder. She noticed that the detective had smooth brown skin, with almond-shaped eyes and teeth as white as snow.

"Tamika, I'm the detective you spoke to on the phone. Detective Ross."

The three went into his office. Once they were seated, he offered them something to drink. Tamika didn't want anything; all she wanted was to know what was going on. The detective pulled out a sheet of paper with a photocopy of Trina's license. He slid the paper to Tamika.

"Is this Ms. Black?" he asked.

Tamika looked at the paper. "Yeah. What's goin' on?"

"Ms. Black was murdered around four A.M. this morning."

Tamika felt her stomach drop to the floor. She started shaking. The detective's words rang in his ears.

"No!" she screamed. "She can't be! I spoke to her . . . We was goin' out for lunch! . . . Where is she?! What happened? . . . I don't undastand what you tellin' me!"

She slipped out of the chair onto her knees. Rob reached down and pulled her up into his arms. He held her tight as she broke down in tears.

The detective continued. "I'm sorry. Your number was the last number dialed on her cell phone. That's how we got in contact with you. Does Ms. Black have any relatives we can inform?"

"No . . . Just her grandmotha and aunt out in Virginia. And her cousin and dem out in Long Island. Her parents aren't living. What happened? I don't undastand."

"Well, it's not much I can tell you at this point, except Ms. Black and . . ." He paused to look through some papers on his desk. "And a Mr. Terry Knoxx, according to the ID that we found, were found shot earlier this morning. Do you know who Mr. Knoxx is?"

Tamika's head was spinning at this point. She couldn't believe her ears.

"Yes, her boyfriend . . . They just got engaged last night," she whispered.

He moved from behind the desk and looked at her. "Would you happen to know his children's mother?" he asked.

Her eyebrows nose. "Why! Did dat crazy bitch have somethin' to do wit' dis!" She became hysterical.

Rob tried calming her down. "Shh . . . Baby, calm down."

Tamika looked up at the detective with red swollen eyes. "Darlene was a troublemaker."

"Excuse me?"

"His baby's mama. She was trouble from the beginning."

"Is that his children's mother's name?" he asked while jotting down everything she said.

"Yeah, dat's her name."

The detective took a deep breath, trying to figure a way to fill her in without letting her know more then she was supposed to. He felt sorry for her. He felt she should know something about her friend's death.

"Well, a young lady made a call to nine-one-one. And in that call, she stated that she had just shot her ex-boyfriend and his new girlfriend."

"Where is she now?"

He took another deep breath. "Her body is still at the house. The body cannot be moved until they finish investigating and gathering evidence. Mr. Knoxx is in the trauma unit over at First General Hospital. He's in a coma."

Tamika began to cry again. "He's still livin'? My girl is layin' dead and he's still livin'! Where's his baby mama?" she asked.

"We are working on locating her now."

Rob grabbed her and pulled her into his arms. "I'm sorry, baby," he whispered.

He didn't know what to say. He just held her in his arms.

Then, suddenly, Darlene's screams interrupted Tamika's mourning.

"I don't know what da hell you talkin' 'bout! I didn't do nothin'! Where's Terry?!" Darlene yelled.

Tamika lifted her head up from Rob's chest. It was Darlene being brought into the police station wearing handcuffs. Four suited-up officers were by her side. She was in a pair of silk pajamas. She had a pink, brown, and white Gucci silk scarf tied around her head. She was followed by a news camera and a reporter.

As the detectives were bringing her through the front doors of the station, she and Tamika made eye contact.

"You crazy bitch! You killed my best friend!" Tamika leaped at her, yelling.

Detective Ross stopped Tamika. He reassured the other officers that Tamika was okay.

In an interrogation room, Darlene was questioned over and over by several detectives. And her answers were the same every time.

"I don't know what y'all talkin' about! Where's Terry at? Y'all keep sayin' somethin' 'bout some attempted-murder shit . . . Where is he?!" Darlene shouted.

Detective Ross sat in a chair across from her and looked her straight in her eyes. "Look, Darlene, let's calm down here. Now, all we want is a little information that you may be able to help us with. Now, where were you this morning between the hours of three and four A.M.?"

She looked him in the eyes and answered, "I told you already where I was! At home wit' my kids!"

"Did anyone see you? Besides your children?" he asked.

"Look, my kids were sleep at dat time! Wait! Wait! As a matter of fact, somebody did see me. Dere was no heat, so I called the oil company twenty-four-hour line," she replied in a muffled voice.

"What time was that?" Detective Ross asked.

"One somethin', almost two. It had to be like one-forty or forty-five."

He took a deep breath. "Okay, but where were you at the time in question?"

"Look, if you let me finish . . . I called at dat time, but they didn't get to my house till over a hour after I called. I remember 'cause da mothafuckas had the nerve to charge me a dollar fifty cent a gallon after I waited over a hour. I called the office and complained. I remember sayin' to the woman I waited for over a hour and I need somethin' to compensate me for bein' inconvenienced. So she only charged me a dollar and twenty-five cent a gallon. The man didn't finish fillin' my boiler and bleedin' it—you know, to get it up workin' again—until round three forty-five."

"Okay, so you mean to tell me that the oil company delivered oil to your home around two forty-five and three A.M., 'cause you said you called them about one-forty almost two A.M., and it took them a little over a hour to reach you. Right?"

"Right."

"So that would put the oilman at your house about three or a little after three A.M. . . . . He worked on your boiler, did what he had to, and in between you had a phone conversation with someone at the oil company and everything was finished at about three-forty?"

He got up out of the chair and grabbed a pen and paper off a shelf in the room. "Okay, what's the name of the oil company?" he asked.

"Speedy Oil, in Hackensack," Darlene replied.

Detective Ross left the room after instructing two uniformed officers to watch Darlene until he returned. He called the oil company to verify Darlene's story. He also told the oil company to have the deliveryman come in for questioning.

While he was gone, Darlene sat in the room, in confusion. Who would want to kill her children's father? she kept asking herself. She began to think maybe it was drug related or something to do with business. As far as she knew, T Mac didn't have any heavy beef in the street. It was hard for her to digest the fact that he was dead.

Detective Ross offered to call Trina's family while Tamika and Rob went out to wait in the car.

Tamika hesitated to call Blossom and Dude at the hotel in Hawaii. She held the paper with their number for a long time before dialing.

"Hello." Blossom was laughing.

Tamika hesitated.

"Hello," Blossom repeated.

"Blossom . . . It's Mika . . ."

"Hey, Mika! I was just going to call you. Girl, we're having a ball! You'll never guess what we just finished doing . . . Hang gliding! And Dude ass was crying like a bitch!"

"Ya sister's lying!" Dude yelled in the background.

"Whatever! But anyway I was going to call you to tell you that we were goin' to pay for you and Rob to come down here with us! We called the travel agent and had everything set up. We tried T and Trina again, but we still couldn't reach them . . . Mika, you have to come—I'm getting married! On the beach! Just like I always used to talk about when I was a little girl. You remember?" she asked.

Tamika took a deep breath. "Baby . . . You have to come home. Now."

"Why? . . . Mika, are you crying, what's the matter?"

"Trina's dead . . . T Mac is in a coma! Please, y'all just come home!"

Blossom stood in the middle of the hotel suite holding the cordless phone with her mouth dropped open. She wasn't sure if she was hearing right. Dude stood in front of her, puzzled.

"What? What happened, Blossom?" he asked.

"What? Wait, what are you saying?!"

Blossom dropped the phone and began to cry. Dude grabbed her.

"What? What happened?!" he asked.

"Trina's been shot. She's dead! And . . . T Mac, too . . . He's in a coma!"

Dude snatched the phone from off the floor. "What is she talking about, Tamika?"

The oil company confirmed that Darlene's story was true. Ross was now waiting for the man who delivered the oil to identify Darlene as the person who actually signed for the delivery. While he waited he talked with Darlene, trying to pick her mouth.

"You sure you don't want anything to eat or drink?" he asked her. "It's been a few hours and you still haven't put nothing in your stomach."

"Naw, I'm straight. I just want to get da hell out of here! What are we waitin' for? I told you I don't know nothin' 'bout what y'all are talkin' 'bout! Why can't you tell me somethin'? Like what's goin' on wit' Terry?" She started crying again.

He replied, "We'll see about that. If you're telling the truth, we will find out in due time. Until then, why don't you tell me about you and Mr. Knoxx's relationship. I mean, he did have a new girlfriend. How did you feel about that?"

She sucked her teeth and answered, "Yeah, and . . . ? How'd you think I felt? We was together since we were young—of course I'm gonna be hurt and a little upset. But dat's life. Dat don't mean I'm gonna go on some shooting spree like a fuckin' loony!"

"Yeah, so who do you think could hate him and Ms. Black so bad? What did you say Mr. Knoxx did for a living again?"

"I didn't say."

"You know, a lot of time we are so burned by abandonment, by our mates, we tend to react without thinking. I mean, if you didn't shoot Mr. Knoxx and his new lover and maybe someone else did. You know, did it for you—"

She cut Ross off. "What?! Are you serious?! What part of 'I didn't do it' and 'I don't know what you're talkin' 'bout' don't you get! And don't I get to make a phone call and don't I have a right to a lawyer?"

Before he could reply, a man walked in and whispered in Ross's ear. The detective got up without saying anything to Darlene and stepped into the room next door. His captain, one of the detectives who'd brought Darlene in, and a tall well-built white man were standing in the room.

"This is Mr. Peters. He's the driver from the Speedy Oil," the captain said to Detective Ross.

Ross reached out his hand and shook the man's hand. "Hello. Thanks for taking the time to come in."

"No problem. Like I was just telling the captain here, anything I could do to help you public servers."

Ross turned around and looked at Darlene in the next room through the two-way mirror. "Do you recognize the young lady sitting at the table?" he asked.

"Yeah!" Peters shouted, with no hesitation. "That's the feisty lady I delivered to earlier. Boy, is she a tough cookie! She kept ranting and raving about how long it took me to come and she wasn't going to pay the full price because it shouldn't have taken me so long. She even called the office complaining to the office manager."

Ross looked at his captain, who just shrugged.

"Are you sure?" Ross asked.

"Sure I'm sure. That wasn't the first time I delivered oil to her home."

"Around what time was that, if you remember?" Ross asked.

Peters looked at a piece of paper and replied, "Well, I have my log-in sheet here. That was at . . . two fifty-two A.M. I arrived at her home and I left at three forty-eight. She insisted I stay until the water got hot to make sure everything was okay. She was a real nerve wrecker, that one!"

"Okay, thank you, Mr. Peters. You've been a great help," Ross said.

"Oh, no problem. What did she do anyway?" Peters asked.

"Nothing," Ross replied, brushing him off and walking him out of the room at the same time.

After the man was out of sight, Ross looked at his captain and asked, "What's next?"

"Well, we can't hold her here. Try and find out what you can about Mr. Knoxx from her. Like if he had any enemies. And have someone escort her to the hospital to see him. Have you contacted his family?" the captain asked.

"As far as I know, he only has his brother. And he's on his way back from Hawaii," Ross replied.

Ross went back into the room where he'd been questioning Darlene.

"Look, Darlene . . . This is very important, are you sure you don't know anyone that might want to harm Mr. Knoxx?"

"Look, I don't know what's going on! I just wanna know where my kids' father is!"

He handed her some tissues to wipe her eyes. "Okay. I'll have someone escort you to General, where Mr. Knoxx is being treated. And please, if you hear or find out any information, let me know." He handed her a card.

She snatched the card. "Dat's it! You hold me in here half da fuckin' day and dat's all you have to say to me!"

As soon as she left the police station, Darlene called her house and told her cousin Tee Tee to take the kids to her sister's house and bring a pair of jeans and sneakers to the hospital. Tee Tee told Darlene that Darlene's cell phone kept on ringing, but she wasn't answering it. Darlene told her to bring the phone to the hospital with her.

Darlene's cousin arrived at the hospital minutes after her. She had a Gucci shopping bag with a jogging suit, sneakers, a baseball cap, and her cell phone. Darlene went into the restroom and changed her clothes. Since cell phones were not allowed on the floor, she went back outside and called Kandi.

Kandi picked up on the second ring. "Darlene . . . Where you at? I been callin' you all day." Her voice was shaking.

"Kandi, somethin' bad happened—"

Kandi cut her off. She started crying. "I know, Darlene . . . It's bad, I know."

Darlene immediately started crying, too. "Where you at?" she asked.

"At a hotel . . . I don't know where to go." She started talking off the wall. "You know I was always there for Dude. Like you was there for T, right? And both of them just turned their backs on us! That muthafucka Dude wit' dat young bitch . . . I showed his ass! Him and her!"

"What da fuck you talkin' 'bout, Kandi?" Darlene asked.

Kandi pulled the ring out of her pocket. "Well, I left dat bitch ringless! Da nerve of him, spending all dat money on a ring for dat bitch!"

"Kandi, what are you sayin' to me?" Darlene asked.

"Look, you of all people know what he put me through! I had no other choice. I tried everything to rid him out of my life, out my mind! Nothin' worked! Well, I found a way. Da bitch just happen to be dere! And . . . And when I saw her lying dere wit' him, like I use to, I lost it!"

Darlene's heart was beating so hard it felt like it was bursting out of her chest.

"Kandi . . . Please tell me you not sayin' what I think you are! Kandi, what are you sayin'?"

Kandi laughed. "Shit, I shot Dude and dat bitch! It happened so fast I'm not even sure how many times. I do know it was a lot of times! I walked into his house and saw the pictures, the champagne, and dis fuckin' ring! And I shot dem!"

Darlene was in shock; it was like her heart had dropped to the floor.

She heard every word Kandi had said, but couldn't believe what Kandi was saying. "Tell me where you at, girl!"

Kandi told her where she was and the two hung up.

When Darlene got back into the hospital, she was crying hysterically. Her cousin Tee Tee tried to figure out what was going on. They still hadn't made it upstairs to see T Mac.

Darlene started dialing on her cell phone.

"Detective Ross speaking."

"Dis is Darlene. I just got a call from Kandi—dat's Terry's brother's ex. Me and her is tight, too. She was real fucked up over breaking up with his brother. She called me, talkin' crazy 'bout how she fixed him and the girl real good."

"Isn't his brother on his way back from Hawaii?"

"Yeah. She thought she was shooting Terry's brother and his girlfriend."

"Where did this Kandi say she was at?" he asked while putting his jacket on.

"She at a hotel," Darlene replied.

"Did she tell you what hotel and where?"

"Yeah, she told me, but look, she's not too right in her head. Maybe I should call her back."

"No," the detective told her. "You should just tell me where she is."

"I knew dat bitch was crazy! I told Trina ta watch her!" Kim shouted, with tears running down her cheek. Tamika was sitting in a kitchen chair rocking back and forth, tears running down her face as well. Shareen held her in her arms, trying to console her. There was no comfort zone for the girls. It was like a piece of them had been taken away from them. Tamika broke down. She jumped to her feet and started throwing everything off the table. Kim and Shareen grabbed her and held her tight.

"Come on . . . It's goin' to be all right, Mika," Shareen whispered in her ear.

Just then the phone rang. Kim answered it while the girls continued talking.

"Tamika, the phone. It's Trina's grandmotha."

The room got silent.

"Hello, Grandma Black."

Tamika answered the woman's questions as best she could before Grandma Black said, "I'll be up there in the morning, baby. You just hold your head and pray, sweetie. You hear me?"

Trina was her baby. She had raised her since she was about six months old. Trina's mother left her at Grandma Black's house one evening and never came back. She called about six months after and never really kept in contact since. Trina told the girls years ago that from what she knew, her mother was young when she had her and just didn't want to be bothered. Trina said her mother had met an older man after having Trina and he did not like kids too much. It never really bothered Trina, though. She was just fine with Grandma Black raising her. And Grandma Black made sure she didn't leave New York until her baby was of age. Now, deep down inside, Grandma Black felt like that was the worst decision she had made in her life. She knew she couldn't help what happened to Trina, but still, a little part of her blamed herself.

"It's almost two in da mornin'. Where is Blossom?" Shareen asked. "They landed hours ago."

"She went with Dude to the police station and the hospital," Tamika answered.

Just as she spoke she heard Blossom's keys opening the door. They all jumped up and ran to the front of the apartment.

The first thing they noticed was Blossom's eyes. She had also been doing a lot of crying.

"What happened? How's Dude?" Tamika asked.

Blossom hugged the girls as they all walked back to the kitchen.

"It's so bad . . . Dude is broken down. His heart is shot! And . . .

T Mac looks so bad, you can't even tell who he is. His head is so swollen and his hair is shaved off. He has all types of tubes coming out of him. It was suppose to be me! Not Trina . . . Me! *Why!*" She hugged her sister tightly and cried.

Kim sat Blossom down at the kitchen table and spoke with concern. "It's okay, sweetie. Have you eaten, are you thirsty?"

Blossom shook her head no and continued crying.

Tamika cried harder. "No! It wasn't supposed to be you! Don't say that! It wasn't supposed to be neither one of you!" Tamika rocked her. "Shh . . . It's okay, boo."

Blossom pulled away. "No, really! It wasn't Darlene! It was Kandi. She thought T Mac and Trina was me and Dude! She killed Trina, not Darlene!"

The girls were shocked. Blossom went on to explain everything to them. It was a sad night for the girls. It hadn't been this sad since Kim's sister passed away.

T Mac woke up from his coma two days later, but went into cardiac arrest after he was told about Trina. T Mac insisted, to his brother, that he leave the hospital to go to the funeral. He was weak and had lost a lot of weight. But he wouldn't have it any other way.

Meanwhile, Kandi was locked up, facing murder and attempted-murder charges. Her lawyer was trying to convince the prosecutor Kandi wasn't in her right state of mind when she committed the crimes. Dude was all but lifeless. He still could not believe that Kandi had gone bananas like that. He kept thinking how it could have been him and Blossom lying in the bed that night. Deep inside, he blamed himself for Trina's murder and his brother's condition. There were a lot of mixed feelings and blame going on among a lot of people. Darlene was angry with Kandi and a little angry with Dude for not being at home that night. Then there was Trina's family. Well, you can imagine what went on at the funeral.

5

The girls could have been mistaken for a singing group, they looked so elegant, all in black, of course. Each of them wore her hair pulled back in a neat bun. Each had a large white flower like Billie Holiday pinned on the side of her hair. Trina had loved Billie Holiday and always told the girls when she got married she didn't care what her bridesmaids wore; she just wanted them to wear their hair pulled back neatly with a big flower pinned on the side. She said if she were living back in those days, she would be like Billie had been.

Trina was well known around the way, so there were about two dozen cars that followed the two stretch limos. One carried Trina's grandmother, her aunt, and her cousins. The other one carried her other family . . . her best friends. And they shed two teardrops for every raindrop that fell that day. They were the last to enter the church. There was standing room only. There were flowers everywhere. T Mac had paid for everything. Everyone in the room stopped when the girls entered the room. They held on to one another as they walked up to the casket and broke down one by one. Dude pushed his brother in his wheelchair and oxygen tank up to the casket. Teddy and Black followed behind them.

"You have the nerve to show your face here, mothafucker! It's all your fault my niece is dead!" Trina's aunt shouted as she leaped at T Mac in his wheelchair. Trina's cousins had to pull her away. Dude pushed T Mac out of the church; he never looked back. Teddy and Black walked out behind them. Trina's grandmother got up and followed; she caught them before they got into their limo.

"Excuse me, son," she called out to T Mac.

He turned around. "Yes . . ."

She walked down the church stairs.

"Hello. I'm Grandma Black. Please excuse my daughter. She's just in a lot of pain. She and my grandbaby were close," she said.

"No problem, I understand . . . I'm really sorry . . . Trina talked about you all the time." Tears came to his eyes. "We were coming down to see you . . ." T Mac could not continue.

She continued for him. "I know. She called and said you all were . . . It was suppose to be this weekend. She spoke highly of you, Terry. I just want you to know I don't blame you for my baby's death, sweetheart. I can't judge you; only God can judge us. Please don't hold blame for this in your heart. If you do, you won't never be able to go on with your life."

T Mac wiped the tears from his eyes and face. He reached his arm up to embrace her. The two hugged and said their good-byes with promises to keep in contact. Just as she got back to the church steps he reached into his pocket and pulled out the diamond ring he had given Trina the night before she died.

"Grandma Black!" he called out to her.

She turned around and walked back over to Dude and Black. "Yes, baby?"

He handed her the diamond ring. "Could you please put this back on her? I gave her this ring earlier that night?"

The two again said good-bye. When she went back into the church, Grandma Black did what T Mac had asked and placed the ring on her granddaughter's finger.

When the casket was lowered into the ground, a piece of the girls' hearts went with it.

Tamika had food and drinks at her house after the service. Another thing Trina had always said was "Shit, when I die, I don't want mutha-fuckas standin' round cryin' and shit! I want to party. Food and drinks.

And don't forget the music! And I'll come back and haunt the person that makes it go down any other way!"

Enlarged pictures of Trina lined the room. One of Trina the night they all went to the mansion party. One of Trina and T Mac on the beach in Aruba. And another of her with the rest of the girls when they were younger. Each picture sat on an easel-like stand in Tamika's living room. People would stand and stare at the pictures, throughout the evening, their eyes filled with disbelief and hearts filled with pain.

6   *A month later*

Blossom was sitting up in the bed; she had tried to go back to sleep but couldn't. She looked over at the clock on her bedroom wall. It read seven-thirty. It was seven-thirty in the morning and she must have had only three hours of sleep. She got out of the bed and put on her house slippers. She caught her reflection in the mirror as she walked out of the bedroom. She walked over to the mirror and got a closer look at herself.

She whispered to herself, "You look like shit."

She threw her housecoat on and went into the kitchen. Tamika was already there, at the kitchen table.

"You know what, Blossom?" Tamika began. "I been thinkin' a lot. And you know what I came up wit'? If ya young ass would've listened to me 'bout fuckin' wit' Dude, just maybe Trina would be alive! Kandi would have no reason ta wanna kill him!"

"I don't believe you, Tamika! You know that girl was crazy! Even if I wasn't with him, she would have been flipping out," Blossom shouted.

"Yeah, but she would've been flippin' 'bout anotha bitch! And if you wasn't in the picture, just maybe he wouldn't have been in Hawaii. And if he wasn't in Hawaii, he wouldn't have needed Trina and T Mac to stay at his place!"

Blossom just stared at her sister. She couldn't believe what she was hearing. Was Tamika really blaming her for Trina's death?

"Are you trying to say it was my fault?" Blossom asked.

"You think about it and answer dat ya'self!" Tamika shouted, and walked out of the kitchen and into her bedroom.

Blossom stood in the middle of the kitchen with tears running down her face. She started to follow after Tamika. But when she heard her bedroom door slam and lock, she returned to her own room.

First, Dude had acted distant with her and now Tamika was flipping out on her. She'd noticed the changes in Tamika's attitude, but she thought she was just still going through it about Trina. Suddenly Blossom felt like she had no one. Nobody was concerned about how she felt or what she was going through. That was supposed to be her and her boyfriend's body filled up with bullets. And Trina had been like family to her, too. Why doesn't anyone see that? she thought.

She picked up her cell phone and dialed Dude.

He picked up on the third ring. "What's up?"

"Nothing. What's up with you?" she asked.

"Just working. I'm at the office, one of the rigs broke down. I'm waiting for the people to come back and tow it to get it fixed."

"Oh . . . So what happened to you last night? I waited until three in the morning for you. You didn't show or call."

"I'm sorry. I got caught up."

"So you don't call or nothing?" she asked.

"I know that was my bad."

"Dude, what's the problem? Is there a problem with us I should know about?"

"No."

"What do you mean, no? You've totally flipped the script on me and you're telling me there isn't a problem?"

"Look, Blossom . . . I'm just going through a lot right now. With my brother, my work—"

"And you think I'm not going through shit, Dude! We're suppose to be there for each other. We're never supposed to turn our backs on one another! We made a pact. Remember that?!"

He paused before answering. "Yes, I remember . . ." He swallowed and said, "Kandi's lawyer called me. He wants me to testify on Kandi's behalf. You know, they're pleading not guilty by reason of insanity. And, um . . . They need me to testify about how I had her going to a shrink. They want me to explain how she took the breakup and everything."

There was a long silence before Blossom spoke.

"And what did you tell him?" she asked.

"Nothing yet . . . I haven't given him an answer."

"Well, what . . . What do you think you're going to do?"

"Don't know."

"Why don't you know? I mean, you can't seriously be thinking on doing it?"

There was a long silence between the two of them before he answered.

"I might—"

She cut him off again. "What! How could you run to that bitch's rescue?! After she murdered Trina and almost killed your brother! And news flash, that bitch was coming to kill me and you, Dude! And now you're telling me something about testifying on her behalf?!"

"You have to look at it in a different way."

"Oh, really! What way is that? 'Cause that's the only way I see it!"

"Blossom, Kandi is really sick in the head. And in a way it's my fault . . . It's the least I can do."

"What the fuck ever, Dude! It's *your* fault 'cause *she* didn't know how to let go! It's the least you could do, you say! So answer me this . . . What if it was me and not Trina? Let's just say Kandi got to me like she wanted to. Would you still feel like you owe her something!"

"Baby, please don't—"

"Please don't what!" Tears came to her eyes.

"Please don't go there. Don't question my love for you or how much I love."

"Well, you have a funny way of showing it! I mean, it was only a month ago we snuck off and almost got married and it seems you're suddenly tired of me. We haven't slept in the same bed more than five, six times since we came back from Hawaii! You know what? Do what you want! I got nothing else to say to you!"

She hung the phone up.

Dude sat at his desk with his mind rattled. Just like Blossom, he felt that nobody knew how he felt. He was truly through with Kandi after this stunt. He felt like he could wrap his hands around her neck and squeeze the dear life out of her. The same way she squeezed them bullets into Trina and his brother. He thought of the past, when he and Kandi had been together. She'd been nothing like how she was now.

He broke out of his daydream and looked at his watch. It read a quarter after eight. He jumped up. Black was downstairs waiting for him in the driver's seat of the Jeep.

T Mac had started having trouble breathing a week ago. The shooting left one of his lungs badly damaged. Despite his condition, Dude wanted to go and speak to his brother about what the lawyer wanted him to do. He needed to see how his brother felt about it. He knew what T Mac's feelings were going to be. He felt like he had to let him know about the phone call from Kandi's lawyer regardless. Out of respect.

Dude headed up to the prison to see Kandi. He was so much in a daze, he barely realized when they arrived.

"I won't be long," he told Black, before getting out of the Jeep.

Dude waited in the visiting room with palms sweaty for ten minutes. Kandi was being held in the mentally disturbed section of the prison. The CO said she was on meds, so he didn't know what to expect once she came out. Then the steel electric doors slid open and there she was. Hair pulled back into one long braid. No makeup, no designer clothes, and no shiny jewelry.

She slowly walked over to the table Dude was sitting at. He could tell she was medicated.

"Hey," she whispered as she sat down.

"What's up, Kandi?" he said.

"Who'da known it would've taken this to finally get you to sit down and talk to me," she joked.

He wasn't sure how to react. "So . . . you wanted to see me."

"Yeah, I did." She smiled. "If only you would've agreed to meet me a month and a half ago. Maybe I wouldn't be sitting here with you."

"Is that what you wanted to see me for?"

"Not exactly," she said, taking a deep breath. "I just came up with that one. Can you tell Terry I'm sorry? And Darlene, too. She won't take my calls or answer my mail."

"Can you blame her?"

"I guess not. But, anyway, tell Terry what I said."

"I don't think my brother really cares about your apology at this point. He's laid up in the hospital with a lung that might have to be removed. Not to mention the metal plate in his head, compliments of the bullet you left in it."

"You know, you really hurt me." She held her head down. "It was like you loved me to death one day and then said the hell with me the next . . . All I knew was you, and you knew that! I was there for you through thick and thin. You said we had a bond! Remember, we had a pact!"

Dude felt like he was having déjà vu. She sounded like Blossom earlier on the phone.

"All you talk about is you. Do you realize what you have done, Kandi? Do you know how many lives you've ruined?"

"Do you realize that you need to share some of that blame with me?" she came back.

He wanted to reach across the table and wring her neck! But he felt like she was telling the truth.

"You're sick!"

"Yeah, I know. That's what my lawyer is trying to make the DA understand." She smiled as if she had no remorse for the crimes she had committed.

She continued. "Since we're on the topic of my lawyer, did he call you?"

"Yeah, I spoke to him."

"Well, what did you say?"

"Say about what?"

" 'Bout testifying on my behalf."

"I didn't say." He got up and walked away.

"Good-bye, Kandi."

The whole ride back from the prison, Dude's thoughts were on over-drive. This whole thing with Kandi, and the problems between him and Blossom. Maybe it was him. Maybe he had bad luck with women. He never had problems when it came to girls he just fucked. He was going through his own shit. He felt like he couldn't tend to Blossom's needs like she wanted. The only thing for him to do was to shut down. He felt like he never thought about himself and always about other people. But deep inside, he knew it was different with Blossom.

"Call Teddy and see if he's ready," Dude instructed Black as they pulled back into the lot of the office.

"I called before you came out and told him to get ready," Black replied.

Teddy pulled up as the two men were going up to the office. Dude waved for him to park around the back.

Dude sat behind his desk. "This is our last pickup for the year. After this one, we won't re-up until about six months. I packed up the dough last night and loaded it onto the truck." He was serious.

"I would've helped you, Dude," Black said.

"Naw, it's aight. I zipped through it in three hours. We're going to take the same route that you took last time. When we pull into the warehouse, you'll stay to the left and go around. Park on the side and walk to the back, to the shipping and receiving."

Black and Teddy nodded yes. Dude got up and went into the bath-room to change his clothes. He returned ten minutes later dressed like a true truck driver. He wore a dingy jeans baseball cap pulled down over his sunglasses, and a pair of gator cowboy boots he called his "lucky pair of feet."

Dude had to drive the truck with the money, since T Mac was in the hospital. They had nearly a million dollars in it. The money was in stacked barrels filled with coffee.

He'd been dealing with Fernando and his sons for years. Dude's supply had grown a lot since he began and he had established a friendship with Fernando.

Fernando was an older Dominican man, in his mid-fifties. He started dealing one-on-one with Dude about two years ago and they hadn't had one problem since. Fernando liked Dude's style. He watched Dude, a young boy who'd run into big money, but instead of going crazy and wasting it, had invested it in a legit business. And that's what Fernando liked about Dude. He had heart. He took a chance most men from his generation would not have taken.

Dude pulled into Fernando's warehouse. Teddy and Black proceeded according to Dude's instructions. Three men walked Dude, Black, and Teddy down a stretch of stairs. Black and Teddy were told to wait outside of the room while Dude went in to see Fernando. This was the routine. Neither Black nor Teddy had ever met Fernando. They wouldn't even have known him if they bumped into him in the street.

Dude sat on the plush leather couch in Fernando's office. Fernando gave him a big hug hello.

"Dude, my man!" Fernando said.

"Hey, Fernando. How's things?" Dude replied.

They both sat down on the couch.

"I no see you face in long time, my friend," Fernando stated in his thick accent.

"I know. I sent my brother last time. And the time before that you were in DR."

"Yes, yes. I need break from dis crazy place!" He paused. "Speakin' 'bout you brotha. I'm sorry what happen to him and his girlfriend. Me and my sons send flowers to church. Dat was no good ting what Kandi has done. How's you brotha?"

"He's back in the hospital. You know, one of his lungs is fucked up bad," Dude told him.

"You and you family is in my prayers. Now, on anotha note. I don't know if my son tell you, but I have to go back to my country for a while."

Dude shook his head. "No, he didn't tell me."

"Well, I leave soon. For longer time den I usually gone for . . . Now, we been doin' business wit' you for long time. And I trust you and you people. I know you type of man dat wouldn't deal wit' no shitty people. Well, reason I'm goin' home for long time is I'm doin' a big big ting in my country! A resort. And I want to give you opportunity to be my partner. I do not know where you stand far as you financially situation. But dis is good ting for you. And I watch how you move for a lotta years and you have good business mind."

Fernando took out a large envelope from his safe.

"Come make me show you sometin'."

He handed Dude the envelope. "Look here, dis is everyting."

Dude looked at the papers in the envelope. It was the blueprints for the resort, a full budget, and copies of all the legal paperwork, liquor licenses, and work permits. After a few moments, Dude put the documents back in the envelope and asked, "Two and a half million, huh?"

"Yes, my friend, but you will make back dat and more," Fernando answered.

"No, don't get me wrong, I trust you. Is it okay if I take this with me and sleep on it?"

Fernando smiled. "Yes. No problem. Dat you copy anyway. Now, down to our otha business."

Dude felt honored that a man like Fernando would even consider giving him an opportunity like this one. He knew Fernando was a very low-key man. Filthy rich, but low-key.

After dropping the money and picking up the load of heroin, Dude went straight home. He let Black and Teddy take care of the load. He sat in his living room thinking. Thinking harder than he had in a long time. He was ready for a change. He thought about calling Blossom.

Any other time she would be the first person he would have called. As a matter of fact, the *only* person he would have called. Something was wrong. He knew it, but he just didn't know what it was. He had created so much distance between them. You know that kind of thing, where you do something but you don't realize what you've done until it's done? And you're so deep into the bullshit you've done, you can't see your way out. Usually with situations like that, we end up digging our hole deeper instead of backtracking and fixing what we fucked up. Well, that's where Dude was. In a tough spot, with his back against the wall.

Dude decided to take Fernando up on his offer. This would mean he would have to go out to the Dominican Republic next week. He wished his brother was able to go with him. He thought of taking Black with him, but if he took him, who would look after things while he was gone? Teddy was the only other person he had on his team that was qualified to handle business. And still Dude needed someone to look over Teddy. It was complicated. Too complicated for him to think about at that moment.

He picked up his Nextel and dialed Blossom's number. He hung up as soon as he heard her voice mail. He tried two more times. He called her town house and got no answer there either. He called over to her room phone in Brooklyn and got nothing. He started getting edgy. He dialed Tamika's number.

"Hello."

"Hey, Tamika, how are you? Is Blossom around?" he asked.

"Naw, she went out a couple of hours ago. Call her cell."

"I tried calling, but her machine keeps picking up."

"She musta left it here. I'll tell her you called." She just hung up in his ear.

He was feeling angry. He could not find Blossom and he was not used to that. He had been neglecting her because he was going through his own shit. He poured a shot of tequila and took it to the head. Four more followed. After some time passed, he looked at his watch. It read 11:41. He figured Blossom should be home in Brooklyn or New Jersey by now. He tried her at the town house again and still got no answer. He was starting to get worried, but as soon as he was about to hang up, his cell phone rang. He looked at the caller ID and saw it was Blossom.

"Oh, now you want to call back?" he asked by way of a greeting.

She sucked her teeth. "What? I left the phone in the car. Besides, you haven't been wanting to be bothered with me anyway."

He just looked at the phone and let out a little smirk.

"Yeah, okay, Blossom. But anyway, where are you?"

"I'm out."

"Yeah? Out where?"

"With a couple of my friends."

"Aight, joke's up. Where you at?"

"I'm in the city about to walk out of China Grill."

"Oh, you taking people to our spots now?" he responded with a giggle.

"Whatever. When I called a certain person, they didn't want to pick up their phone."

"I was busy. I been trying to call you all night. Why weren't you picking up your phone?" he asked.

"I was in the restaurant."

"All night?"

"No. I went to Macy's earlier. You might have called while I was inside of the store. What's up, baby?"

"Nothing. I want you to come over here now."

"What's the matter?"

"Why does something have to be wrong? I just need to talk to you."

"Okay, I'm on my way now."

After she hang up, Blossom turned to Lil' Richie and said, "I have to go. I'm sorry."

Lil' Richie knew what was up. He knew Blossom was not ever going to be his. He just smiled and kissed her on the cheek. The two went their separate ways.

7

When Blossom walked into the house, Dude was on the living-room couch asleep. The only light came from the television. She went over and kissed him softly on the mouth. He opened his eyes and smiled. He grabbed her gently and began to kiss her passionately. He slowly undressed her. She hadn't been touched by him in a while, so it didn't take much for her to come out of her clothes.

As soon as he entered her they both wanted to explode. He tried to hold back. With each stroke, they almost let go.

"I love you, baby," she whispered in his ear as she rode him.

He held her hips and guided her movement. "I love you, too, baby," he whispered back.

"Please don't never leave me, baby . . . Oh . . . Oh. I'm coming, baby. I'm coming!" she shouted.

"Me, too, baby! I'm coming, too! You better not ever give nobody my pussy!" he shouted back.

They both reached their climax together.

The two lay in each other's arms after making love. He stroked her back with his fingertips. He was waiting for the right time to tell her his decision about Fernando's offer.

"I might be going away for a while," Dude whispered.

Blossom sat up. "Go where?"

"To DR with Fernando."

She jumped up. "To DR?"

"Yeah," he answered.

"For what? I mean, when you say for a while, do you mean a long time?" she asked in confusion.

"The first trip may be only for a couple of weeks—"

"Wait a minute. What do you mean, first trip? How many times are you planning on going down there?"

"Look, a good business opportunity has been presented to me. I mean a really good one and I'm going to jump on it."

"Like what?" she asked.

He got up and retrieved the paperwork Fernando had given him. He turned on the light and handed it to Blossom. After a few minutes, she set the papers down on the table.

"Are you sure this is something you want to do?" she asked.

He paused for a minute before answering. "Yes. I'm sure. What do you think?"

She sat silent for a minute. "Well, from a business aspect, it is a good thing. It looks like a good investment. But from a personal level, it sucks. I know that I won't be seeing you as much once you take this on."

He knew that she was right. But he also knew that this was an offer he couldn't refuse.

"Do you think you'll be able to deal with it?" he asked.

"I guess so."

She knew she wasn't telling the truth. But it was what sounded good at that moment.

8 *A month later*

Dude was rushing around his house trying to pack. Blossom was in the bathroom gathering his toiletries.

"Baby, you seen my passport!"

She walked into the bedroom and opened the top drawer of one of the dressers.

She pulled out the passport and handed it to him. "It's right where you put it last night."

He took it and kissed her on the mouth.

"I'm going to run to the hospital to see T real quick. I'll be right back," Dude said.

Blossom looked at her watch. "You think we'll still be able to eat before you leave?"

He went over to her and pulled her into his arms. He hugged her tight for a few moments and then kissed her on her forehead.

"I promise I will be back in time."

She watched him through the bedroom window as he got into his car and pulled off. Blossom sat on the bed in tears. She was not sure why, but she felt like her world had been crumbling since that night of the shooting. Dude hadn't been the same, but she knew that she had to let him do what he had to do.

When Dude arrived, T Mac's room was empty and his bed was made. He immediately rushed to the nurses' station.

"Where's my brother?"

The nurse hesitated.

"Where's my brother?" He shouted louder this time.

"Here is the doctor. Maybe you should speak to him."

"Doctor, what's going on? Where's my brother?" Dude asked.

The doctor gestured Dude to follow him. "Come over here where we can talk."

Dude followed him down the hall and into his office. The doctor got a beep and excused himself from the room. Dude sat in the office and looked around. He read all of the certificates framed in expensive frames. He noticed the photos on the doctor's desk. There was a big picture of a young woman. She had long thick curly black hair. She was sitting on the beach with big round glasses. He knew the glasses were Chanel. He had bought the same pair for Blossom. The frame had seashells on the bottom. It had HAWAII written in script on the bottom. There were many pictures on the desk, but the one that really caught his eye was of the doctor and the young woman with the thick black hair. In that same picture, three children sat in front of the couple. Three children—two boys and a girl—sitting in front of them with huge smiles.

The doctor came back into the room, interrupting Dude's thoughts about his future with Blossom.

"I'm sorry about that," the doctor began. "Terry had to be moved back to ICU. He's developed a very bad infection in his chest and is unable, at this time, to breathe on his own. The one lung that was strong is now weak. As I suspected, the type of head injury your brother had was very uncommon."

Dude was confused. "But I thought that the metal plate was supposed to help?"

"Yes, and it has. It's just that when you're dealing with injury and damage to the head and brain . . . well, it's tricky. Terry has a little fluid in his brain that we have to drain. All of this has taken a big toll on your brother's body. And even though he is a strong young man, his body is just not strong enough now. This morning he began having seizures. I don't want you to see him and be thrown off by all of the machines. He's in a lot of pain, so we had to sedate him. You can talk to him, but he can't talk to you."

Dude couldn't believe what he was hearing. His brother had been making progress and now everything was falling apart. His heart started beating rapidly.

"Can I lose him?" Dude asked.

The doctor took another deep breath and Dude knew the answer.

"Yes, it is possible. But not likely."

Dude stood to his feet. "Can I see him now?"

Once they got to the ICU, Dude suited up in a gown, cap, and mask. This wasn't a new procedure to him. He'd been to see T many times before, but this time tears were streaming down his face. He saw T's lifeless body. He stood over him and T Mac slowly opened his eyes. T Mac smiled at his brother.

He tried to talk, but the long tube in his mouth prevented him. Dude got a piece of paper and pencil for T Mac. T Mac's hand shook as he tried to write.

I thought you was leaving, he wrote.

Dude shook his head up and down.

"Yeah, I am supposed to leave later on, but I can't leave with you back in ICU."

T Mac reached for the paper and pencil again. *Nigga, please. If you don't get on that plane! I'm gon' be straight. Trina told me so. I saw her and I wanted to go with her, but she wouldn't let me. She said I couldn't go with her. I had to come on my own. She just wanted to say she loved me.*

Dude didn't know what to say. He thought his brother was hallucinating from the medication.

Dude tried to reason with his brother. "Man, you just high off them painkillers. If the shit you taking was on the street . . . Shit! I don't feel right breaking out with you in here."

T Mac shook his head. He wrote to Dude pleading for him to go because it was a good opportunity. He asked how Blossom was doing.

After thirty minutes, T Mac fell back into a deep sleep. Dude held his brother's hand and kissed him on his forehead good-bye.

Blossom was waiting for Dude on the living-room couch when he came back to the town house. He headed toward the stairs without speaking.

"What happened?" she asked.

He told her and then continued upstairs to get his bags. When he returned to the living room, he noticed Blossom was still sitting in the same place he had left her.

"What's the problem? You don't want to get something to eat?"

She took a deep breath. "You mean you're still going?"

"Yes, I'm still going. You don't think I should go?"

She stood up and put her hands on her hips. "What do you think?"

"I spoke with my brother. I told him I was going to stay and he insisted that I continue with my plans."

"Just because he said you should go don't mean that you should still break out while he's in ICU."

"What are you talking about?"

She began to speak louder. "I'm talking about you being selfish! I'm talking about this person you've turned into! I'm talking about you being an inconsiderate motherfucker!"

He looked at her like she was crazy. "Yo, what the fuck are you talking about, Blossom! If you feel like you want to say something to me, please say it! But don't try to use me and my brother's situation as a smoke screen! It sounds like you have some type of anger you're holding in. Let it out!" he shouted.

"Don't try to use reverse psychology on me! Don't you think I should be a little bitter—"

"Bitter about what?" he asked.

She screwed up her face. "About what? You have the nerve to ask me about what! Um . . . for starters, how you've been treating me. We went from sleeping next to each other almost every night to barely seeing each other! You have completely turned your back on me. How did you think I felt after? You didn't even bother to ask me! Then all of a sudden you're just up and leaving out of the country."

"You ungrateful, inconsiderate bitch! Listen to you! All you're spitting out your mouth is about you! You are not the only one going through shit, you know! And how dare you use my brother and your selfish-ass wants me to stay! This has nothing to do with me leaving T Mac! I don't know what you rampin' and ravin' about: you have everything and you didn't have to work for nothing! You have your own crib and car! Shit, you got a man with five cars! You have what most girls would die for!"

"What most girls would die for, Dude? Like Trina?"

He just looked at her for a few moments. Then picked up his bags and opened the front door.

He turned to her before walking out. "The number to where I'm staying is on top of the dresser. I left five Gs for you up there, too. Call Black if you need more."

He walked out, leaving Blossom sitting on the couch in a rage.

She jumped up and ran upstairs to the bedroom closet. She grabbed a shoe box from the top shelf. She sat in the middle of the bedroom floor going through papers in the shoe box. She found a stack of letters Kandi had sent Dude. She jotted down Kandi's inmate ID number. She put the box of letters back on the top shelf and left the house.

Then she raced toward the correctional facility where Kandi was being held.

Blossom sat in the car for a half an hour before getting out. She did not know why she'd come to the prison. She needed to see Kandi face-to-face; the person that was responsible for turning her life upside down.

Blossom filled out the registration forms and showed her photo ID to the CO. She took off all her jewelry and put it in a locker. She emptied everything out of her pockets and put it in the same locker, along with her pocketbook. Her heart pounded rapidly as she walked through security and down to the visiting area. She didn't know how Kandi was going to react when she saw her face. A CO explained the rules to Blossom. Being that Kandi was a mental inmate.

It felt like a long time that Blossom sat in the waiting area. Her palms were sweaty. Finally, she heard the steel doors open. There she was face-to-face with the person who had murdered one of her best friends. Kandi looked nothing like she had the night of the mansion party. She wore no makeup and not one piece of jewelry. Her hair was braided into two cornrows. She sported a bright orange jumpsuit instead of a designer getup. Her hands were cuffed in front of her.

Kandi stopped in her tracks when she realized who her visitor was. She sat down and looked Blossom directly in the face.

"What you here for, girl?" Kandi asked.

Blossom didn't answer for a few moments. "Not too sure yet. I guess I just wanted to see you . . . Ask you some questions."

Kandi laughed at her. "Are you serious? Dude know you up here?"

"No."

"Aight, so what you wanna ask me?" Kandi cut to the chase.

"What would make you do something like that? I mean, do you have that much hate in your heart that you would want to take my life? Why would you want to ruin your own life?"

Kandi looked Blossom in her eyes. "Love. It wasn't about you or me."

Blossom squinted her eyes in confusion. "What?"

"You asked me what would make me do something like dat? I said love. You asked me if I had that much hate in my heart for you? I said it wasn't really about you. You asked me why would I want to ruin my own life? I said I wasn't thinking about my life."

Blossom sat in silence again. She'd had so many questions in her head when she was on her way up to the jail. And now she couldn't remember any of them.

"Look," Kandi went on. "I'm sorry about your friend and T Mac. Shit, he's my best friend's baby daddy. It was suppose to be you and Dude . . . But honestly, at the time I was not in my right state of mind. You will never understand how I feel 'cause you don't know about the love that we once shared. He was all I knew. Could you imagine that?

And then, out the blue, from left field that person just flips the script on you. Trust me; it was a slow process that sped up before my eyes. It was Dude that drove me crazy. Not me who drove me crazy. I have to live with what I've done."

Some of the things Kandi said sounded familiar to Blossom. They reminded her of her own thoughts.

"How's Terry? Darlene won't take my calls or answer my letters."

"Terry's back in ICU."

"Damn! I really fucked up this time! I thought me taking my own life would fix it. It would bring some sort of satisfaction to those that I have hurt. That's why they have me cuffed like this. They say I'm capable of harming myself."

"And are you?" Blossom asked.

"What you think?" Kandi paused, then asked, "Has Dude flipped the script on *you* yet?"

Blossom just sat there. She didn't understand how Kandi's attitude could change so quickly.

Kandi was on a roll. "Oh, yeah, watch out, 'cause he has a temper. He will knock you upside your head. Yeah, I know him well. I was with him when he didn't have as much as he does now. I watched him grow. And he thinks materialistic things can substitute for love and time. Watch out 'cause you can fall victim to that materialistic bullshit. And you best believe dat he's a ladies' man. He'll have you think it's all about you. And next thing you know, he's got two other chicks on the side. But he'll think just because you are wifey, it's suppose to be okay with you."

With that, Kandi stood up and started to walk off. But she suddenly turned back and said, "Girl, you got your hands full with that one dere. Yup, he's a doozy."

And as a parting shot: "And please don't come back up here again. I don't never want to see your face again in my life!" Kandi shouted.

Blossom sat and watched Kandi disappear behind the heavy steel door.

• • •

The day was sunny in the Dominican Republic. It was set up for Dude to get through customs quickly and efficiently. He got his luggage and two officers escorted him through the checkpoint and out to Fernando's sons, Junior and Ricky, who were waiting with two other men dressed in linen clothing and sunglasses. Neither Fernando nor his sons looked Hispanic; they could all have passed for light-skinned black men.

"Dude, my man! How was you trip? You no have problem wit' custom?" Ricky asked.

Dude hugged Ricky and Junior. "No, everything was straight."

Ricky walked Dude to a tinted black Cadillac. They drove off, followed by Junior in a tinted silver Cadillac. Dude took in the scenery as they drove to their destination.

En route, Ricky turned to Dude and announced, "My papa cancel you hotel suite. He say you must stay at our home wit' da family."

"Naw, I don't want to be a bother. I can stay at the hotel," Dude insisted.

"No botha! You stay wit' us at house," Ricky insisted with his heavy accent.

It was settled; Dude did not debate anymore. When the two cars pulled up on top of a hill, Dude's eyes almost popped out of his head. The large house was guarded by a solid-gold gate. Four men with machine guns hanging from their shoulders stood on the other side of it. It looked like a hotel resort! Dude thought he was in front of a set from *Lifestyles of the Rich and Famous*. He noticed other armed men scattered around the house. The cars pulled in front of the huge house. There were two men outside waiting to retrieve Dude's luggage. Dude and Fernando's sons entered the house and were greeted in Spanish by two female servants.

Ricky and Junior spoke in Spanish to the women.

"I told her you no speak Spanish," Junior said to Dude. "She's instructed to speak to you in English. Come, we go to Fernando out by pool."

Dude had seen some nice cribs but none like this. The ceilings were high. The windows were as huge as a department store's. The drapes were ornately patterned and rich-looking. Each room had its own color scheme and theme. Dude looked at the decor in the long hallway that led to the back, where the pool was located. Fernando's backyard was the size of Dude's whole block. There were beautiful women everywhere. Most of them were topless with bikini bottoms. There were just as many men with guns guarding the pool area as there had been out front. Dude spotted Fernando sitting at a table made out of crystal. He had a tall well-shaped female massaging his back as he talked on a cell phone. When he spotted his sons and Dude, he hung up and walked over. He had a huge smile on his face.

"Hey, you here, my man!" Fernando said, hugging Dude tight.

Dude hugged him back. "Yeah, I made it."

He pulled Dude over to where he was sitting. Ricky and Junior walked over to a couple of ladies sitting by the pool.

Fernando signaled the females sitting at the table to leave. He and Dude talked about the resort for a while. Fernando said that they would go over to the work site in the morning. He let Dude know that the rest of the day would be spent chilling out. They would go out for dinner later at Fernando's favorite spot. Fernando also told him that if he got lonely, he had a huge variety of women he could choice from. Dude turned down his offer. He assured him that he was appreciative, but he had to pass. The two talked over champagne and cigars for a couple of hours. Their conversation was put on hold when a young woman approached the two men. She was tall and perfectly built. She had long straight jet-black hair. She was wearing a white linen sundress. The mole that sat over the left side of her top lip stood out. She walked over and kissed Fernando on the cheek. Her smile was wide and her teeth were perfect.

"Excuse me for interrupting. I'm leaving for the salon now," she said to Fernando.

Fernando grabbed her hand softly and kissed it.

"Dis early?" he asked.

"Yes. Today I have lots of deliveries coming in," she replied.

Dude tried not to stare at the woman, but her beauty overwhelmed him.

"Oh, forgive my rudeness. Dude, dis is Maria. Maria, dis is my good friend Dude."

She smiled and reached her hand out. "Hello, pleased to meet you. I've heard so much about you."

Dude smiled back. "It's nice to meet you, too."

"You will join us for dinner later, yes?" Fernando asked.

"Yes. What time?" she asked.

"We will be pulling out at eight-thirty."

She assured him she would be on time and kissed him once more on the cheek before leaving. Fernando continued his conversation with Dude where they left off. He didn't say anything about the young lady, so Dude did not ask.

It was about three and a half hours after Dude arrived at Fernando's palace that Ricky showed him to his room. It was more like his own floor. The bedroom suite was double the size of the second floor of any of Dude's homes. The room was all white. It had a living room sectioned off by a beautifully draped set of double doors that led to a balcony. The balcony looked over a set of stairs that led to a beautiful stone pool. Outside of the main entrance of the suite was a long hallway.

There was a huge wood door at the end of the hallway that opened into a large kitchen. Ricky told Dude that he would have his own cook 24/7. He'd also have his own maid and personal assistant. If he needed anything from town, he also had his own personal driver. He had an entire staff with living quarters on the same floor as himself. Ricky opened a closet door and Dude saw that it was filled with an entire wardrobe.

"Papa sent out for you some tings," Ricky said. There was everything from shoes to designer sportswear. Ricky pointed to three pairs of shoes. "Papa bust his ass getting these. He said he hear you mention a lot about them. He say you say this is you favorite sneaker ever made. He say you say you still have you original pair, but they no good, too old. Now you have new."

Dude couldn't believe Fernando had remembered something like this. He walked over and picked up one pair of the sneakers. He smiled and nodded.

"The motherfuckin' Gucci original! Goddamn, these was the shit in the eighties. How did he get his hands on these?" Dude inquired.

"Believe me, he had to pull strings," Ricky answered, and left Dude to get settled in.

Dude unpacked the few items he had thrown in his bags, figuring he would shop when he got out. But thanks to his friend Fernando, he was straight. Fernando even had a huge selection of cologne and toiletries for him in the bathroom. Dude took a long hot shower and then lay down for a nap.

A knock at the door woke him up. His personal assistant, Elda, told him that someone was waiting in the car to take him to dinner.

He walked back over to the closet and pulled out a soft smoke-gray suit. His favorite color when it came to suits.

The driver came and got Dude at 8:25 on the dot. He was well groomed, but Dude could not help but notice the bulge in his hip. It was like everyone in Fernando's camp was packin'.

They walked to the garage. The setup was like a stable, but instead of horses, there were rows of cars, all types. Dude lost count after about thirty! He also noticed there were three more homes on the property.

Fernando was sharp as an arrow! So were Ricky and Junior. Even the bodyguards were sharp. Four bodyguards got into a silver 600 Benz. The other four got in a silver G Wagon Benz truck, and two more rode off in a Black 600 Benz coupé. Fernando and Dude rode in the back of a white Bentley. Both Junior and Ricky rode in separate Bentleys, one black, one silver.

"So how you like you quarters? Is it comfortable enough for you?" Fernando said.

"Yeah, everything is perfect. Actually, the shit is off the hook! And man, the Gucci sneakers . . . Thanks! I felt like a kid on Christmas," Dude exclaimed.

Fernando laughed. "Boy, those was someting to get my hands on! I had to get me a pair, too. I had to see fo' myself what was so good about them. I see you like the suit, too."

"Yeah, man, you have good taste!" Dude told him.

Fernando smiled. "No me! You have to tank Maria for dis. She shop for everyting."

When they pulled into the parking lot of the large restaurant, Dude noticed there were no cars in the lot besides theirs. There were some men standing outside the restaurant as if they were waiting for them.

"Fernando, it's so good to see you." The man who seemed to be the owner of the restaurant hugged Fernando tight.

"I know, I know! And trust me, I've missed the food!" Fernando said.

The entire restaurant was filled with Fernando's crew.

Within minutes of their entering the spacious dining room Maria appeared. Maria was mind-blowing! Dude had dealt with many women in his time; however, none was as beautiful or exotic as Maria. All the young ladies she was with were beautiful, but there was something about Maria that caught Dude's eye. He felt uncomfortable looking at her with Fernando sitting next to him.

The women walked over to a long, well-appointed table. Maria took her seat next to Fernando. By the time the drinks were brought to the table, Dude had set his mind and eyes on another woman seated nearby. She was not as tall as Maria, but her beauty was as overwhelming. He even went as far as trying to imagine giving her a back shot. Plus, their eyes had caught when he was being introduced to all of the women.

The food was excellent and the wine was like no other he had ever tasted. His head was feeling nice. He didn't know if it was the wine, but Dude thought Maria was cutting her eye at him. It seemed like the two kept catching eye contact.

"Listen, everybody, can I have you attention, please? I wanna make toast to my friend Dude. Dude, come stand up," Fernando said.

Dude stood and grinned.

Fernando continued. "Dis man here is a very good friend of mine. He is a good man, too. For all you here who no know him. And you know if he is dis close to me, he must be good man. So, I wanna toast to our business venture and our friendship!"

Everyone raised their glasses and made a toast. Dude couldn't help looking at Maria with a loving smile. As he did so he was reminded of Blossom. He wondered what she was doing at that moment. His day-dreaming stopped when he saw Fernando handing him a box.

"Dis is something for you from me and my family," Fernando said.

Dude hugged Fernando and took the box. He removed the silver wrapping paper and found a watch. It was the same watch Fernando had given both his sons and was worth about $300,000.

Dude felt like he couldn't take Fernando's gift.

"I know you know about dis watch. So you must know what our friendship means to me," Fernando whispered in Dude's ear as he hugged him again.

After dinner, the men went to a gentlemen's club. Once again, they had the place to themselves. Maria and the rest of the girls soon joined them. They all danced and ate some more. Dude could not believe the bodies on the women. He had seen women in these kinds of clubs before, but none like these. Fernando told Dude he could have one or all of the women if he wanted. Ricky had slid off with two of the women to a back room. Maria and the rest of the girls were drinking and talking among themselves. Dude took phone numbers from three of the women and told them he would give them a call before he left town. Dude knew that was a lie. In some sick way, he felt like he was not a real man. Anybody else in his position would have been leaving the club with all of those women. But for some reason, Maria was stuck in his head. He was thinking about what she would think of him if he left with any of the women.

During the drive home, Fernando lit a cigar and offered Dude one.

Fernando took only two pulls before putting the cigar out. He turned to Dude and looked him in his eyes.

"Dude, you make a lot of money in da streets 'cause of me, yes?"

Dude agreed.

"I help a lot of people make lots of money. I am a businessman. But never I make friends with da people I help make money. Never let people even see my face. A lot of people in you country can't even see my sons' faces. But you, I watch you grow even when you don't know I see you I see you. I watch you money and you business. Before you meet me, I know you from you business. My son Junior tell me about dis young black boy who do good business wit' me. Junior say, 'Papa, dis boy is different. Dis boy reminds me, Papa, of the stories you tell me about you when you was a young man.' And I trust my son's judgment. Now you make three times what you started with."

For a minute Dude caught himself wondering if Fernando knew how he'd been checking Maria out or something. "Thank you, Fernando. I look up to you and I appreciate all you have done for me. Especially treating me as if I was part of your family. I've been in the streets all of my life. And I had to teach myself a lot, but what I learned from you is loyalty. You have one hundred and ten percent loyalty when it comes to me. You letting me into where you rest your head means a lot to me. I want you to know you can trust me. And thank you for giving me this business opportunity."

Dude couldn't help adding, "So, Maria is that special lady, huh? You two make a good couple."

Fernando laughed so hard he almost choked. "Couple? You tink Maria is good woman for me!"

"What? She's not your main chick?"

"Maria is my baby girl! You know my daughter! She is my last born!"

Dude felt like an ass.

Fernando stopped laughing and got serious. "My wife, God rest her soul, passed away giving birth to Maria. I raise her wit'out her mother. Sometimes, when I look at her, I see her mother." He reached into his pocket and pulled out his wallet. He showed Dude a picture of him and his wife on their wedding day. Both of them looked so young. And you could tell from the picture that Fernando hadn't been as rich at the time.

"Boy, those was da days! Me and my Maria, dat's my wife. My daughter is name after my wife. We didn't have much. As a matter of fact, we basically didn't have not'ing. But, we had each other. And Maria believed in me and my heart. She was such a wonderful woman. Money never matter to her. All she wanted and loved was me and our boys. I wish you could've met her. She would have liked you a lot."

9

*B*lossom jumped up and grabbed her cell phone. The clock read 10:34 in the morning. She hadn't had a call since Tamika phoned the night before. She climbed out of her bed and got the paper that had Dude's hotel number written on it. She picked up her house phone and dialed the number.

A woman's voice answered on the other end.

"Yes, Mr. Knoxx's room, please," Blossom said.

The woman checked. "Sorry, no have him here," she said.

Blossom was confused. "Are you sure? He was supposed to arrive yesterday. You don't have a record of this person?" Blossom asked.

"Please hold. I check again."

Blossom paced the floor with butterflies in her stomach. She grabbed the remote and turned the television on. She started having crazy thoughts. She turned to the news channel to see if there had been any report of a plane crash. Just as she got to the news channel the lady returned to the line.

"*Hola. Sí.* Mr. Knoxx was supposed to check in yesterday, but his reservation was canceled."

She hung the phone up and called Black.

"Hello."

"Hey, Black, what's up? Have you heard from Dude yet?" she asked.

"Yeah. He called when he landed yesterday. Is everything aight? You need anything?" Black asked.

"No, I'm straight. Well, if he calls you back, can you tell him to give me a ring, please?"

Black agreed and the two hung up. Blossom was pissed. Dude called Black and hadn't called her. All kinds of things started to go through her head. Maybe he had a chick on the side and he took her with him, she thought. But she quickly axed that thought from her head. She knew that if Dude was going down there for business, he would not take a bitch with him. She didn't know what to think. She sat on the bed for a few minutes. Then she picked up the phone again to call Tamika. She hoped maybe he called there looking for her. But he hadn't. She was angry. She jumped in the shower and got dressed. To go where? she thought. She just had to make moves, 'cause the more she thought, the more fed up she would've gotten. She jumped in her car and hit the highway toward Brooklyn. She picked up her cell phone and dialed Lil' Richie. His machine came on. She left a message. She decided to make a detour into the city.

She turned her cell phone on anxious to see if Dude had called. She had three messages, two from Lil' Richie and the other from Tamika. Her heart dropped. He still hadn't called her. Maybe that was why Tamika had called the night before, she thought. Maybe Dude had called there looking for her. But that bubble burst when Tamika told her that Dude hadn't called. After calling Tamika, Blossom returned Lil' Richie's call.

"What's up, stranger?" Lil' Richie asked.

"Nothing much. What's up with you, shorty?"

"Not too much. Where are you?"

"In the city. I'm getting ready to come to Brooklyn. What you getting into tonight?" she asked him.

"Not too much. I'm supposed to be going to the movies, but I'm waiting on a callback."

"Oh, let me find out you got a hot date!" she said jokingly.

When her shit was poppin' with Dude, it was easy to tell Lil' Richie they could still hang out but they could only be friends. That's why she couldn't understand why she felt a little jealous when he told her he might have a date.

He laughed. "Yeah, something like that. Being you don't want me."

He agreed to give her a call if his movie plans did not go through.

Blossom stopped at Duncan's Fish Market. She bought fish and Red Alizé and called Tamika again. She felt like being around her sister and her friends.

After she hung up with Tamika, her cell phone rang.

She answered.

"What's up, Blossom?" It was Dude on the other end.

"Oh, you still breathing? You tell me what's up. Why didn't you call me yesterday?" she asked.

"I got caught up once I got here," he replied.

"Caught up? You had time to call Black, though. And where are you staying? When was you going to call and tell me about changing hotels?" The questions came flowing out.

"Look, it was nonstop for me as soon as I got off the plane. And I had no idea I would be staying at Fernando's house when I got here. Sorry. How are you anyway?" Dude asked.

"I'm okay, I guess. I'm on my way to Tamika's. We're going to have a girls' night. What are you up to?"

"Nothing much. I'm about to go take care of some business. I'll try to call you when I get a break."

"Try? Why can't you just make it your business to call?" she asked.

"I will. I'll call you later," he said.

The two hung up. Blossom felt like their conversation had been dry and shallow. They had departed on bad terms and it felt like he was still holding a grudge. She wasn't used to his new behavior. He hadn't even mentioned her meeting him down there for a couple of days. He didn't even give her the number to Fernando's house.

The girls were all in the kitchen. Tamika was at the stove frying her famous whiting and porgies. Shareen was sitting at the kitchen table cutting up potatoes. They had already started drinking. The women's road-to-recovery album was playing in the background—Mary J. Blige's *My Life* album.

Shareen started on Blossom almost immediately. "So da nigga startin' da bullshit already, huh?"

"Why you say that?" Blossom asked.

Shareen sucked her teeth. "Girl, you ain't foolin' nobody! Whenever a nigga start actin' stupid, we run to our friends. And the first thing we pop into da CD player is my girl Mary! Now, she knows how it feels to be a woman."

Blossom did not want it to look like Dude was playing her. Even though that's how she felt. She did not feel like hearing a bunch of *I told you so*s.

"Where's ya hubby at anyway?" Kim asked.

"Out of town," Blossom answered.

"Grandma Black called this morning," Tamika said as she flipped the fish.

The mood changed in the room.

Kim tried to bring some humor into the situation, to loosen up the tension. "She still ain't give me my flows for dat Juicy sweatsuit," she said, referring to the piece of clothing she had stolen for Trina.

Shareen smiled. "I miss dat crazy girl."

It was silent; everyone was lost, having their own memory of Trina.

Tamika took the last batch of fish out of the grease. "She sounded so happy dat last night." She paused. "Grandma Black said Trina took out life insurance. She said she wanted to give us some of the insurance money."

The girls were silent. Tears started to fill their eyes. Blossom wondered whether she should tell the girls about her visit with Kandi. She decided not to mention it.

Shareen switched the mood back. "Come on now, you know Trina wouldn't want us sittin' here sad and shit!"

Shareen jumped up and started singing along with Mary J. Blige's CD and everyone wiped their eyes and joined in. The bell rang, interrupting their flow. "Who is it!" Tamika shouted into the intercom.

"It's me!" Rob's voice shouted back.

"What you want!"

"Don't fuck wit' me, Mika! Buzz da fuckin' door!"

Tamika just walked away from the intercom without answering.

"Trouble in paradise?" Shareen asked.

Tamika sucked her teeth. "Trouble, yeah. Paradise not! I'm sick of dat nigga!"

Kim laughed. "Yeah, we heard dat one before."

"No, I'm serious! I gotta get my shit together. All Rob do is stagnate me. I'm sick of his ass!" Tamika informed her.

Rob kept ringing the bell for about ten minutes. And before they knew it, he was banging on the door. "Tamika, don't play wit' me! Open dis fuckin' door!"

The music was blasting, so the girls did not hear him at first.

"Tamika, I think Rob bangin' on ya door," Shareen said.

Kim turned down the music. They sat quiet for a few seconds.

Bang! Bang! Bang! Rob continued hitting and kicking the door. "Don't fuckin' play, Mika! I'll kick dis fuckin' door down!"

Tamika rushed to the door. "Nigga, you betta stop bangin' on my door like dat! You don't pay no bills up in here!"

"Who you think you talkin' to, bitch! Oh, ya homies probably in dere, so now you wanna show off! I'll fuck you and dem bitches up!"

Tamika was furious. "We wasn't bitches when we put the dough togetha and bailed ya crab ass out! Get da fuck away from my door, nigga! Before I go in my kitchen and mix some shit up!"

He kicked the door with force. "Yeah, and so da fuck what! I'm gon' give y'all ya paper back! And since we talkin' 'bout givin' back, give me my fuckin' truck back!"

"Yo, you can have ya fuckin' whip, you bitch-ass nigga! I'm tired of you every minute takin' dat shit back anyway! You fuckin' crab! I'm gon' throw da keys out da front window! Anything I got in it you can throw dat shit away, BITCH," Tamika screamed.

Tamika snatched the keys off the counter and went over to the window. She waited until Rob got back downstairs and she saw him look up. She opened the window and threw the keys out. She tried aiming for his head, but just missed by a few inches. Rob got into the Jeep and sped off. For the first time in ages, she felt relief. She was usually stressed out when he pulled a stunt like this, but this time was different. She really was sick of him. Him taking the Jeep again was like a relief. She didn't want to have any attachments.

She went over to the counter and poured another drink.

"He'll be bringin' da shit back later tonight," Shareen stated.

"I won't be takin' it! I don't want dat shit! I rather take public transportation or a cab! He always tryin' to hold dat fuckin' truck over my head. I don't want da fuckin' headaches!"

At that moment Blossom wished she was half as strong as Tamika. She wished she could write Dude and all of his stuff off.

The girls went back to talking and drinking. The phone rang and Tamika let it go to voice mail. It was Rob. He decided to leave a message.

"Aight, Mika! You wanna play games? Let me catch you in the street, I'm gon' break ya fuckin jaw! You watch, bitch!" he screamed into the phone.

"Damn, girl! What you did to dat nigga? Got him losin' his mind! You musta gave him dat ass!" Shareen said.

The girls burst out laughing.

"Must be dat head game got dat nigga buggin'!" Kim added.

"Yeah, brain will have a nigga flippin' out!" Blossom said.

The girls paused and looked at her like she was crazy.

"What da fuck you know 'bout givin' brain?" Shareen asked.

"What?" Blossom asked.

"Yeah, what you know 'bout suckin' some dick, girl!" Tamika asked.

"Hello . . . I know the same thing y'all know!" Blossom replied.

"Yeah, she a grown-ass women now!" Kim said, coming to Blossom's rescue.

Tamika handed a bottle of Corona to Blossom.

"What?" Blossom asked.

"Show me ya skills," Tamika said.

Everybody started laughing.

"Show ya skills! Show ya skills! Show ya skills!" all the girls shouted, banging on the table.

Just as Blossom was about to pick up the bottle, there were three loud bangs at the front door.

The girls hit the floor.

"How 'bout dat, bitch!" Rob screamed through the door.

Tamika jumped up off the floor.

"I know dat muthafucka didn't bust shots at my door!" she screamed.

She ran to her room and reached into her nightstand drawer. She pulled out her Glock and ran to the front door. The girls tried to stop her, but couldn't.

Tamika snatched the door open and saw Rob and his homeboy running down the steps. She cocked back and started busting shots at them.

"You muthafucka! You don't scare nobody, nigga! I'm not ya punk-ass baby mama!" she shouted.

Rob and his friend just ran off. Tamika stood outside her door looking at the three bullet holes. Her neighbors started opening their doors and looking out. Blossom took the gun from her sister's hand and hid it in the apartment. The girls quickly came up with their story. They had to make sure their stories were the same.

The police came and went. The girls told the officers they'd heard some guys arguing and then heard a few shots. They convinced them that their door must have caught some of the shots.

After the cops left, Tamika packed up a couple things. Shareen packed up the food and liquor. The girls decided to go to Kim's apartment for the night. Ten minutes or so later, Rob started calling. Tamika just ignored his calls. As he screamed through her answering machine, the girls hurried around, gathering Tamika's things. After Rob's sixth attempt to get Tamika to pick up, she finally gave in.

"Girl, you a stupid ass if you pick up dat phone!" Shareen shouted at her.

Tamika ignored Shareen's advice and picked up the phone.

"Yo, you really OD'd dis time, Rob," she said into the phone.

Blossom looked at her sister like she was crazy. She could not believe her sister was talking to Rob after he just finished shooting through their door.

Tamika continued to talk to Rob. The girls stood and stared at her like she had lost her mind. The conversation between Tamika and Rob seemed to be in riddles, so the girls did not know what he was saying. Tamika hung up and took her coat off.

"What?" Blossom asked.

"I'm not going," Tamika answered.

Kim's jaw practically dropped to the floor. "What you mean, you not going? What happened?" she asked.

"Nothin'. I'm straight, he ain't comin' back here," Tamika answered.

Kim shot her a look of total disbelief. Tamika gave her back a warning look.

"Look, da nigga just shot through ya fuckin' door!" Shareen yelled at Tamika. "He could have hit anybody in dis crib! And you mean you trust him enough to believe him if he tells you he ain't comin' back!"

"Look, don't start wit' me, Shareen!" Tamika yelled back.

"You fuckin' dummy, dat nigga da one who startin' wit' you! You really done lost ya' fuckin' mind if you stay here," Shareen said.

Blossom intervened. "Tamika, what did he say?"

"It ain't got nothin' to do with what he said. I just know he ain't gon' come back here. And I can protect myself if he does try some stupid shit," Tamika replied.

"Yeah, but you was just ready to go to my crib. And now all of a sudden you wanna stay here," Kim said.

The girls got into a screaming match. Blossom tried intervening numerous times, without success.

"You stupid, Tamika! A fuckin' fool!" Kim screamed at her.

"Fuck you, Kim! Ya shit ain't no betta den mine!" Tamika yelled back.

Kim jumped up out of her chair. "What! At least I don't have no nigga beatin' my ass and fightin' me! A mothafucker shootin' my goddamn door up! You think dat shit is cute! You fuckin' dummy!" she screamed at Tamika.

Blossom was confused. "Beating your ass? That nigga been beating you?" she asked her sister.

Kim didn't give Tamika a chance to answer. "Tell her, stupid!" she shouted.

Tamika reached over Shareen and tried to punch Kim in her face. But Shareen blocked the blow.

"Oh, now you wanna fight me over dat crab-ass nigga! Over a motha-fucker dat don't really give a fuck about ya ass! Over a slouch-ass E-head nigga!" Kim yelled in Tamika's face.

Shareen looked at Tamika like she was crazy.

"Bitch, dat nigga on Ecstasy? I know dat nigga ain't fuckin' wit' dat dumb shit," Shareen said to Tamika.

"Yeah, dat nigga on dat shit!" Kim yelled with tears in her eyes. "Bitch wanna talk about my shit ain't no betta den her shit! Yo, fuck you, Tamika! You wanna get funky wit' me ova dat nigga! *Me?* I had ya back, bitch!" She put her coat on and walked out of the apartment.

Shareen and Blossom stood speechless in the kitchen. Tamika poured another drink and went into her bedroom.

After the other girls had left, Blossom cut off the kitchen lights and went into her bedroom. She turned on the flat-screen television. Dude had fixed up her room before he got her the town house. She looked at her cell phone; there were no missed calls. She looked at the phone on her nightstand and noticed she had two new messages. Neither of them was from Dude. Both of them were from Lil' Richie. She looked at the clock and realized that it was probably too late to call him back. She lay down on her back. She'd been tired just minutes ago, but all of a sudden she couldn't fall asleep. She wanted to pick up the phone and call Dude, but didn't have his number. This was the first time since they'd been together that she wasn't able to contact him. She was used to being able to pick up the phone at any given time to reach him. She started to wonder if they were broken up and she just didn't know it. She began to fall asleep, but her phone rang.

"Hello."

"Hey, sorry if I woke you. You want me to call you in the morning?" Lil' Richie said.

She cleared her throat. "No, it's okay. What's up with you?"

"Nothing much. Just checking on you. I heard some shit went down at your crib."

"How you know what happened?" she asked.

"Come on, this is the hood. How am I not going to know?" he replied.

"So, what are you doing up this time of night?"

"Nothing much."

"Don't tell me you're just finishing up with your hot date?"

"Something like that. I just left her crib."

Blossom sat all the way up in her bed. She had a funny feeling in her stomach. She was really jealous. It was more like, if she couldn't have him, she didn't want anyone else to have him either. Even though she and Lil' Richie never got far, she had liked him at one time. Before Dude came along, he was the only person she had any interest in. But Dude came along and swept her off her feet and Blossom left Lil' Richie hanging.

"Hello . . . Earth to Blossom," Lil' Richie yelled through the phone.

Blossom had drifted off into thought. "Oh, yeah . . ."

"Are you falling asleep on me?" he asked.

"NO! No. I wasn't. But, anyway, what's up?"

"I'm a little hungry. I might go to Jackson Hole."

"Oh, you and your hot date didn't go out to eat?" she asked with a sarcastic tone.

He laughed. "You're funny! If I wouldn't know better, I would think you were a little jealous!" he joked.

"Wouldn't you like that." She paused. "You driving?"

"Yeah. I have a rental."

"Come get me. I'll ride with you."

Lil' Richie agreed and the two hung up.

Blossom jumped up and went to the closet. She had a full wardrobe at the apartment. She decided to look a little sexy but not overdo it. She threw on a pair of tight Cavali jeans with a T-shirt to match. She snatched a pair of gator boots out of a box as well. She had never worn them before. It was August, and there was a light breeze outside. She snatched a butter-soft leather jacket out of her closet and left to go meet Lil' Richie. He was in front of the building waiting for her when she got downstairs. She jumped into his car and gave him a hello kiss on the cheek. He sped off and drove toward Jackson Hole.

Blossom felt kind of funny. She didn't know if going with him to the restaurant was wrong. It was just two friends grabbing something to eat. She wondered if Dude was doing something he was not supposed to.

When they got to the restaurant, Blossom ordered a cappuccino and cheese fries.

"So where's your Prince Charming tonight?" Lil' Richie asked.

"Out of town."

He smiled. "I guess that's why you're here, huh?"

She turned her lips up. "Whatever!"

"Naw, I'm just playing. Seriously, how's everything going with you and him anyway?"

She hesitated. "Everything is cool."

He knew she was lying.

"Look, Blossom, no matter what, we are friends and I got ya back. I'm always here if you want to talk."

She gave him a warm smile. "I know."

He dropped her home after dinner. As she lay in her bed looking up at the ceiling, she thought Lil' Richie was a real cool guy. She thought about how her life would have been if she had never gotten with Dude.

The sun was just coming up when Blossom's cell phone rang.

"Hello."

"You sleep?" asked Dude.

She opened one eye and looked at the clock. It read 6:15 A.M.

"Yeah, I was. What's up with you?" she asked.

"Nothing much. What's up with you?"

She sat up. "Dude, is there a problem or something?"

"No, why you ask that?" He sighed.

" 'Cause your whole disposition has changed. You didn't even call to let me know you were not at the hotel. And when you do inform me, you still don't leave a number for me to call back. So basically my husband is away in another country and I have to sit and wait for him to call me. It's just not fair, Dude," Blossom told him.

"Blossom, I'm out here on some serious shit. I don't mean to sound bad, but I really don't have time to call you as often as I do when I'm home. I thought you would understand that. And as far as the whole thing about not having a number to reach me, I just got a cell phone today. I was calling you now to give you the number."

"Well, it's about time. When are you coming home? I miss you."

"I'll be back soon. I miss you, too."

"What happened to you sending for me?"

"I said when I got situated. Most likely on the next trip down."

"So, how's everything going?" she asked, changing the subject.

"It's been mostly work since I got down here. We went out to eat the first day. That's about it. What about you?" he asked.

"I'm going to see T Mac later on. I'm in Brooklyn; I stayed here last night. I'll probably stay here again tonight."

"I was going to ask you to check on T for me. I should be home in a couple of days. If you need anything, call Black; he'll take care of you."

"All I need is you, baby."

He gave her the number to the cell he had for down there and the two said their good-byes. That lump that was in Blossom's stomach disappeared. She closed her eyes and fell back to sleep.

10

Dude took a long shower and put on a jogging suit and his fresh Gucci sneakers. He was about half an hour ahead of schedule. He walked over to the intercom and rang for Elda.

"Good morning, Mista Dude. How can I help you dis morning?" she asked.

"Good morning, Elda. You think I can have an omelet with Cheddar cheese and onions?"

"Sure you can, sir. You no want any meat wit' that, sir?" she asked.

"No, thank you. Just a cold glass of orange juice, please."

"No problem, sir. Right away, sir."

He heard a ring.

He answered.

"Rise and shine, mister. I know you no still sleeping!" a woman said on the other end. He instantly recognized the sexy voice.

"Hey, good morning. No, I wasn't still sleeping. I'm dressed already. I'm waiting for Elda to bring me breakfast. Then I have to meet your father." He felt like he had given up more info than was needed.

"This is good thing. You being woke. 'Cause my papa wants you to come with me."

"Where?" he asked.

"What, you don't trust me? You tink I'm goin' to kidnap you?" she said.

Dude laughed. "No, not at all, sweetie."

"He say someting about coming up and he's running behind sched-ule. So you stuck with me dis morning. I must take you to my salon and

105

you must have facial, massage, manicure, and tings like that. My papa insists. So you ready in thirty minutes, yes?" Maria asked.

"Yeah, I'll be ready."

"Good! Papa tell me to ask what car you feel to drive in today."

"It doesn't matter."

"Okay, I'll choose, then. I tink I have good taste, yeah?"

"Sounds like a plan. I'll be ready."

Maria couldn't wait to see Dude. She liked his relationship with her father. She had never been with an American before, let alone a black American. She knew that Dude was off-limits because he was her father's business partner. But she figured a little flirting wouldn't hurt. She jumped up and walked into her huge closet. The closet was a little larger than Dude's entire bedroom. She looked through the rows of clothing. She wanted to look sexy, but still wanted to look classy. She decided on a Cavali miniskirt suit. She pulled out a pair of four-inch pumps to match. She pulled her hair up in a ponytail with a diamond clip. Fernando had bought it for her when she was seventeen years old. She looked at herself with satisfaction. Then she picked up her pocket-book and went to meet Dude.

When Dude got down to the car lot, there were three cars lined up in a row. A cream Bentley, a black BMW truck, and a silver Benz limo. Maria was smiling, standing in front of the row of cars. Dude wasn't sure how he felt. He looked at her and chills ran down his body. He tried hard not to get an erection!

Maria's smile grew wider. "Good morning, Mr. Dude. I couldn't choose which one. You tell me what you tink."

"It doesn't matter. You choose."

She decided on the silver Benz limo. Two security men drove behind them in a black Cadillac jeep. The inside of the limo was stocked with juice, soda, and champagne. The limo was custom made inside.

Dude couldn't keep his eyes off of Maria's smooth legs. She smiled at him with her big brown eyes. Her eyelashes curved long, landing a little below her eyebrows. She knew Dude was checking her out. She closed the partition to give her and Dude privacy.

"I hope you no mind?" she asked.

"Naw, naw, I'm straight," he replied.

She shook her head. "What is dis ting you say all the time? A New York slang? 'Naw, naw, I'm straight,'" she mimicked.

He laughed. "Yeah, something like that!"

"I like dis saying. It's really cool. I like to learn more of New York slang. Like I know 'Dat shit is off da meter, son,'" she said.

"Where do you know that from?" he asked, laughing harder.

"BET video show, and I go to you country to shop and tings."

Even the way she spoke turned him on.

"BET! What you know about that?" he asked

"I know music, I love music! Papa no know about me in New York sometimes at clubs. I love to dance and party! What about you?"

"I like to party sometimes. I can't go to too many spots in New York, 'cause people where I'm from are what you call 'haters.'"

"Yes, I know about dat slang, too. Those kind of people are no good people. But, you no go to otha place for party?" she asked.

"Other places like where?"

"You know, like Jamaica, Paris, you know?"

"No, not really. But that's a good idea."

She reached out and put her hand on his leg. "Good! Den it's final. When you and Papa are finish wit' resort, I will take you away somewhere to party and have fun. A place where no player haters will be!"

It was one of those moments when it feels like the world just stops. There was silence between the two of them. Dude did not want to do anything to disrespect Fernando. He felt that sticking his tongue down Maria's throat would not sit right with her father.

But it seemed like Maria was not thinking about her father. She pressed her lips against Dude's. Her sweet tongue maneuvered into his mouth. He didn't know what to do, so he just followed his body and kissed her back. The kiss lasted a long time. Afterward, they just sat silent.

Maria broke the silence. "Papa must not know," she said.

"Sure, I agree."

The rest of the ride passed in silence. And once they got to Maria's salon, things between them were kind of weird. Neither one knew how to react to the other. Dude got his facial, pedicure, and manicure. He didn't see Maria once his treatment started. It wasn't until he was walking over to the massage room to get his massage that he saw her. She was talking to a tall man. He was handsome and a little lighter than Dude, but he was clearly Dominican. It looked like they were having a deep conversation. Maria looked over to Dude and smiled. He was escorted into a massage room. The whole time he was lying on the massage table, he thought about Maria. She was different from any other female he had been with. She had her own. She did not need anything from him. But then Fernando popped into his head and that made all of his thoughts turn sour.

When Dude finished his massage, he saw Fernando at the front of the shop talking to one of the hairdressers. He looked around for Maria, but there was no sign of her. Dude walked into the lobby of the huge salon.

"Here's my boy! How you like you treatment today?" Fernando asked.

"Good, everything was good!"

"Good! I'm sorry about this morning. Some tings come up wit' da resort. I had to run and settle some tings! But anyway, come, let us go over to da property."

The two got into Fernando's Bentley. Dude wondered where Maria had gone.

When they got to the property, Dude noticed there were triple the number of workers than he'd seen there before.

"I have more men to work now. We should be finished much earlier," Fernando said, as if reading his mind.

Dude looked around. He really hadn't digested that he was part of a major operation here. He had taken a huge chunk of his savings and invested it in this operation. He knew it was going to be worth it. He thought about his brother and wondered how things were going back home. He excused himself to make a call.

"What's up, boy?" Dude said when Black answered.

"What's the deal?"

"I can't call it. How's everything going on that end?"

"Everything is everything. The nigga Teddy disappeared for two fuckin' days. So I had mad shit on my hands, son!"

"Where the fuck was he at?"

"The nigga said he had food poison. He showed me the hospital papers. 'Cause you know I was ready to break that mothafucker's shit wide open!"

"Where's he at now?"

"I'm waiting for him now. If you ask me, the nigga acting crazy. I think that new chick he fuckin' with got his mind bugging. Either that or that nigga fuckin' with that shit!"

Dude laughed. "He still fucking with that light-skin chick?"

"Yeah. That bitch is weird, too! I'm telling you, son, she ain't got it all!"

"Yeah, I know. I don't care for her too much. I told the nigga don't bring the bitch around me! When you get up with him, tell him I said to call me. But anyway, boy, you got to see the ass out here! Nothing like you ever seen before!" Dude said.

"I could imagine!" Black exclaimed. "Man, they need to import some of them hos out here, 'cause these chicks are busted! I went to this little spot last night. Shit, the bitches were so broke down in there. I just got me a couple of drinks and broke out."

"Well, these chicks out here are exotic-looking broads! You spoke to Blossom?" Dude asked.

"Naw. Not since she called that first time. You spoke to her?"

"Yeah. She suppose to go see T Mac. Look, I got to go. Don't forget to tell Teddy to hit me."

The two said good-bye and hung up. Dude returned to Fernando and the workers. There was a translator to repeat in English what any of the workers said. He was explaining that the materials they needed for most of the plumbing had not gotten there. This upset Fernando. He went off. He asked how could this be when they were supposed to have ordered these things a month ago. The worker he was speaking to tried to explain that they had ordered the materials to get there at the right time. Fernando told the worker not to worry about it. He would take care of it and what he needed would be there within two days. Dude had never seen Fernando lose his cool. But he knew. A man with the kind of money and position in life like Fernando had to have some type of dark side.

After taking care of business at the property, Fernando and Dude were riding back to the house talking about what they were going to eat. Dude said "anything but pork," which made Fernando laugh. Then, all of a sudden, Dude's phone rang.

"Hello, Mr. Dude. Is my papa around you now?" Maria asked on the other end.

Dude was surprised. He hadn't remembered giving her the number. "Yes . . . Why, you need—"

"No! Do not let him know I'm on phone. Are you on you way to house?" she asked.

Dude looked over to Fernando, who was busy talking on his own cell phone.

"Yeah. Why, what's up?"

"Oh, not'ing. I just like to kiss you again. Is dis okay, yeah?" she asked.

He hesitated. "Sure. I think that could work."

"Dis is good! So I will see you tonight, yeah?"

"Sure will, sweetie. Okay, bye bye." He hung up.

Fernando, who seemed like he was in his own heated conversation, soon finished speaking, hung up, and then looked at Dude. "I will call Maria and tell her to dine wit' you. I'm going to get—how you young

Americans say? Nukkie, I'm going to go get me some nukkie. You know, get my groove on, get my swerve on!"

As Dude's eyes widened in amusement, Fernando continued. "What! You tink I don't like pussy!" Dude shook his head. "You tink only you young men get pussy! Listen, I have a women. Each one have purpose for something! Spanish, Japanese, Chinese, American, white, even black. Black girls are my favorite! Not half-breed black women. Black! West Indian women very good!"

"You're serious, aren't you?" Dude asked.

"Yes, I am! Tonight I have my special lady dat fly in from Trinidad! But I will make sure Maria will sit and eat wit' you."

Dude didn't have a problem with that. It was settled: he was having dinner with Maria and it was all okay with Fernando.

After they arrived at the residence, Dude went straight to his quarters and took a shower. He got nice and fresh and sprayed some good-smelling stuff on. His cell rang.

"Hello."

"Hey, Mr. Dude. Are you ready for dinner?" Maria's sweet voice asked.

"I sure am. And I'm starving."

"Good! I will be ova in a few minutes. I told da staff to serve dinner at you place. I know you have a long day. We can eat out by you pool," she said.

"That sounds good!"

"I can't wait."

She hung up. A half hour later, a man rolled in with a cart full of food, wine and champagne in chilled buckets, and beautiful flowers in a crystal vase. But there was no sign of Maria.

The staff set everything up out by the pool area and left. Minutes later, Maria knocked at the door. Dude ran to the mirror to make sure he looked presentable. He felt like a bitch! He went over and opened the door. And once again her beauty blew him away! She walked in and went straight out to the pool area. She inspected everything. And everything, including him, seemed to meet with her satisfaction. The two sat down to have dinner. They drank champagne and laughed for what seemed like hours.

"So, Mr. Dude, who do you have back in America?" she asked.

He took a sip of his champagne. "Well, my mother and father passed away when I was a kid," he replied. "My grandmother raised me and my brother, T Mac. So I don't have too much family. Yeah, I have aunts and uncles that live out of town, but we're not close."

"No girlfriend or wife?"

He knew what would be the right answer; he just didn't know if he should say it.

She continued. "What—you do not know if you should say da truth?"

"Yes. I do have a girlfriend at home."

"Just one or many?"

"Naw, just one."

"No children?"

"No, not yet."

"So, how does you girlfriend feel about you being away in another country filled with a bunch of beautiful women?"

"I guess she feels a little neglected. But she knows I'm out here taking care of business."

He explained how he met Blossom and their age difference. He even told her how she'd been a virgin when they met and about crazy-ass Kandi and what went down with Trina and T Mac. After he finished, she poured him another drink.

"You life is very interesting. You have done good for yourself, like my papa said . . . Tell me someting?" she asked.

Dude gulped down the whole glass of champagne before answering, "Shoot. You can ask me anything."

"Would you like to sleep wit' me? Make love to me?" she asked.

He almost choked!

"You no hurt my feelings if you say no," she said.

He leaned over and started to passionately kiss her. It was even better than the first time they kissed. Maria stood up and pulled him close to her. She felt his bulge. And it was all that she thought it would be. She took his hand and guided it up her skirt. She placed his hand on her ass. He kissed her harder as he gently squeezed her butt. She guided his hand to the front of her wet panties. Dude could feel the heat coming from between her legs. He stopped kissing her for a moment.

"Yes, I do wanna make love to you. I wanted to from the first time I laid eyes on you."

They slowly walked inside the bedroom suite while kissing. Once they were in the room, she began to undress. Her body was flawless. She had a birthmark on her right hip. She had a matching purple lace thong-and-bra set on. That turned him on even more. He loved a woman who took pride in the underwear she wore. After undressing herself, she undressed him. Kissing his body in between. Within minutes, they both stood naked in the middle of the bedroom. She kissed his chest and arms. Then she kissed his stomach and hips. Her touch turned him on. Then, that moment came. She dropped to her knees and started to kiss his penis. And before he knew it, she had all of him in her mouth. He wanted to come instantly, but he tried his best to hold back. She sat him on the edge of the bed. He moaned and rubbed her soft, thick black hair until he couldn't take it anymore.

He started to softly push her away. "I'm coming, baby. I'm coming."

She pulled him back into her mouth and whispered, "It's okay, baby. You don't have to take it out, just come, baby."

She was giving him permission to ejaculate in her mouth. And that's just what he did. And it drove him crazy! He felt that it was only right for him to return the favor. He laid her on her back in the middle of the bed and went downtown on her. And just like him, it drove her crazy! After she came, she got on top of him and started riding him. He again wanted to come instantly, and that was not like him. She was tight and warm. And she didn't have an unpleasant scent coming from between her legs. Not even a scent of sweat. Their lovemaking session lasted for hours. They did it in all types of positions until neither one could take it any longer. They both fell asleep in each other's arms. Moreover, they both fell asleep a hundred percent satisfied.

Dude opened his eyes. His body was worn out from last night. He rolled over and noticed Maria was gone. He then looked at the clock and it read nine-forty. It was early in the morning, and yet it felt like late afternoon to him. He saw a note on the nightstand. He picked it up and read it. It basically said thank you for last night, I enjoyed it. Hope you enjoyed it, too. See you later today. And for him not to mention what happened last night. He ripped the note into pieces and threw it in the garbage. His cell phone rang, but by the time he found it he had missed the call. He saw that he had missed five other calls. He listened to the messages. They all were from Blossom. She insisted that he call her immediately. He walked back over to the bed and lay back down. He set the phone on the nightstand. He closed his eyes and recapped last night. He wondered what time Maria had left. He hadn't heard her leave. She'd pulled a nigger move on him. That made him smile. His phone rang again. He rushed to answer it, thinking it could be Maria.

"Hello."

"Yo, you didn't see me calling you earlier!"

He wasn't up for her bullshit.

"What!"

"What, what! Which part did you not understand!"

"Yo, who are you talking to like that!" he barked.

Blossom sucked her teeth. "Look, I don't have time to go back and forth with your inconsiderate ass! You need to come home, Dude. T Mac is not doing good and he keeps asking for you. So I think you should come back. But then again, my opinion doesn't mean nothing! Call your brother's doctor, Dude! And thanks for calling me back yesterday!" She then hung up.

He grabbed his wallet off of the dresser and called T Mac's doctor.

His machine came on. He started packing and called Fernando. He thought about calling Maria but didn't have her number.

My friend, is everyting okay?" Fernando asked.

"Hey, Fernando. I have to go home. I got a call from New York. My brother's not doing too good. Do you think you can make flight arrangements for me?"

"I make some calls. I will have a flight for you immediately, my friend."

When Dude was in the shower, his cell rang again.

"Yeah, hello!" he shouted.

"Yes, Mr. Knoxx, it's . . ." It was T Mac's doctor.

"Yes, how are you? Is everything okay with my brother?"

"I do not think he wants to fight anymore. It is my experience that a person's mental state has a lot to do with a situation."

"So what you're telling me is my brother wants to die?"

"He says so, over and over again."

"Okay, I'm trying to get a flight back into the country. I'll be there as soon as I can."

This was not like T Mac, Dude thought. His brother was a fighter!

11 Back home

Darlene was sitting in a chair next to Blossom at the hospital. Both of them felt uneasy. A few minutes had passed before Darlene broke the silence.

"I'm sorry 'bout your friend."

Blossom forced a smile. "Thank you."

She was not forcing a smile because she was not appreciative of Darlene's sympathy. It was the mention of Trina that made her sad. The doctor came out of T Mac's room. Darlene stood up.

"Hello, Darlene," he greeted her.

Darlene shook his hand. He also greeted Blossom. He knew her from her visits to T Mac with Dude.

"Has Mr. Knoxx arrived yet?" he asked.

"Not yet, but he's on his way," Blossom told him.

"Has anything changed yet, Doctor?" Darlene asked.

"No. It's the same as I told you earlier on the phone. I'm sorry. He asked for his brother again before he went back to sleep."

Darlene held her head down and cried. The doctor let the women know they could go in and visit if they wished.

T Mac had just been given pain meds and was probably out of it. Blossom put her arm around Darlene and consoled her. At that moment it was not about the beef and ill feelings Darlene had against Trina when she was alive. It was about a woman possibly losing the father of her children.

"I don't know what to tell his kids if he doesn't pull through," Darlene said.

"I'm sorry, Darlene," Blossom replied, consoling her. Darlene stood up and put her head on Blossom's shoulder, crying and wiping her eyes with a tissue that Blossom had given her. Then Darlene proceeded to walk to T Mac's room alone.

He was hooked up to so many machines, Darlene could only stare and shake her head as she stood at the door for a few moments before walking over to his bed. His head was shaved bald. You could see where his head was stitched up from the insertion of the metal plate. He was skinny- and weak-looking. Darlene walked over to his bed, a look of worry and disbelief on her face.

"Damn, T . . . I can't believe . . . The doctor said you actin' like you don't wanna fight. Come on. Dat's not like you."

She reached into her pocketbook and pulled out a folded piece of white paper.

"Look, da kids made dis for you."

She unfolded the paper and taped it to the wall over his bed.

"They miss you so much . . . I know I gave you a hard way to go and always stayed beefing wit' you. But I take all dat shit back. I neva meant none of the bullshit I ever said to you. Just please come out of this bull-shit, baby . . . I know I beefed 'bout Trina and shit, but I'm sorry 'bout her. I would neva wish dat shit on her," she said, rubbing his hand.

He slowly opened his eyes. He was too weak to hold them open all the way.

"Hey," he said in a raspy dry voice.

"Hey . . ." Darlene smiled.

"Is Dude here yet?"

"No. Blossom is outside in the hall. She said he's on his way."

He moaned in pain. "I need to see him."

She rubbed his hand again. "Don't worry, he'll be here in a few."

"It's over now . . . No more pain. You and my kids will always be straight," he managed to say as a hot tear rolled slowly down his face.

Darlene couldn't take what she was hearing. "Come on, T, don't talk like dat. Everything's gon' be aight. You just have to be strong. You got ta be here for ya kids."

He was not trying to hear what she was saying.

"Man, where's Terence?"

At the sound of that name, Darlene's heart almost jumped out of her chest. Her head started to pound and her stomach went into knots. T Mac had called Dude by his birth name. Something he never did. She had almost forgotten that it was his real name, she hadn't heard it in so long. T Mac using the name now was somehow not a good sign.

"Huh?" Her voice shook and cracked as she spoke.

"What's taking Terence so long? I need to talk to him." When he was able to speak again, he demanded, "Call Blossom in here."

Darlene didn't ask any questions. She got up and left the room. Blossom was sitting in the same spot she had left her in.

The two walked back into T Mac's room. They both stood over his bed in silence.

Finally, Darlene whispered, "Baby."

He opened his eyes weakly and whispered, "Hey, Blossom. I'm sorry 'bout Trina. But she's okay. I saw her and she's okay. She loved her farewell party you guys gave her . . . Look, I tried waiting for my brother, but I can't no more. Tell him I said love is love. He'll know what I mean. But I can't live da way I would have to if I ever did get out of here. I love you, Darlene. Tell my kids dere daddy will always be dere for dem no matter what."

He closed his eyes. And everything stopped at that moment. Not just the machines that were hooked up to him. It seemed like the world had just stopped.

Darlene dropped to the floor. The noise from the machines echoed in the air. "NO! Mac, no!" Darlene cried, out of control.

Blossom held her tight and rocked her back and forth like she was holding a baby.

The doctor and nurses rushed into the room and tried to resuscitate T Mac, but they had no luck. Darlene and Blossom sat on the floor of the hospital room as if they were the only two people in there. It wasn't until Dude walked in fifteen minutes later that the two lifted their heads.

Dude felt like his life had been sucked out of him. He heard the doctor and the nurses talking, but it was like little voices ringing in his head. He heard the doctor telling a nurse the time and date of his brother's death. He heard the doctor giving him his condolences. And even when the doctor asked him if he wanted a few minutes alone with T Mac before they moved the body, all Dude could do was nod numbly.

Tears were streaming down his face. His other half was gone for good. His silent tears soon turned into loud cries.

"No! I'm sorry, I tried to get here . . . Come on, man, wake up. I'm here now . . . Wake *up*!" Dude shouted, and began crying like a baby.

Blossom walked over to him and put her arms around him. It was just a short time ago that he had been consoling her in the same way when Trina had passed. He stood in her arms for a few moments. He then turned to Darlene with bloodshot eyes.

"What did he say?" he asked.

"He said love is love and you'd know what he meant. He said he couldn't live the way he would have to live if he got out of here. He said he tried to wait for you, but he couldn't." Then Darlene broke down. The three of them looked at T Mac for the last time and left the room. Dude walked ahead of the girls like a zombie. He walked straight out of the hospital, leaving Blossom and Darlene behind. Blossom called out for him, but didn't get a reply. She and Darlene exchanged numbers and promised to call each other later.

Teddy and Black were outside of the hospital when Blossom got downstairs, but there was no sign of Dude. The two men rushed over to Blossom.

"Yo, what up?" Black said in greeting. "Where Dude? He called when he got off da plane and said T wasn't doing good. He said he was comin' straight over here."

Tears started to run down her face again. "You just missed him. T Mac's gone and Dude's not doing good at all."

Black's face went blank.

"What you mean, gone?" he asked.

"He died a short while ago," she answered.

Black banged his fist in the palm of his hand. "Naw! Can't be!"

Teddy's face was flushed with emotion. "Where Dude go?" he asked.

"I don't know. Probably to the house."

Teddy and Black walked back to the car. Blossom watched the two pull off before walking to her car.

She dialed Dude's cell phones, but both kept going to voice mail. Then her phone rang. She hoped it was Dude.

"Hello."

"What's up?" Tamika asked on the other end.

Blossom sucked her teeth in disappointment. "What's up?"

"Damn! Don't sound so disappointed," Tamika answered.

"I'm sorry. I was hoping you were Dude . . . T Mac just passed 'way and Dude is fucked up."

Tamika didn't know what to say. For a split second, she was kind of happy. She knew it was wrong, but she felt like it was justice for her best friend's death.

"Hello . . . Mika?" Blossom said.

"Damn, dat's fucked up."

"And Dude is twisted out his mind," Blossom said.

"Well, I'm gon' let you go. I was just calling to let you know dat some lady from TCI called and said classes ain't gon' start until next week. She said somethin' about some electrical problem in da building and they was fixin' it."

"Okay. I'm going to call you back later."

Blossom drove off toward one of Dude's town houses.

• • •

Dude had been sitting for a couple of hours in the hotel suite. His cell phone was ringing off the hook. He didn't have any family to call. Their grandmother had passed away years ago and she'd been their only real family.

He only picked up when he noticed that it was Fernando calling.

Fernando began without preamble: "I need to speak wit' you. It's very important, but no good to talk on phone. Tomorrow I fly up dere to see you. Okay?"

Instead of answering the question, Dude said, "My brother didn't make it. He passed away earlier today. I didn't even make it to the hospital on time . . . They said he tried to wait for me, but couldn't hold on. Ain't that some shit? I wasn't even there for him."

"You need anyting, you know me and my family is here for you."

An hour later, Dude got a call from Blossom.

"Yeah," he said.

"Where are you? I've been calling you for hours . . . Are you okay?" Blossom asked.

He wanted to act like Blossom was his family and confide in her, but he couldn't.

"I'm all right . . . I'm just chillin' for a minute."

"Where are you? I'll come and meet you."

"Naw, that's okay. I just want to be alone for a minute."

She felt bad. She would have thought that he wanted her support. She was itching to push the issue, but she knew it was not the right time. Hard as it was, she let it go.

"Okay, then . . . I guess you'll call me when you feel like being bothered."

She knew something wasn't right between them and it had nothing to do with T Mac's death. She was up on Dude's shit for a minute. Woman's intuition made the situation clear, but it wasn't the kind of thing she wanted to admit to herself. So like most women, she just went with the program and acted like nothing was wrong.

As for Dude, he was feeling guilty because he couldn't stop thinking about the night he and Maria got it on. He felt bad having dirty thoughts running through his mind at a time like this. Then he laughed to himself because he could hear T Mac's voice condoning his thoughts.

It was 6:40 A.M. when Blossom's phone rang, waking her up from a long sleep.

"Hey, girl. I'm sorry if I woke you up." Darlene sounded tired and hoarse. "I don't know if I'm comin' or goin' . . . Are you around Dude?"

Blossom felt embarrassed to tell her no, she hadn't seen Dude since they'd left the hospital the day before.

"Oh, I wanted to know what he wanted to do about burial arrangements," Darlene said, and began to cry. "I'm a mess. I can't eat or sleep . . . I can't even look in my kids' face! And that goddamn Kandi called me all last night!"

"What did she want?" Blossom asked.

"Hell if I fuckin' know! I let my cousin answer the phone. I have nothing to say to her right now . . . Are you gon' be busy later dis mornin'?"

"No, why? What's up?"

"You think you could come over here when you get up and get yourself togetha?"

"Sure . . . I'll be there at about . . . noon? Is that good?"

Darlene answered, "Yeah, that's good. Thanks, Blossom."

Blossom sat in silence. Her mind was blank and her heart ached. She looked around the picture-perfect living room. She had a fifteen-thousand-dollar television hanging on the wall. Thin as a huge picture frame. She thought about the day she and Dude bought the dining-room set. It had caught her eye as soon as they walked into the furniture store.

"You like this?" he had asked her.

"Very much," she answered.

"Okay, well, get it."

"But you didn't ask how much it cost."

He'd looked at her like she was crazy. "And? I said if you like it, you're gonna get it."

That was that! The salesperson had come over and Dude told her they wanted the dining-room set. And he gave her the same look he had given Blossom when she'd asked him if he wanted to know how much all of the pieces cost. By the time they had added the china cabinet and two extra chairs—as if she was ever going to have a large dinner party— everything came to fourteen thousand dollars. It was the only piece of furniture she had picked out herself for the town house. Dude had furnished the place from top to bottom. The dining-room set was the only thing that felt like it was really hers. Everything else she had came from Dude. He was her whole world. She had lost her own identity. And now she felt like what they had was slipping away. All of the crazy stuff going on in Dude's life was her excuse for not acknowledging it. She just kept telling herself that his life was upside down and she should keep quiet. She felt she owed him the benefit of the doubt that he wasn't cheating, since he had done so much for her.

Just then, Dude walked in and headed for the stairs.

"Dude, is that you?" she yelled.

"Yeah. What's up?" he shouted from upstairs.

She got off the couch and walked up the steps.

"Hey, how you feeling?"

"It is what it is."

"You hungry? I can make you something to eat real quick."

"Naw, I'm straight."

He was standing inside the walk-in closet, pulling money out of the large safe. Blossom didn't know what else to say, but she felt like she needed to talk to him.

"Darlene called. She wanted to know what you wanted to do about the funeral arrangements," she said.

"Aight. I'll call her when I get back in the car." His back was to Blossom.

She suddenly felt like an outsider.

He began to change his clothes. Blossom stood watching him, hoping he would say something to her. His body was smooth. She hadn't seen, let alone touched it in a long time. She walked over to him and rubbed him softly on his back.

"Baby, you know I'm here for you . . . I just feel like . . ."

She staggered, hesitating to express how she'd been feeling. Dude turned around and wrapped his arms around her.

"I know, baby," he whispered in her ear. "I just have a lot on my plate right now. Please bear with me for a minute."

She took a deep breath of satisfaction. "Okay . . . I love you."

He kissed her on her forehead. "I love you, too, baby. I promise once I'm finished with everything today, I'll come straight home."

"Thank you. I need that."

He knew he hadn't been doing home base right. It was just something that just happened. He felt bad every time he looked at her. His guilt about his affair with Maria overwhelmed him.

"You know what? As a matter of fact, I could use something light and quick to eat before I hit the street."

"Okay, I'll make you a breakfast sandwich. I picked up a new juicer. I'll make you a glass of fresh orange juice, too." She kissed him on the cheek.

He knew he had something special.

On his way to his office, Dude bumped into Teddy.

"Hey, man wha's the deal? I been trying to reach you since yesterday . . . Are you okay?" Teddy said.

"I'm straight. I just had to fall back for a minute to collect my thoughts and shit. What up wit' you, though?"

"Nothin' much. Tryin' to see if you need me to do anything," Teddy answered.

"I'm straight for now. I got to go take care of some BI right now, so I'll hit you when I'm finished."

"If you need me to do anything, just let me know."

Dude wondered why Teddy would say this to him. Teddy knew there were no pickups to do. But he just brushed it off, figuring with everything going on, Teddy might have forgotten.

There were two cars parked in the lot of his office. A black-on-black Cadillac and a silver 500 Benz with tinted windows.

Ricky and Fernando got out of the silver Benz with the same bodyguard Dude remembered from earlier meetings.

Junior and Maria got out of the black Cadillac. There was a lot of security, Dude noticed.

Damn, she's beautiful! he thought to himself. He tried not to reveal his feelings.

He walked over to Fernando and hugged him. Fernando held him tight for a few seconds before letting him go.

"My friend, how are you?"

"I'm okay," he lied.

Fernando gave Dude a pat on the back. "No, you not. Let us go inside and finish talk."

The family went into Dude's office. The bodyguards waited outside.

"Man, I so sorry about T Mac, Dude," Ricky stated.

"Thanks, man."

"I know you must be a wreck right now. I don't know what I would do if I lose Ricky or Maria," Junior said.

"Dude, I know you feel you have to hold it in," Fernando began. "But trust me, dis is no good ting to do. I know how it is to lose the closest ting to you. I lose my Maria and my whole world crumble down. So, we know what you going through. And, you a good man wit' good heart, so God will always bless you. Me and my family, we here for you. Maria, where's the card?"

Maria dug into her pocketbook and pulled out an envelope. She walked over to Dude and handed it to him.

She kissed him on his cheek. "I'm so sorry for you loss, Mr. Dude."

He gave her a friendly hug. "Thank you, Maria."

"This is from me and my family. Go on, open it," Fernando stated.

Dude opened the envelope. Inside was a beautiful card, two checks, and a note.

The first check was written to him, for sixty thousand dollars. The other check did not have a name on it, but was for a hundred thousand dollars.

"I did not know you brother's children's mother name," Fernando explained. "So I leave it blank. But dat's for her and the kids. I know you will always make sure dey are okay. But still we wanted to give someting."

"Thank you so much," Dude said as he unfolded the note and began to read. Everyone in the room sat quiet as Dude read the note to himself.

My dear friend Dude,

As this may not be a good time to mention this type of thing . . . with the loss of your brother and everything, but this kind of thing must be addressed. You know I have friends in many high places and it has come to my attention that you have a rat amongst you. And as close as you and my family are, that is no good for us. Your friend Teddy is secretly working with the FBI. He is a snitch! Sorry I could not speak to you one-on-one like a man. But we do not know if your office is bugged and we cannot take a chance. We will help you to our best ability to rid of this problem. You are family to us. Never forget that.

Yours truly,

Fernando and Family

When he'd finished reading the note, Dude's mind went blank. He looked around the room at Fernando and his family. This was not the time for this bullshit, he thought. His heart started to fill with rage. After all he had done for Teddy, he'd stabbed him in the back like that!

"So, you make all of the funeral arrangements yet?" Fernando asked.

Dude was in a daze. "He asked to be cremated." There was going to be a viewing of the body before the cremation and then a little memorial party afterward. T Mac had always said he wanted a party when he passed. He didn't want people sitting around crying and sad. He said he wanted people eating and drinking, thinking 'bout the good ol' times they'd spent with him. Trina had said much the same thing.

Fernando insisted that Maria help Dude with the party arrangements.

Darlene was sitting outside talking on the phone when Blossom pulled up to her house. "My cousin took the kids over to her house. Come inside," Darlene said.

Blossom could tell she must have been crying all night long. Her eyes were bloodshot and swollen. Her voice sounded hoarse and scratchy.

"You hungry?" Darlene asked Blossom when they got inside.

"No, not really. I made a breakfast sandwich for me and Dude earlier. I'm still kind of full from that."

Darlene giggled. "What, an egg with Cheddar cheese, and turkey bacon, on a bagel?" she asked.

"How you know?"

"Oh my God! I can't believe he still eats dat shit!" Darlene said.

"Yeah, he'll eat that all day if he could. I could cook dinner, and he'll still eat one of those sandwiches in the middle of the night."

"Girl, him and Terry used to make me make those goddamn sandwiches all the time back in the days. I'm talking ten or more years ago!"

"You guys were together for a long time."

"We grew up together," Darlene said.

"You grew up with Kandi, too?" Blossom asked. "I'm sorry—that wasn't a good thing to ask."

"No, it's okay . . ." Darlene said. "We didn't grow up together. We became cool 'cause I was T Mac's girl and she was Dude's girl."

"So, was she always crazy?" Blossom asked.

Darlene paused and sat with her thoughts for a minute. "Well, I guess she would have to be crazy from the start. I don't think people just bug out like dat out the blue. I think she might have had some hidden issues we didn't know about . . . But, den again, Dude must of known somethin'."

"Why you say that?"

" 'Cause he was sending her to therapy. I just found dat out the other day when her lawyer called me tryin' to get me to be a character witness. He said he wanted it to be known dat she was trying hard to overcome her mental illness. I don't know—some fuckin' crap like dat. Then he startin' talking about Dude sending her to therapy for a while. She ain't never mention it to me. Waste of fuckin' money; shit ain't work."

Suddenly Darlene started breaking down again. She started sobbing. "Shit ain't work! My kids' daddy is dead, ya friend is dead, and she's sittin' up in prison tryin' to find a way to justify what she did!" She dropped to her knees.

Blossom bent down and held her in her arms.

"I'm sorry . . ." she whispered while rocking Darlene like a baby.

At that moment Darlene wasn't T Mac's baby mother, the one Blossom and her friends had been fighting the night she'd met Dude. She was Blossom's friend. And they both shared a common pain, caused by the same person. Finally, Darlene calmed down and stood up.

"I'm sorry. I've been trying to hold up, but it's hard. I just don't understand. Terry and me been together since kids. He's all I ever known, more than Dude and Kandi. And Lord knows he put me through some shit! But, I would never flip out the way she did! She just didn't know how to let him go," Darlene said, with tears running down her face.

For a minute, Blossom felt like Darlene was talking about her when she said Dude was all Kandi knew. Maybe this was his MO, Blossom was thinking just as the house phone rang.

"Hello," Darlene answered.

"Hey, it's me. How you holding up?" the voice on the other end of the phone asked.

Tears started running out of her eyes again. Her voice cracked when she replied. "Hey, well, I'm doin' the best I can. How you doin'?"

"I guess I can say the same. Where's the kids?"

She cleared her voice. "Wit' my cousin."

When Darlene hung up, she turned to Blossom. "That was Dude. He called before you came. He said he'll be here in a little while."

"How did he sound?" Blossom asked.

"Like he's holding too much in. I know Dude; he's dying inside. T Mac was his other half."

"It's like he's just clammed up," Blossom acknowledged.

"He's good for that. You just have to pry ya way in. Don't give up too easy. Trust me; he may act like he doesn't need you, but he does."

"I just feel like I should fall back and give him room."

"Naw, dat's how I lost T Mac. Fallin' back when I needed to be moving closer. Next thing I know, we were two people living separate lives. He always did good by me and my kids. We never had to ask for nothin'. We knew we still loved each other, we just couldn't get it together. We were too stubborn to admit our faults. Too ignorant to say, 'Let's try and make this work again.' "

After speaking with Fernando on the phone and agreeing to meet him and his sons early the following morning, Dude jumped into his car and sped toward the highway on his way to meet Maria at the catering hall. She was standing outside of the car with her bodyguard when he arrived.

She gave Dude a hug. "Hey, Mr. Dude. How you holding?"

"I'm good . . . Especially now that I've seen you."

"You someting else, you know." She smiled.

She directed the security to get her gator briefcase from the backseat of the car. She sat on the hood of the car and popped it open.

"Now, the very good ting is dis date you wanted is good. You say you expect about one hundred to one hundred and seventy-five people. Yes?"

He nodded yes.

"Well, what you tink?" she asked.

"I think you are beautiful. And you can't even imagine how much you've been on my mind. And I wish your people weren't behind us so I could kiss your lips. That's what I think . . . I love everything you decided on, baby." He rubbed her leg.

She smiled and blushed. He said just what she had wanted to hear. He had been on her mind constantly since their night together. She wanted to reach over and gently put her tongue into his mouth. But she knew she was being watched.

Dude and Maria got into his car and drove to Darlene's house. When they arrived, he rang the bell.

"Who is it!" Blossom called as she answered the door. "It's probably Dude!" she shouted to Darlene, who was in the kitchen, and fixed her hair real quick with her fingers. She was excited about seeing him.

Blossom snatched the door open with a huge smile on her face. That smile dropped when she saw Dude and Maria standing practically on top of each other.

When Dude realized who had opened the door, his forehead wrinkled up with confusion. Blossom was the last person he would have expected to be answering Darlene's door.

"Blossom . . ."

He caught himself when he realized he was making himself look guilty about something.

He walked in and kissed her on the cheek. Maria followed him.

"What you doing here?" he sweetly asked.

"Darlene asked me to come over for a while. She wasn't doing too well."

"Where is she?"

"In the kitchen . . ." She reached around him and stuck her hand out to Maria. "Hello, I'm Blossom."

"Oh, my bad," Dude quickly said. "Blossom, this is Maria. Maria, this is my girlfriend, Blossom."

Darlene came out of the kitchen. "Who was it, Blossom—"

When she saw Dude and some female, her words cut short.

"Oh, Dude, it's you."

She gave him a hug.

Dude introduced Darlene to Maria as his sister-in-law.

Blossom had never known that T Mac and Darlene were actually married. And Darlene hadn't heard anyone refer to her as T Mac's wife in so long, it kind of threw her off.

Maria stuck her hand out to shake Darlene's. "Please to meet you. I hear so much about you," she said with her thick accent.

"Nice to meet you, too," Darlene told her. There was an uncomfortable silence before Darlene continued. "Well, let's go into the kitchen."

"Mmm, smells good in here," Dude said. He couldn't look Blossom in her face. He could feel her eyes piercing at him and Maria.

He began describing the funeral arrangements. Blossom sat listening, trying to figure out when he was going to explain who the fuck the bitch with him was.

"Maria went over to the Carriage House for me and set up something for the party. Just how Terry would've liked. Food, music, drinks. She's even ordered gold rose key chains with Terry's name, date of birth, and death engraved on them for the guests. So, write up a list of people you want there so I can get invites out to them."

Darlene nodded. "Thank you. Dat's somethin' Terry would've wanted. To go out wit' a bang."

"You welcome," Maria replied.

Blossom got up from the table and threw her empty wine cooler in the garbage. "Yeah, sounds real nice."

Dude ignored her and continued talking to Darlene.

"Oh, yeah. This is for you and the kids," he said as he went into his back pocket and pulled out the envelope with the check Fernando had given him earlier.

Darlene took the envelope. "What's dis?"

"Something from Fernando and his family," Dude told her.

She opened the envelope and looked at the check. "Wow . . . um, dis is . . . um, very generous. But I haven't even met him before . . ." Darlene stated, pleased but startled.

Maria spoke up. "Yes, but my papa was very fond of you husband. And me and my family give this gift to you and you children, from the depths of our hearts."

Darlene hugged her. "Thank you. Tell ya father I said thank you so much."

She suddenly realized she shouldn't have hugged Maria in front of Blossom, but what else was she to do? The woman and her family had just given her a hundred thousand dollars.

"So, ya Fernando's daughter?" Darlene asked, still flustered.

"Yes."

"I never met him, but I understand he's a good man," Darlene continued.

"Well, I should be going now," Maria said.

"Okay, I'm going to walk her outside. I'll be right back," Dude said.

Blossom pulled out her cell and started dialing Tamika.

"Nice meeting you, Blossom," Maria said.

But Blossom kept dialing her cell phone, pretending not to hear Maria.

When they were gone, Blossom peeped out the curtain on the low to see them say good-bye.

"So, you'll call me later, right?" Dude asked Maria.

"Oh, don't get me wrong, Mr. Dude. I would love to, but I don't want to get you in trouble wit' you girlfriend."

He laughed. "I'm sorry. I don't know what that was all about in there."

"Is that so?"

"She doesn't know anything about our night together. She had no right acting like that."

Maria smiled. "Woman's intuition, Mr. Dude. It just wasn't—what do you people in America say? It just was not a good look. Not cool at all. And very uncomfortable, I must say."

"I'm sorry for putting you in an uncomfortable situation. I didn't know she was here."

"I need you to give me the dates of the party so I can order the key chains. And I will have a sample of the invites by tomorrow evening."

"Okay, fine. So that's it?"

"I guess for now."

"Let's talk later on, maybe get a drink or something."

"Maybe; we'll see."

He hugged her tight. He wanted another night like the one they'd had in DR. He kissed her softly on her cheek then watched her drive away.

Dude went back into the house. Blossom was sitting at the table flipping through a magazine. Dude went to the fridge and took out a bottled water.

"Where's Darlene, Blossom?"

"I think upstairs." She never looked up from the magazine.

He stood in the middle of the kitchen looking at Blossom, whose back was turned.

"What's your problem, Blossom?"

She ignored him. He walked over to her and asked her again. This time she looked up from the magazine and rolled her eyes at him.

"What was that for?" he asked.

"Don't patronize me, okay."

"I don't understand."

"You played yourself! I don't give a fuck who you say daughter she is, I'm not stupid! You gave yourself away when I answered the door. You looked like you seen a ghost. You didn't even know what to say, Dude. The vibe that was coming from you told it all. So, that's why you couldn't call me while you were in the Dominican Republic, huh? You are a piece of work! You have some fuckin' woman help you plan something for your brother? I'm your girl and you don't even ask me to do anything. I can't even get a decent conversation from you! And FYI, my woman's intuition is telling me something just ain't right about this situation. And frankly, I'm tired of trying to push my way into your life . . . and trying to gain back my spot, which I didn't even realize I had lost! I haven't done nothing to you, Dude, for you to treat me the way you have been treating me. This last month or so you've been treating me like I was a stranger! And I'm sick and tired of feeling like—" She stopped and stared at him.

Her voice trembled.

"I'm just tired of feeling the way you've been making me feel. I don't deserve it and you know it, Dude. I'm going back to Brooklyn for a while, to give you your space. I won't bother you; I'll let you mourn your brother's death. When you're ready, you know where I'll be." Her eyes were flooded.

She left the room to tell Darlene that she was leaving.

Darlene saw what was up. "Just remember what I said earlier, 'bout letting go and being too stubborn to fight for ya relationship."

A lump grew in Blossom's throat. "Yeah, that's what I've been doing and it hasn't been working in my favor. I just refuse to lose a piece of myself along the way. You need to share that advice with Dude."

Blossom left and Darlene walked into the kitchen. "You better not fuck up wit' dis one," she said to Dude.

He shrugged his shoulders. "What are you talking about?"

"Come on, don't play wit' me," Darlene said. "You know I know. I'm talkin' 'bout Blossom. She love you to death and you just don't see it. I know how you can give somebody the cold shoulder. I know how you can clam up and throw up that brick wall."

"And when did you and her become such good friends anyway?" he joked.

"When did you start fuckin' Fernando's daughter?" she spat.

He almost choked on his soda. "What!"

"Don't even try the bullshit wit' me! I know you, Dude! And you fuckin' dat girl! And I don't know what makes you think Blossom can't figure that one out! I'm tellin' you, woman's intuition is a muthafucka!"

"You crazy, girl!" he exclaimed.

"Look, Dude, you know me and ya brother been through a lot of shit in our day, but you know I always had his back no matter what. You two were—I mean, are my family. I only want the best for you. Like I always only wanted for Terry."

She began to cry. He held her and cried, too.

Darlene's house phone rang.

"Hello."

"Hey, it's Blossom. Do me a favor, look on top of your counter and tell me if you see a set of keys on a Gucci key chain."

"Okay, hold on a minute. Let me check," Darlene told her.

Darlene spotted the set of keys on the counter.

"Yeah, I got dem. You gon' come back by and pick dem up?"

Blossom didn't answer right away. "Um . . . Is Dude still there?"

"Yeah, he's right here. You wanna talk to him?" she asked.

"No! I'll get them tomorrow or something. My sister's probably home. If not, my girlfriend has a spare."

"Are you sure? You don't want me to give them to Dude?"

"No. Don't do that. I'm not going to see him."

"Okay. I'll hold them for you."

Darlene hung up the phone.

"What?"

"Blossom left her keys," Darlene replied. "I thought she maybe was pulling a stunt. But she's not coming to get them while you're here. You fucked up big-time!"

"Whatever! Trust me, she's just having a tantrum. She'll be over her shit tomorrow. Just give me the keys. I'll give them to her tomorrow when I see her."

Teddy crossed over the Benjamin Franklin Bridge into Philly. He drove to Broad Street and pulled over. He looked at his watch and sucked his teeth.

"Come the fuck on!" he mumbled to himself.

He looked over his shoulder. He took a cell phone out of the glove compartment and powered it on. He dialed Dude.

Dude did not recognize the number.

"Yo," he answered anyway.

"Hey, what up, man?" Teddy asked on the other end.

Dude's heart started pounding. Teddy's voice threw him off. It took everything sensible in him not to flip on Teddy.

"What's up? What number is this?" Dude asked.

"Oh, dis is my new number. I still got the other jack, but I ain't fuckin' wit' it too much."

"Word. Why not?"

"Nothin' really, just bitches playin' on my jack actin' stupid. Plus, it just time to change up."

"I hear that. So, how you?"

"That's what I'm callin' to ask you. How you holdin' up? You need anything?"

"Naw, I'm straight. I made the funeral arrangements today. I'm going tomorrow to pick up something for him to wear. It is what it is."

"Well, if you want, I'll run around wit' you tomorrow. You spoke to Black? I tried to call him, but he's not pickin' up."

"Not since this morning." In fact, Dude had just spoken to Black when he was at Darlene's house. Fernando had assured him that Black had nothing to do with Teddy and his dealings with the feds. Dude felt it was only right to put Black up on what Fernando had told him about Teddy. So he knew why Black wasn't answering Teddy's calls.

Just then, Teddy noticed the people he was waiting for pulling up. He rushed Dude off the phone. "So, hit me tomorrow and let me know if you want me to run wit' you. And give Black dis number. Tell him to hit me."

"Aight, will do."

Just as Dude was hanging up Teddy added, "Oh, and if you need any runs to be made, I got you. I know you kind of hectic right—"

Dude hung up on him without letting him finish. That wasn't something he was trying to hear. He knew everything Teddy said had a bad motive behind it.

The two men Teddy was meeting walked up to his car, one to the front passenger window and the other behind the driver's side. Teddy hit the button to unlock the doors, and the men got in.

"So, how are you, Teddy?" the man who sat in the front seat asked.

"How am I suppose to be doing, in a position like dis?"

The man in the back laughed. "As if it's our fault."

Teddy turned around and looked at him. "Man, fuck you!"

"Come on now," the man up front said. "Let's be nice. We're all suppose to be on the same team here."

Teddy and the man sitting in the back stared each other down, ready to go at it at any given moment. The man in the front seat gave Teddy a pat on the shoulder. "Come on now, let's take it easy."

Teddy slowly turned back around. "You need to check ya boy," he said to the man sitting next to him.

"Lighten up, man. So, how's that cell phone we gave you working?" he asked Teddy.

"It's aight, I guess. I just started using it today."

"Well, did you get anything good on it?"

"Not much."

The man in the back broke his silence. "What's not much?"

"Not much . . . Which part of 'not much' don't you get?" Teddy shot back.

"You do understand we are working in a time frame, don't you?" the man sitting up front asked.

"Yeah, you told me dat, but you gotta understand dat his brother just passed away. He's not gonna be doing too much. And he damn sure don't want to talk about no business."

The man in the back spoke again. "And what part of that has to do with us? The way I see it, you don't want to go to prison for the rest of your life. So, we give you an opportunity to make your situation a little better. It's like an even trade, except you seem to be having a problem holding up your end of the bargain. Whereas we, on the other hand, are prepared to fully hold up ours. And just to let you know, our offer will not sit on the table forever, so you need to start doing whatever you need to do."

Teddy held his lips tightly together. But he knew the agent was telling it like it was.

"He's right, Teddy," the man sitting in the front seat stated. "We need to be able to make some type of move by next week. I mean, your friend's shit is so tight we cannot even pick him up for tax evasion. So we need you. We need him on tape . . ."

The agents exchanged looks, then the one in the front said, "We got word from our boss that you might have to take the stand."

Teddy turned red. "What! Y'all ain't never say shit about testifying! Where the fuck did dat come from? And what does 'maybe' mean? Either I am or I'm not."

The agent in the front seat continued. "Well, maybe means most likely . . . And we're going to need you to sign some papers."

The agent in the backseat pulled some papers out of a leather briefcase. He handed them to Teddy, saying, "You should go over these with your lawyer and get them back to us as soon as possible."

Teddy looked down at the papers.

"Very soon, like in a day or two."

Teddy didn't respond. He just looked up from the papers and put them in his armrest compartment. The agents got out of the car and pulled off. Teddy sat there for a while. He could either chuck it up and do his time or take the easy way out and rat out his friend. Dude had been nothing but a friend to him from day one—treated him like family and always made sure he was all right. And now he had to cross him. His back was up against the wall. Taking the stand was going to be a problem.

"So, did he ever say who the girl was?" Shareen asked Blossom as she put the fish in the pan of grease.

"Yeah, where the bitch came from!" Kim asked.

"Fernando's daughter," Blossom replied.

"Who the fuck is Fernando?" Tamika asked, pouring the girls another round of Alizé.

"I don't know. Darlene didn't get into all that. But him and his family gave Darlene a hundred-thousand-dollar check for her and her kids."

Shareen started choking. "What! You can't be for real! You sure dat bitch ain't lyin' 'bout dat money?"

"No, she ain't lying! I saw the check. I was there when Dude gave it to her."

"So, you mean to tell me dat dis girl is the daughter of the man who gave Darlene the money?" Shareen asked.

"Yeah."

"Shhhit, girl! I be fuckin' her, too! Wit' a pops wit' paper like dat! I be—"

"Shareen! Ain't nobody say he was fuckin' her!" Kim cut her eyes at Shareen. "You so triflin'!"

"No, it's okay," Blossom said to the girls. "He probably *is* fucking that bitch! That's the vibe I got."

"Man, you don't know that, Blossom. You might just be paranoid." Kim was trying to keep the peace and avoid drama.

"No, I'm not. You had to be there to know what I'm saying. Trust me, if he hasn't fucked her yet, he has plans to. It's something going on. I don't care what he says."

Tamika shook her head and took the fish out of the grease. She placed another batch of fish into the pan.

"Girl, welcome to the real world," she said to Blossom. "Dat's a man for you. And I say dat not to say Dude isn't a good guy, but he's still a man. And a man is capable of doin' almost anything!"

Kim held her drink up. "I'll drink to dat one, sister!"

Shareen lifted her drink up, too. "And I'll second dat!"

Tamika lifted her glass. "And I done lived it!"

They looked at Blossom. Blossom lifted her glass up to the girls' glasses. "And I'm learning it!"

The girls all toasted and took their drinks to the head. Shareen put on their favorite CD—*My Life,* Mary J.

This was just what Blossom had needed, some moral support. The lobby doorbell rang and the girls all looked at one another waiting for one of them to get up and see who it was. Nobody moved. They just kept on eating and talking. The bell rang again and the girls once again ignored it.

"Kim, won't you go to the intercom?" Tamika suggested.

Kim sucked her teeth. "Shit, you go. It's your crib."

"You closer," Tamika answered.

This time it was the front doorbell that rang. The person had found a way into the building, without the help of any of the girls.

"I'll get it," Blossom said, and walked down the long hallway to the front door.

"Yeah, dat's a good idea!" Tamika shouted toward the hallway.

The rest of the girls laughed.

Blossom looked through the peephole. It was Lil' Richie. She took a deep breath, fixed her hair, and opened the door.

"Hey, what you doing here?"

"Damn, is it a problem?"

She smiled. "No . . . I'm sorry. I'm just surprise to see you. Come in; we're just here drinking and eating fish."

She let him in and they walked back to the kitchen.

"Look who's here, everybody!" Blossom announced to the girls.

The girls looked up and smiled.

"Hey, what's up!" they chorused.

"Hello, how y'all doing tonight?" Lil' Richie asked.

Tamika smiled. "Look at my real brother-in-law."

"You crazy, Mika," Blossom told her.

"No, I'm tellin' the truth. You hungry?" Tamika asked him.

"Yeah, I'll take a couple of pieces of fish."

They all sat down, ate, drank, and talked. Every now and then Blossom and Lil' Richie would have eye contact and chills would run through her body.

•   •   •

Dude was heading toward the Holland Tunnel when he got a call from Maria.

"Hey, you. What's up?" he said.

"Not'ing much, what's up wit' you?"

"Just driving."

"Driving where?" she asked.

"Nowhere really. I didn't have no real destination. Why, you have somewhere for me to go?"

"It depends." She chuckled.

"Yeah? On what?"

"It depends on where you feel like going."

"I think you know the answer to that."

"Okay, then come pick me up."

He agreed to meet her. He wasn't going to make it to the Brooklyn Bridge like he initially had planned. Instead, he was heading toward a penthouse on Park Avenue.

12 *The next morning*

Dude woke up to the sight of Maria's flawless naked body and snatched his pants from off of the floor. To his surprise, Blossom had never called him. He dialed her number in Brooklyn.

"You still sleep?" he asked when she picked up.

"Yeah, I'll call you when I get up, okay?"

He hadn't expected that. "Huh?"

She cleared her throat. "Yeah, I'll call you back when I wake up."

"Yeah, aight."

She hung up the phone and turned over. She looked at Lil' Richie sleeping. She wanted to talk to Dude, but she didn't want Richie to make noise and have Dude hear him. She hadn't had sex with Lil' Richie, but still, she didn't want drama with Dude. Her head was pounding. She sucked her teeth and plopped her head back down on her pillow. She and Richie had sat up talking for hours. She told him everything that was going on with her and Dude. And he told her everything that was going on in his life. She wondered if he felt just as jealous about hearing her and Dude's business as she was jealous about the girl he was with. She wiggled closer to him and pushed herself up under him.

Dude lay on his back staring at the ceiling, trying to comprehend what had just gone down with Blossom. After a few minutes, he closed his eyes and tried to get a little more sleep.

Maria's phone rang and broke his attempt. Maria didn't budge. The phone would ring out for a few seconds and stop. Then it would ring again. This happened for about five minutes straight. Finally, he couldn't take any more. He tapped her gently and tried to wake her up.

"Hey, baby, your phone is ringing."

She spoke without opening her eyes. "I know. I hear it. I know who it is."

He lay back down and the ringing continued. After about another five minutes, Maria reached over and picked up her cell from her pocketbook.

"*Sí.*"

Dude was trying to act like he was asleep. Maria spoke in Spanish and he couldn't pick up on what was being said. But he could tell by her tone that she was angry.

"Look, you need to let me be right now!" she said, switching suddenly to English. "Because I no want to talk wit' you right now! I am sleep and can't handle you headaches! I will talk to you when I get back home. Until then, please do not bother me wit' you stupid phone calls!" She hung the phone up.

She looked over at Dude, who still had his eyes closed. She leaned over and kissed him softly on his lips.

"I know you no sleep," she whispered.

He opened his eyes and smiled. She's perfect, he thought to himself. Even when she wakes up in the morning, she's beautiful. And she didn't even have morning breath!

"Sounds like you got your hands full early in the morning."

"No really . . ." She rose and walked into the bathroom.

He could hear the water running for a minute or two. Then she came out of the bathroom with her hair pinned up. Dude sat up and looked at her naked body as she stood in the middle of the room.

She teased him. "You like what you see?"

He got up from the bed and walked over to her.

"I love what I see."

As if last night wasn't enough, the two started kissing and making love again. They had gone four rounds last night, but he just couldn't get enough of her. It wasn't that he felt Maria's sex was better than Blossom's. They were on the same level as far as satisfaction went. They were just two different people making him feel good in different ways.

A half hour or so later, Dude and Maria were lying in the middle of the floor, out of breath. Dude looked at his watch; they had been going at it for forty-two minutes. He gathered his strength and went to take a shower. When he came out, Maria was lying across the bed. He gathered his clothes and got dressed. He sat on the bed and gave her a kiss on the cheek.

"I have to run. I have a lot to do today. I have to go shopping for my brother's clothes and stuff. What are you doing today?"

"Not'ing much. I'm going to pick up the invites . . . Oh, don't forget to leave the information for the key chains. And I'm going to do a little shopping."

"Okay, I'll call you later." He kissed her again, this time on her mouth, and walked out.

He waited until he got into his car to call Blossom.

Blossom's phone rang three times before she bothered to look at the caller ID.

She put on an extra-sleepy voice and answered. "Yeah, hello."

Dude sucked his teeth. "Don't give me that sleepy shit. You got caller ID, you knew it was me."

She sighed. "First of all, I am still sleep. Second of all, I answered without looking at the caller ID, so I didn't know who it was."

"Yeah, whatever. Why are you still sleep?"

" 'Cause I'm tired. And I went to bed at like five-thirty this morning."

"Where were you at all night?"

"I was hanging out."

"What?"

"I said I was hanging out . . . Look, I'm going to call you soon as I get up."

He hung up on her. He dialed Black and told him to meet him. The whole ride to meet Black, his mind was on overload. There was too much going on in his life at one time. And this shit with Teddy was really throwing him off track. He had never had to think about killing a man before. But the situation with Teddy was giving him no other choice. He always played fair when it came to business, so he never had any beef about money. Everybody he dealt with respected him for that. His brother, on the other hand, had taken somebody's life before, and if he was still alive, he'd probably take Teddy's, too.

Dude pulled up to the cemetery and cut the car off. Black was already there. Dude walked over to Black, who was setting a beautiful flower arrangement in front of a huge tombstone.

Dude gave him a pat on his back. "What up?"

This was the first time they had seen each other since T Mac had passed.

"Man, I'm sorry . . ." Black began.

"It's okay, man."

"Naw, it's not aight, kid. You got to stop sayin' dat. It's aight to hurt, man. Dat was ya brother, ya best friend. It's no way it's aight. Next to this woman right here." He pointed to the tombstone that read HATTIE MAE KNOXX, A LOVING MOTHER AND GRANDMOTHER. YOU WILL BE TRULY MISSED AND YOU ARE UNCONDITIONALLY LOVED.

"He was ya only real family left. And the more you hold in your pain, the worst it's gonna be when you finally let it out."

Dude just stared at his grandmother's grave. He knew Black was right. Black had been through a similar tragedy. His girl had been eight months pregnant with their first child when she passed. They had been out driving one day when a car had suddenly pulled up on the side of Black's and opened fire. She'd been killed instantly. Black took three bullets and was in a wheelchair for almost a year. As Dude remembered that awful time tears started flowing like a faucet from his eyes. Black quietly stood next to his friend and let him cry.

When Dude had cried his cries, he turned to Black and hugged him. Then he knelt down to say a prayer for his grandmother.

"No need for thanks," Dude said. "So, what we gonna do 'bout dis fuckin' rat?" ·

"Mirk dat nigga," Black answered. "It's either dat or we fall back and end up locked for life."

"Yeah, but we just have to do it right. 'Cause them boys are on our heels. And besides, if that nigga shows up dead or ends up missing, trust I'm the first one they gonna look at."

Black nodded. "Oh, no doubt. I know we gotta be straight clean wit' it."

"Man, I felt bad when Fernando was telling me about Teddy's punk ass. All that Fernando did for me and here I come jeopardizing his shit. That man been doing him since forever and never got caught up. And here I come bringing heat around him. Not to even mention all I did for Teddy's punk ass. I mean, what would even make a man want to rat a nigga out just to save his own ass. Ain't nobody hold no gun to that faggot's head and make him do nothing."

"Everybody ain't built for consequences," Black observed.

Dude thought about what Black said. Many cats are good at pursuing a certain lifestyle, but when it brings havoc . . . they don't want to face it. He and Black both agreed to sit for a day or two and try to come up with a good plan to smoke Teddy without causing any problems for themselves.

They both got back into their cars and jumped on the highway. Dude picked up his cell phone and dialed Blossom's number again.

"What's up?"

"What you mean, what's up? How you know who's calling on the other end?"

"Caller ID."

"Oh, so now you decided to look at the caller ID . . . Anyway, what are you doing?"

She inhaled deeply and let the air out. "Nothing much. I was getting ready to lay back down for a little while."

"Didn't you get enough sleep?"

"Not really. I wasn't feeling too good."

He jokingly replied, "Let me find out you laid up with some nigga over there in Brooklyn."

"Yeah, let you find out."

He paused for a minute.

"Well, tell that nigga it's time to break out. I'm on my way to pick you up."

Even though she was upset with him, she couldn't help but feel good. She hadn't heard him say he was coming to pick her up in so long.

"Hello . . . You still there?" he asked.

"Yeah, I'm here. Where we going?"

He sucked his teeth. "Man, since when it mattered where we were going when I said I was picking you up?"

"I'm just saying—"

He cut her off. "Look, you want me to pick you up or what? So I'll know which way to go."

"Aight. I'm going to jump in the shower and get dressed. Call when you get downstairs."

She hung up and rushed into her room. Lil' Richie was sitting on her bed with the television remote in his hand.

"So what are you doing for the rest of the day?" she asked him.

He stood up and grabbed his jacket. "That must be my exit music."

"What are you talking about?"

He kissed her on her forehead. "Just call me later. I'll be around."

"Okay. Maybe we can go check out a movie or something."

"Sounds like a plan."

She walked him to the door then ran back into the room and started sorting through the clothes. She tried to find something sexy but not too overboard. She wanted to remind Dude of what he had been missing, but she didn't want to overdo it. She found a pair of black leather pants that had a nice, waist-length jacket that matched. She dug deep into a plastic bin in the bottom of her closet and pulled out a leather Chanel pocketbook adorned with beads and pearls. She looked down at her fingernails and sucked her teeth. She hadn't had a manicure in a while, and she knew that Dude was big on nail maintenance. She looked at the clock, hoping she'd have enough time to make it to the salon before he got here. She grabbed her towel, washcloth, and her toiletries bag and rushed into the bathroom.

Dude let Black know about his detour to Brooklyn to see Blossom. Just as he hung up his cell rang. He noticed the new number Teddy had used to call him before. He hesitated about answering, but he didn't want to act too shady. He needed Teddy to think everything was still all good.

"Yo!"

"Hey, what's going on, man? Everything's okay?" Teddy said.

"What up? I was just getting ready to call you. Where you at?"

"Up around the way. Why? What's up, you need me?"

"Um . . . Yeah, I might. You think you could drop off T's clothes to the funeral parlor?"

"Yeah! Come on, man, you got dat. I told you if you needed me, I would be there. Where you at now?"

"I'm on my way to Route 4 to cop T's clothes. I'm going to hit you soon as I'm done and we can hook up."

Teddy agreed and the two hung up. Dude didn't want to give him too much info on his whereabouts and destination. He didn't know what Teddy could've been up to. As far as he was concerned, the nigga could've had them boys waiting at the mall for him. He didn't want to take any chances. Bad enough he had to hold a normal conversation with Teddy. 'Cause only God knew how bad he wanted to explode on him. The thought of telling Teddy to meet him somewhere so he could blow his head off had been running through his mind during their brief conversation.

Meanwhile, Blossom went to Maribel's, the best Dominican hair salon in Brooklyn, and got her hair cut into layers. She hoped Dude would like it. She had her hair wrapped and in pins when he had seen her at the hospital. She took her M-A-C chestnut pencil and lip gloss out of her bag and did her lips.

She had just spoken to Darlene. Darlene told her that Maria was on her way to her house to show her everything she'd planned for Terry's going-away party.

Blossom had a funny feeling in her stomach. Who the fuck was this Maria bitch! And why the fuck was Dude pushing her in the family like that? Yeah, she understood the relationship Dude and Maria's father had, but Dude was handling this bitch like she was his girl or something.

"I know you fucking her . . ." she whispered to herself.

Her phone rang; it was Dude. She was pissed off all over again, but tried to maintain her sanity. She didn't want to start beefing with him at a time like this.

She took a deep breath. "You downstairs?"

"Something like that."

"What's that suppose to mean?"

"I'm upstairs at your front door. Open it."

She was confused. He never came upstairs. He hadn't been upstairs since they'd first met. She went to the front door and peeked through the peephole.

"What you peeping for? Open the fucking door," he said through the door.

She opened the door with her hand on her hip.

"Excuse me. I thought you were going to call when you were downstairs. You never come up no more."

He pushed his way in, brushed past her, and headed toward her room. She rushed behind him.

"Why you runnin' behind me? What you have to hide up in here?" he demanded.

"Nigga, please!"

He stood looking around the huge bedroom. He went over to her dresser and picked up a crystal picture frame. He stared at the picture of the two of them on the beach in Hawaii. A bright smile came across his face. He thought about something his brother had said about Blossom when he had first hooked up with her.

T Mac had said, "Man, I'm tellin' you, you got ya'self a winner, partner! No matter what, don't let her slip away and don't corrupt dis one. I like her for you. That's your wife, man."

Blossom walked over to him and wrapped her arms around his waist from behind.

"Are you okay, baby?"

He set the picture back on the dresser and turned to her. "Yeah, I'm good."

He stepped back and looked at her for a few seconds.

"Did you cut your hair?"

"Yes. You don't like it?"

"I do like it. A lot. It makes you look mature and sexy . . . So who you had up in here earlier?"

She tried brushing him off. "Please, Dude!"

They walked toward the bedroom door. Dude grabbed her arm tight and swung her around.

"You know if you ever sleep around on me, Blossom, I'm going to leave you and never come back."

She looked him straight in his eyes and shot back, "Ditto! And don't you forget it. Now, can we leave?"

Dude decided to let it go for now. He knew in his heart that she was only his. What scared him was that he didn't know how long that was going to last.

There wasn't much conversation between Blossom and Dude the whole ride into the city. Blossom was itching to mention Maria to him. But she kept telling herself that it was not the right time to bring it up.

Dude put his hand on her lap and began to rub her leg. She gave him a smile of satisfaction.

"So, what do you have a taste for? We can get something to eat after we go shopping," he told her.

She just couldn't help herself. She replied smartly, "What I have a taste for, it seems like you have no interest in anymore."

"What's that suppose to mean?"

She sucked her teeth. "If you don't know, then it doesn't matter."

He knew what she meant, but decided not to pursue the subject just at that time. And Blossom didn't bother pushing it. She knew him well enough to know when he was not interested in talking about something.

At that moment, his cell rang. He reached into the armrest and took the phone out.

Darlene's number appeared on the screen.

"Hey, what's up?"

"What's going on, how you doing?" Darlene said.

"I'm good. I'm on my way to pick up Terry's stuff for the viewing."

"Make sure you don't get no dress suit. He hated dress suits. Remember, he used to always say, 'And don't y'all put me in no corny-ass suit if I die!' "

Dude laughed. "I know . . . Did Maria get there yet?"

Blossom cut her eyes at him, with her face screwed up.

At the other end of the line, Darlene passed the phone to Maria. "Dude wants you."

Maria pulled off her diamond clip-on earring and put the phone to her ear. "Hello."

"Hey, how's everything?"

"Good. I tink de invites come out nice. I hope Darlene likes them." She turned and smiled at Darlene.

Dude knew he had to be careful of what he said and how he said it. He knew Blossom would take the littlest thing and blow it out of proportion.

"Hello, Dude?"

He snapped out of his thought. "Yeah, I'm here . . . I was just calling to check up on how everything went today."

"Oh, everyting is runnin' smoothly. The key chains will be ready on time and I will have sample tomorrow morning."

"Sounds good! So, give me a call later if you need me."

Blossom sat in the passenger seat with sweaty palms. Dude could feel the tension. After hanging up with Maria, he reached to return the cell to the armrest. But Blossom held her elbow down tightly on the top of the lid. He just laughed under his breath and set the phone in the ashtray. Just when he was going to say something to her, a little voice told him not to even touch it.

"I knew I should've drove my car," she mumbled.

"What?"

She ignored him and he didn't bother to repeat himself. He was trying to keep the peace. Blossom unhooked her seat belt as soon as Dude pulled into a parking garage.

The parking attendant walked over to the car to open the door for Blossom, but she had already gotten out of the car.

"You'll have to excuse her, she's in one of those moods," Dude told the attendant. "It's a female thing, I think."

The man laughed. "Oh, believe me, I know. I've been married for thirty years! You can just leave the car here and give me the key."

Dude gave him the keys. "Make sure you park—"

The parking attendant cut him off. "I know, make sure I park your car and your buddy's car next to each other and park it close to the front."

Dude laughed. "No doubt, you're on your job."

Dude and Black, who had been following them and arrived at the same time as Dude and Blossom, walked out of the garage. Blossom was leaning up against the wall with her arms folded. Black gave Dude a curious look. Dude shrugged, letting Black know he wasn't paying her attitude no mind.

Everything Dude picked up for T Mac, he would ask Blossom's opinion. Trying to make her feel like she was part of the process. But of course she was still acting tight. All of her answers were bland. Eventually, she loosened up and picked out T Mac's whole outfit. By the time they got to the cash register, Dude and Black both had two outfits apiece.

Just when Blossom was getting comfortable, Dude's cell phone rang. His phone was in her pocketbook; she'd taken it from him earlier when he was in the dressing room. She walked to the side and sneaked a peek at the caller ID. It read *Maria*. He had actually put an exclamation mark after her name! Blossom's whole attitude changed in a heart-beat.

She stormed back over to Dude and Black and handed Dude the phone.

"What happened, why your face screwed up?"

She rolled her eyes and walked away. He looked at the phone and saw Maria's number.

Dude handed Black the bags and walked over to Blossom. "Yo, what's your problem, Blossom?"

"I don't have a problem."

"Look, I've been trying to ignore your ignorance. But now you're getting a little beside yourself. Now is not the time for your little hissy fits, and I'm honestly not in the mood for your shit! You bugging out about this Maria shit!"

"Naw, I'm not bugging. And you just confirmed that I'm not."

He stood stuck. He knew she was right. But he also knew she had no proof, so all she was doing was assuming.

"Man, you're trippin' for nothing." He waved her off.

The whole ride back to Brooklyn was quiet and tense. Dude's cell kept vibrating on his hip. He refused to answer it; he didn't feel like hearing Blossom's mouth.

Blossom was feeling a need for revenge, when T.I.'s "Let's Get Away" rang through her cell phone. She snatched the cell off her hip and looked at the screen. It was Lil' Richie. Revenge had just arrived.

"Hello."

"Hey you, what's up?" Lil' Richie asked.

Blossom had a huge smile on her face. "Nothing much. On my way home. What's up with you?"

"Chillin'. Checking to see what you up to. What you doin' later?"

"I didn't really have anything planned."

"Well, you wanna catch a flick or something?"

"Sounds like a plan to me. I'll call you when I get to the crib."

She hung up. Dude looked at her out of the corner of his eye. She felt his eyes beaming on her. She ignored his glares and continued singing along with the radio. She unhooked her seat belt as soon as they turned onto her block. She reached in the backseat and got her bag. She was halfway out of the car before Dude had even pulled in front of her building.

Before she walked out, she reached over to kiss him.

"You going to call me later?" she asked.

"Go get anything you need from upstairs and come back down. Follow me home in your car," he said with calm authority.

She was confused.

"What? You're looking at me like you don't know where you live. Something changed and I don't know about it?" he asked her.

"I don't know. You tell me if something changed. 'Cause that's what I'm feeling and there's nothing you can say to make me think any different. Therefore, I think you need to tell me the truth so we can deal with it and make some decisions."

He turned the car off and reclined his seat back a little. The two stared at each other without speaking.

She wished he'd just fess up to his shit so they could deal with it and move on. She knew she wasn't going anywhere anytime soon, no matter how much she souped herself up.

She cleared her throat. "Okay, give me a minute. My car keys are up on the dresser."

She got out of the car and walked toward her building with a feeling of satisfaction. His action told her he was not only jealous, but he also had feelings of guilt.

"Yo, Blossom!" a voice yelled from down the block.

With one foot in the door, she stopped in her tracks. Her heart began to beat fast. She knew the voice; she just couldn't decide if she should turn around and answer. Or if she should simply keep walking in the building like she didn't hear him.

Just when she decided to keep it moving, the voice caught up to her.

Lil' Richie was trying to catch his breath. "Yo, you didn't hear me yelling your name out?"

Blossom spun around. "Hey, what's up? You were calling me?"

She peeped over his shoulder, trying to see if Dude was watching.

Lil' Richie turned around, following her eyes. He figured it was Dude sitting in the dark-tinted truck. He turned back around and faced Blossom with a blank look on his face.

"I'm sorry, my bad . . . Um, I think I dropped something in your room earlier."

She smiled, trying to play it off. "No, it's nothing. Where you think you dropped it?"

"I'm not sure. It was folded up in my jacket pocket. It's a small white envelope . . ." He paused before continuing. "But it probably wouldn't be a good idea for me to come up with you to look, huh?"

"Probably not, but I'll go up and look around the room for it . . . It's just that he knows about our little childhood thing and—"

"Naw, you don't have to explain. I understand. I'm waiting for somebody anyway. I'll be right on the corner."

"Damn it! What fucking timing," she whispered to herself.

When Blossom arrived upstairs and walked through the apartment, it was clear to her that Tamika wasn't home. She searched around her room until she saw a little white envelope at the other end of the bed. She tucked it into her back pocket, but curiosity led her to take a peek, being that it wasn't sealed. When she opened it, her eyes got wide and her jaw hung low.

"What the fuck . . ." she whispered to herself.

She read the name Jackie Roberts out loud. Then it hit her! Jackie was the girl Lil' Richie was dating. Dude honked the horn. She placed the paper back in the envelope and left the building. Lil' Richie was standing on the corner talking on his cell phone. She walked toward the corner, but Dude's horn stopped her in her tracks. She reversed her steps and walked over to the truck.

He rolled down the window. "Yo, where you going?"

By the time she got the envelope out of her pocket, Lil' Richie had walked up.

He extended his hand to Dude. "Hey, how you doing? I'm Lil' Richie."

Dude returned the handshake. "What's up, man? Dude."

Blossom spoke quickly. "Baby, remember I was telling you about my friend Lil' Richie?" She pulled the paper from out of the envelope and showed it to Dude. "He forgot this at the crib the other day. See, it's a sonogram picture of him and his girlfriend, Jackie, baby. Isn't that sweet?"

She handed Lil' Richie the envelope. "I'll catch you later."

Blossom jumped into the passenger side of the truck with a feeling of relief. She wanted to make sure Lil' Richie knew that she had known all about the baby.

"Baby, I really don't feel like driving," she said. "Can't I just leave my car in Brooklyn and ride with you?"

Dude kissed her on the forehead, "Sure."

She immediately put her seat back and closed her eyes. Dude finally felt at ease.

He made sure Blossom was asleep before he removed the vibrating phone from his hip. He had a feeling it was Maria.

"Hey, what's up?" he whispered.

"Not'ing much. What's up wit' you, Mr. Dude?"

"Had a long day; on my way home."

"Okay, I won't hold you long. Everyting is complete. Everyting for party is finalized. The key chains are ready. I left all of the invites with you sister-in-law."

"Thank you so much. I'll be out early tomorrow, so if you need me, you can reach me from early."

He was trying to keep the conversation as short as possible, without coming across rude. The two said their good-byes and Dude turned his phone off.

Two days later, Dude sat at the edge of his bed wearing his twenty-five-hundred-dollar Italian suit and matching gators. His head down, buried in his chest, he hadn't felt this cold and empty since the day he got to the hospital too late.

"Dude! Are you okay?" It was Blossom, standing by the closed bedroom door.

"What you want, Blossom!"

"Are you okay? Why is the door locked?"

"I'm straight! You go ahead to the party. I'm just going to chill here."

"What you mean, 'go ahead'? How . . . why aren't you going? You can't just not go to your brother's going-away party—"

"I don't feel like fucking partying and celebrating my brother's death! Now go ahead. Tell everybody I wasn't feeling too good."

"But, Dude—"

"Look, Blossom, leave me the fuck alone! What part don't you understand! I said I'm not going and that's that!"

She stood outside of the door, confused. Should she keep trying or leave him alone?

"Baby, can I come in, please?"

He walked over to the door and unlocked it. Blossom slowly turned the knob and opened the door. He had returned to the spot on the bed where he had sat for the last two hours. Blossom walked over to him and knelt down.

When she reached out to touch his face, he backed up and pushed her hand away.

"Don't touch me!"

She shot to her feet. "What's the matter?"

He pointed to the bedroom door. "Just go! I don't want to be bothered! I want everybody to leave me the fuck alone! Ain't nothing none of y'all can do for me! Motherfuckers don't know me! The only person that knows me is gone! And I've been sitting here for the past couple of hours thinking, and you want to know what I came up with?"

She stood staring him eye to eye. He had a look in his eyes she had never seen before.

"Well, I figured, if I would have never picked you up, my brother would be living today! So, trust me, you can go ahead and break the fuck out, 'cause your face is the last face I want to see right now!"

Her heart was crushed. She walked slowly out of the room, still staring at him. Guilt filled her as she thought about what he'd just said. He wasn't his usual self, she repeated in her head.

When she was gone, Dude dialed Darlene. No answer.

He threw the phone down, took the rest of his clothes off, and lay across the bed. His cell began to vibrate. He ignored the call until he noticed Darlene's cell number on the screen.

"What's up, Darlene?"

"No, it's Maria. Darlene's busy taking care of someting at the door."

"Just tell her to call me back. It's important."

"Okay. Where are you?"

"I'm at home. I can't explain right now, but I'm not going to make it tonight."

"Is everyting okay?" Maria asked, concerned.

"Yes . . ."

"Um . . . I need to see you. It is very important."

"Okay. I gotta go. Please don't forget to tell Darlene to call me."

He hung up before she could get another word out. He raced to his walk-in closet and began changing into black sweats and a black hoody. He reached into a shoe box and snatched a 9mm out. He tucked the gun in his waist and dialed Black's cell. Before the first ring could end, he hung up. He dug a new prepaid cell phone, still in the box, out of the nightstand drawer and dialed Teddy's number.

Teddy answered on the second ring. "Yo!"

"Yo, Teddy man, I'm stressed, kid. I'm not dealing with this T Mac shit too good . . . Where you at?"

"I'm at my crib down the way, man. You want me to meet you or something?"

"Naw, I'll come by your crib. If anybody calls you looking for me, you haven't spoken to me. I don't feel like being bothered right now."

"Not even Black?"

Dude replied firmly, "Nobody."

• • •

Teddy paced his living-room floor, trying to decide if he should set up the equipment the two federal agents had given him. He went into his bedroom closet and took a crystal clock out of the safe. He walked back into the living room and set the clock on top of the mantel over his fireplace. Then he sat on the couch and smoked a blunt to ease his nerves. Moments later, the front doorbell rang. He jumped to his feet and looked at his watch. He hadn't expected Dude to get to his crib so quick. The doorbell rang again, followed by two hard knocks on the door. Teddy ran over to the mantel and pushed a button on the back of the clock. He stood still for a minute, dealing with the reality that there was no turning back now. He knew once he turned on the minicamera that was built into the clock, he was officially a rat.

He pulled himself together and opened the door. His facial expression changed when he saw who was standing on the other side.

"Man, what y'all doin' here?" Teddy asked, blocking his guest from coming in.

The two men ignored him and walked inside. Teddy closed the door and followed them into the living room.

"We was just in the neighborhood and thought we'd stop by," one of the men said, looking around the single-level home.

"What da fuck y'all was doin' around here?" Teddy looked down and noticed the other man holding a roll of thick plastic. "And why da hell y'all dressed in fuckin' rain suits for? And what da fuck you walkin' round wit' dat big-ass roll of plastic for?"

The man laughed. "Well, we wasn't sure if we were going to hack you to death, so we wore these suits. We didn't want to ruin our clothes. And we brought the roll of plastic just in case we decided to shoot you. We figured we would wrap your body in the plastic and dump it."

The three men stood in the middle of the living room in silence for a few seconds.

The first man spoke again. "You're the only one here?"

What da fuck is going on here? Teddy asked himself. By the time he had come close to figuring it out, it was too late. One of the men pulled

out a gun with a silencer attached while the other rolled the plastic out
on the floor. Teddy stood staring at the man, in shock.

"What da fuck . . . Y'all can't be fuckin' serious, man! What da fuck
is all dis about!"

The man stood pointing the gun at Teddy's face. "It's not personal
. . . Just business. I personally thought you was an all-right cat."

Before Teddy could reply, the man put three bullets in his head.
Teddy's lifeless body dropped to the floor, landing perfectly on the plastic. The men had begun rolling the body up in the plastic, when the
sound of a car door closing distracted them. The two men jumped up.
One signaled with his hands for the other to look out the window. The
man looked out the window and shook his head from side to side. He
signaled the other man to follow him into the kitchen. The two men
stood in the corner of the huge kitchen with their guns out.

"Who is it?" one of the men whispered.

"It's Dude, man."

"What! What's he doing here?"

"Just chill for a minute. We might not have a problem."

Outside, Dude checked his waist for his gun before ringing the bell. He
rang the bell twice, but there was no answer. He knocked on the door,
but Teddy still didn't answer. Dude walked over to the garage and
peeped through the glass at the top of the garage door. Teddy's cars were
parked inside, both of them. Dude pulled out the prepaid cell he had
called Teddy from earlier. He walked back over to the front door and dialed Teddy's cell. He could hear the phone ringing inside of the quiet
house. Dude hung up when the voice mail picked up. He twisted the
doorknob and tugged at the door. To his surprise, it opened. He slowly
walked into the house calling out for Teddy. The two men in the kitchen
waited patiently before making a move. Dude continued to walk
through the house.

"Yo, Teddy, it's Dude. You here, man?"

He walked straight to the living room. He froze as he saw what looked like a body rolled in plastic. He backed out of the living room. He wiped the doorknob off on his way out. He looked around before getting in his car. He didn't want to be seen leaving Teddy's house. He pulled away with his lights off and didn't look back.

He spoke to himself out loud. "What the fuck was that about? Somebody must have been reading my mind."

He picked up his cell and dialed Black's number, but quickly changed his mind. He decided he'd keep the Teddy situation to himself for the time being. A million and one thoughts raced through his head while he sped home.

Back at Teddy's house, the two men continued wrapping up his body.

"I think you should make that call now," one of the men suggested to the other.

"Yeah," the other replied, taking out his cell and dialing.

"Hey, it's me, It's done . . . Yeah, everything went smoothly. We had a slight interruption."

"What kind of interruption?" the voice at the other end asked.

"Dude showed up as we were wrapping the body up, but he didn't see us. He saw the body, though."

"What about your car, did he see your car?"

"No, we parked away from the house."

"Okay, I don't think he's going to be a problem. Call me in a few hours and I'll tell you what I want you to do about Dude."

The phone line went dead and the men finished their job.

Dude paced his bedroom floor, drinking Rémy out of the bottle. He tried to figure out what type of shit Teddy had been into to get his shit pushed back like that. Although a part of him didn't mind that somebody got to do the job before he did. But who? he wondered. His cell rang; it read private.

"Hello."

"Hey, Dude my man, how you feelin'?" Fernando asked on the other end.

"Hey, Fernando, what's going on?"

"Oh, not'ing, my friend. I'm just checking on you. How you holding up?"

Dude took a deep breath. "I'm holding."

"Wha's a matter, you no go to you brother party tonight?" Fernando asked, with his thick accent.

"Naw, I'm not up to it. The memorial service, earlier, was enough for me. I'm just going to sit here with my thoughts for the rest of the night."

"I understand, my friend. Well, you know I'm here for you. I tink it would be good idea for you and you girlfriend to come to my country for a vacation."

"Yeah, that might be a good idea. Plus, I'm ready to get back to work on the resort."

"You sure it's no too soon?"

"I think that's the only thing that's going to take my mind off of my brother."

"Okay, if you are sure, I'm behind you one hundred percent. So, tomorrow you tink you be up to havin' lunch wit' me? I want to discuss some tings wit' you."

"Yeah, I'll give you a call around noon. You can tell me where to meet you when I call."

The sunlight beamed in through the bedroom window, waking Dude up. He opened one eye and looked at the clock; it read 8:23 A.M. He looked over to his right. Blossom was fast asleep. He hadn't heard her come in last night. He sat up, but his spinning head laid him back down. He looked at his cell, lying on the nightstand. He saw he'd missed four calls from Maria. He peeped back over to Blossom, still asleep. He picked up the cell phone and went down to the kitchen. He poured a glass of juice and dialed Maria back.

"Good morning, Mr. Dude," she answered.

"Good morning, sweetie."

"How you feel today?"

"I'm okay, and you?"

"I'm good also . . . Look, I need to talk to you about something very important."

"I'm listening."

"No, not on phone. Face-to-face, please."

"Is everything okay?"

"I can better explain in person."

He didn't like her tone. "Sure, I'm suppose to have lunch with your dad. You want to hook up afterward?"

"Yes, please."

"Okay, I'll call you when I'm done."

He hang up and stood looking out of the glass sliding doors. Then went back upstairs and took a shower. When he got out, Blossom was awake. He walked over to her and gave her a tight hug.

"What you doing up so early?" he asked her.

She turned from looking through the long rack of clothes.

"I have a doctor's appointment today."

"You okay?" he asked with concern.

"I'm not sure. I have been getting the worst headaches and I've been really short-winded. It's probably nothing. My blood pressure might be a little up again."

"Again? When did you ever have high blood pressure?"

"It hasn't been up for a while now." She kissed him on the cheek. "Trust me, it's not that serious."

She walked out of her walk-in closet, a jogging suit and sneakers in her hand. Dude followed her, not satisfied with the answers he was getting.

"Wait a minute, Blossom. Do you know how serious high blood pressure is? My grandmother suffered from high blood pressure for many years and eventually it took her life."

Blossom turned and looked at him with a serious expression. "Well, I strongly believe that you won't have to worry about that with me, baby."

He kissed her again. "I hope not. You want me to come with you?"

She liked that he was concerned; it felt like old times.

"I wish you could, but you don't remember you told your aunts you would take them around to a couple of places today?"

"Shit! I forgot about that. I got a lunch meeting with Fernando this afternoon. They're going to have to wait until I'm finished."

"Oh, yeah! Your lil' girlfriend, Maria, was there last night. Yup! All night. Look like she was looking for you to walk in all night, too."

She walked into the bathroom and closed the door. Dude could hear the shower running through the door. He considered asking her what she'd meant. He decided to let it be. He plopped down on the bed with a pen and notepad. He needed to start getting his brother's business in order. He wrote down a to-do list. He needed to get T Mac's cribs in order. Darlene's house was straight. He figured he would put his condo in Fort Lee up for sale and maybe rent out his town house in Edgewater. The week before Trina got killed, T Mac had bought some land and hired a home developer to build a house for him and Trina. Dude jumped off the bed and grabbed a business card out of his junk drawer. He stuck the card into his money clip so he'd remember to give the developer a call later. He made a note to go through all of T Mac's clothes and stuff later in the week. Whatever Darlene didn't want, he would donate. Then there was T Mac's furniture. He made a note to call a moving-and-storage place to make arrangements for that. Then there was his financial business that needed to be handled. He figured he would leave his brother's "rainy day" stash where it was and any other hanging money he'd put to the side for Darlene and the kids. He called one of the real estate agents he did business with and left a message for her to give him a call.

When Blossom came out of the bathroom, Dude was already dressed. She walked around the room like he wasn't there. He snatched his car keys off the dresser and stuck his to-do list in his back pocket.

"I'm out. I'll hit you on your cell later."

Blossom ignored him and continued getting dressed. Dude back-stepped into the bedroom.

"And I'm sorry for that shit I said to you last night. I didn't mean it. I was just going through something."

She nodded. "Uh-huh; it's okay."

Outside, he called Fernando and they decided to meet at the usual Italian restaurant. As he walked to the garage he noticed Blossom standing at the window looking down at him in the driveway. He could tell by the look on her face that she was assuming he was on the phone with a chick.

Dude rolled down his window, license and registration in hand. "Is there a problem, Officer?"

The officer on the driver's side said, "Mr. Knoxx?"

"Yes, is there a problem? I was going under the speed limit."

The officer on the passenger side of the car looked around.

He flashed a wallet with his ID and a badge. "Agent Stokes. This is my partner, Agent Fletcher. We're going to have to ask you to please step out of the car and come with us."

Dude looked at the man's ID; it read FBI.

Shit! He thought.

Dude hesitated before getting out of the car. "Sir, can you please tell me what this is about?"

The agent on the passenger side spoke firmly. "Mr. Knoxx, let's not make this any harder than it has to be. Please remove the keys from the engine, hand them to my partner, and step out of the car with your hands in the air."

Dude debated if he should try to make a move and snatch his heat from under his seat. He didn't know if these cats were really who they claimed to be. For all he knew, they could be trying to stick him. Then he thought about Teddy's rat ass! He knew this was all a result of Teddy's working with the feds. Knowing Teddy was dead made him feel a little at ease. He didn't want to give these men the impression that he had something to hide. He was a taxpaying workingman and he had the paperwork to prove it. The only tool they had to show different was dead.

Dude followed the agents' orders. The two men walked him to their dark-tinted black Impala and placed him in the backseat. The men stood outside talking to each other for a few minutes. The tints were so dark, Dude had a hard time seeing them. It looked like one of the men pulled a cell phone out. Dude leaned into the window to hear, but couldn't.

The agent turned his back toward the car and spoke in a low tone into the phone. "Yes, we have him and we're on our way to location B."

The men got into the car and sped away. Dude sat in the back wondering if he should have followed his first instinct and tried to make a move. He peeped up to the passenger side of the car and saw the agent looking through some papers.

"So, Mr. Knoxx, you have had some kind of extraordinary life, buddy."

Dude ignored him.

"Yeah, your story is one of those once-in-a-blue-moon stories. You know, you growing up poor and everything. Then one day you have this life-threatening accident, and all that changes. You got you a nice piece of change from that lawsuit. But I must admit, you were a smart one. You knew what to do with your money and you got a free college education out of the deal, too. If that's not hitting the jackpot, I don't know what is! Started you a fast-growing business, bought you some property, and started raking in the dough. Very smart man, so smart you have made my life a living hell for the past three years! Three years of trying to catch you slipping, and you just wouldn't slip."

Dude sat with the agent's words—*three years*—ringing in his head. He couldn't believe these motherfuckers had been watching him for three years. He looked out the window and saw they were at the end of the Jersey Turnpike, heading toward Delaware. Dude closed his eyes and tried to put his thoughts in order. He pulled his lawyer's name out of his memory bank. When he opened his eyes, he saw that they were on a back road, surrounded by open land. The car took a left turn onto a long dusty road. At the end of the dusty road was a huge deserted barn. They parked in front of the barn and the two men got out. At this point, Dude really began to wish he'd gone with his first instinct. The agents took him from the car and walked him into the barn.

"Man, what the fuck is going on? This doesn't look like no FBI headquarters to me!"

The men tugged at his arms, pulling him farther into the barn. There was a folding table and chairs set up in the middle of the room. They sat Dude down and pointed to several pictures laid across the tables.

"We just need to ask you a few questions, Mr. Knoxx, aka Dude. Starting with your partner Teddy."

Dude gave no response. He sat in the chair, silent, staring straight ahead.

"So tell me, what was it? You finally figured out Teddy was working with us?"

Dude looked at him like he was crazy.

"Oh, come on, Mr. Knoxx! Don't tell me you didn't know about Teddy turning over on you!"

Why is this fed cat sounding so convinced, Dude wondered, like he knows for a fact that I know about Teddy. Could they know about Fernando knowing and sharing it with me?

He decided to play the fifth and not respond to anything the man said.

"Come on, why try to lie about the obvious? I mean, what other reason would you have to do him the way you did? Three shots to the head? Now, that displays some serious anger, but I could step out of the box and look at it from your point of view. You did do a lot for him. Hell, if it wasn't for you, he'd probably never gotten to live the life he did. You take him up under your wing, treat him like family, and he stabs you in the back! If I was you, I would want to kill him, too."

"I don't know what you're talking about. What I do know is I don't have nothing to say until I call my lawyer."

The second agent came from the other side of the table. "We know you know Teddy's dead. And we also know that you did it. So why don't you stop the bullshit and come clean!"

Dude turned and looked him in the eyes. "Look, I said what I said . . . I don't know nothing about Teddy being dead. The last time I spoke to him he was alive! Now either you're going to let me call my lawyer or you're going to take me back to my car."

The first agent said calmly, "Look, we know you were at Teddy's house last night."

This was almost impossible for him to know. Dude knew they were just trying to pick his mouth.

"Look," the agent continued, "me and you both know that murder is not your thing. I mean a murder charge will get you way more than what we have on you. With Teddy gone off the scene, me and my partner figured you might want to go with our plan. Only the three of us know you killed Teddy, and if you cooperate, it can stay like that. With Teddy gone, we don't have too much ammunition to come after you. So we're forced to go after bigger fish. And you're going to help us reel in that big catch."

Dude stared the agent in his face, without blinking. He knew off the bat what the man was talking about. Rather, *who* he was talking about.

"Like I said, I don't know what you're talking about!"

The agent laughed. "Oh, I think you know what we're talking about . . . Your overseas partner, Fernando. The big mystery man that nobody sees. You know, your large-and-in-charge drug connect! I'm sure you remember him, the man who's made you a very wealthy individual. Oh, so you mean to tell me that you're denying having any business with Fernando? Or are you trying to tell us you don't even know a Fernando? Which one is it?"

Dude sat in the chair with no emotion and no response. The agent began to get aggravated with Dude's passivity. He turned to his partner and shouted, "I told you this motherfucker wasn't going to cooperate! I told you he would fuck everything up! If he doesn't cooperate, we have no case against Fernando! And that will send two career-making cases down the drain!"

"Calm down!" the other agent told him. "He *will* cooperate! Isn't that right, Mr. Knoxx? Why wouldn't you? Why would you want to throw your whole life away, when you have a choice. Do you really think that if the tables were turned, Fernando would even think twice?"

Dude sat clenching his jaw, angry with himself for even giving the agent's statement about Fernando any thought. He couldn't even imagine Fernando getting caught up in any shit like this; he was too good. But then again, he thought he was good, too, and still here he was sitting in the hot seat.

"What if Fernando was the one sitting in this chair instead of me?"

Just as he mentally answered that question, the other agent pulled out his gun and pointed it to Dude's temple. And still he sat firm, without letting the agent break him. He refused to fall victim to the same shit that had had him ready to smoke Teddy.

The agent shouted to his partner, without taking his eyes or gun off of Dude.

"I'm telling you, man, I'm tired of playing with this motherfucker! I say he don't talk about Fernando, he dies! Make it look like a robbery! How about that, Mr. Knoxx, you ready to die for a motherfucker that probably wouldn't return the favor!"

Dude responded with anger. "I told you I don't know nothing about Teddy's death. I didn't smoke him. And there's no way you can prove that I did something that I didn't . . . And on all that other shit you talking about, helping you nail some drug connect that I don't even have! I'm a businessman, not a drug dealer! I think you might have me mistaken for someone else!"

The agent cocked back his gun. "You're not as smart as I thought you were. It's too bad for you that you're not. And what did you think you were doing, wiping off the doorknob? You watch too much Court TV."

When he heard these words, Dude said a quick prayer, repented for all his sins, and prepared to meet his Maker . . . With no regrets for living his life the way he did. He only wished he had made it in time to be by his brother's side when T Mac took his last breath.

Then a loud bang echoed in his ear followed by a crushing feeling in his head. It happened so fast he couldn't tell which came first, the loud bang or the crushing feeling in his head . . . Then everything slowly faded to black. The agents voice began to get lower and lower, like Dude's eyelids. Soon he neither heard nor felt anything . . .

Black was racing down the turnpike at top speed, not giving any thought to possibly being pulled over. He reached the end of the turnpike in forty minutes or so. He reread the directions in his hand and drove into Delaware. He drove slowly as he rode the dark back road. There were no houses to his left or his right, just dark endless land. He slowed up when he saw lights shining from a distance. He turned right, like he was told to do, and drove up the dusty path. The closer he got, the brighter the light became. He slowed down and picked up the Tec-9 from his passenger seat. He hit his chest, making sure he had his vest on. He pulled to the side of the barn, away from the three construction work lights that were set up outside it. He grabbed the flashlight that the caller had instructed him to bring, then slowly exited his car and walked into the barn. He waved the flashlight around, to get a better view. The light finally hit Dude's body, lying in the middle of the barn. He couldn't tell from where he was standing if Dude was breathing. He swung the flashlight around the room, looking for any unexpected guest, before walking over to Dude. It wasn't until he got up close that he noticed dried-up blood on Dude's head and on the floor. Dude's chest was barely moving up and down. That was good enough for him; he was still breathing. He picked him up, threw him over his shoulders, and walked out backward, gun in one hand and flashlight in the other. He laid Dude in the backseat and drove off. He didn't know what kind of injuries Dude had suffered. The caller hadn't said much when he phoned Black. He just said Dude was left for dead in an old deserted barn. The caller gave directions and hung up.

Black heard mumbling from the back.

"Yo, you aight, man! I'm going straight to the hospital. I got you!"

Dude tried sitting up, but became overwhelmed with dizziness. He lay back down and began to talk clearer.

"Where'd you come from . . . ? Where are we?"

"It's a long story how I got to you, and we're on the turnpike. I'm taking you to the hospital—"

"No . . . No hospital. Take me to my crib and call the doc."

Black strongly disagreed. "You need to go to the hospital. We don't know what kind of injuries you have."

"I don't think I was shot in my head; it doesn't feel like I've been shot."

"Nigga, you crazy! How you suppose to know what it feels like to be shot in your head and you ain't never been shot in the head!"

But Dude insisted. "Trust me. I need to go home and call the doc."

As much as Black disagreed with Dude, he had no other choice but to follow his orders.

"Which crib?" he asked.

Dude paused for a few seconds, catching his breath. "As a matter of fact, take me to my brother's spot in Edgewater."

Black put the call in to the doc and gave him directions to T Mac's town house in Edgewater.

Black looked around before pulling into the two-car garage. He waited for the garage door to close fully before taking Dude out of the car.

Dude handed him the keys. "The big silver one is the key for that door."

Black took the key and opened the door of the house. Black picked Dude up and carried him into the house.

Black slowly walked up the stairs and into the guest bedroom. When he laid Dude on the bed, he noticed there was blood still leaking out of his head.

"Man, you still bleeding. What da hell happened?"

Dude spoke slowly. "Two dudes took me out of my car, said they were FBI agents. Showed their IDs and badges, drove me out to that farm . . . Start asking me questions about Teddy, saying they knew I was the one that smoked him."

Black's forehead wrinkled, "Smoked? . . . Teddy's dead?"

Dude was not sure what was going on and who had any involvement, so he decided not to tell Black the whole story about Teddy's murder.

"Yeah, that's what the agents said. They said something about him getting three shots to the head."

"So what da fuck they wanted wit' you?"

"I don't know. For some reason they think I'm the one who popped him. They said they knew I knew about Teddy rollin' over on me. They claimed that's the reason I killed him. Then they start telling me about some other bullshit about Fernando . . . Man, I told them pussies I didn't know what they were talking about. Talking about working a deal out with me; they wouldn't tell anyone I murdered Teddy and I would help them bring down Fernando. I told them cocksuckers I didn't know nothing about Teddy getting popped and I didn't know nothing about no big-time drug dealer named Fernando."

Black sat in confusion. "Teddy's ass got smoked? Where, when?"

Dude ignored Black's inquiries. "But something doesn't make sense. Why didn't they kill me? He had the gun to my head ready to kill me, but he didn't."

Then Dude remembered the agent making weird remarks. It was like the agents knew for a fact that he was up on Teddy's snitching. And why did the agent mention Dude wiping the doorknob off. How'd he know about the doorknob? Had somebody been watching him last night, and if so, who was it? And why did Fernando's name come up? As far as Dude knew, besides the feds themselves, he and Fernando were the only ones who knew about Teddy's dealings with the FBI.

At that moment, the bell rang. Black grabbed his gun and started downstairs. "That must be Doc."

Dude's mind was on full throttle. What the hell was going on?

Black returned to the bedroom with a tall, well-aged, brown-skinned doctor. The man walked over to Dude and immediately began taking his vitals. He slipped on a pair of plastic gloves and proceeded to examine Dude's head.

"Are you feeling dizzy?" the man asked.

Dude struggled to speak; he began to feel weak. "Yes. It's worst than when I first woke up."

"Well, by the looks of things, you should be dizzy. You lost a lot of blood, young man. And you've had major trauma to the right side of your head. You're going to need an MRI of the brain to see if you have any damage. You also need some fluids. I have what I need to start you an IV in the car. I want to put you on some antibiotics. It looks like your head's been open for a period of time. I want to kill any infection you might have gotten. And you're going to need a number of stitches."

Dude fussed at the man. "Come on, Doc, you know I hate stitches and there's no way I'm going to the hospital for a MRI. Not tonight. I'll go tomorrow."

Ten minutes later, the doctor had started Dude's IV. Within minutes, Dude felt relaxed and pain-free. The doctor laid out everything he needed to stitch up Dude's head. All Dude felt was the pressure from the pulling and tugging.

By the time the doc sewed the last stitch, Dude was barely awake.

The doc turned to Black. "You should really bring him down to the hospital tomorrow for an MRI. I don't like this kind of trauma; it has its way of sneaking up on you and biting you in the ass. I'd just rather be safe than sorry. I'll have him in and out."

As Black accompanied the doctor to the front door, he assured him Dude would be at the hospital in the morning. The doctor gave Black a bottle of Demerol, just in case Dude woke up in pain.

"Black!" Dude shouted from the upstairs bedroom.

Black shot up the stairs. "You aight, man?"

"Yeah, I just remembered I was suppose to meet Fernando earlier.

That's where I was on my way to when I got picked up. My cell phones are in my car. I want you to call over to Tommy's, have one of his drivers pick my car up and tow it here."

Black wrote down the location of Dude's car and took off. Dude picked up the cordless from the nightstand and dialed Blossom. When it went straight to voice mail, he hung up and dialed the house phone.

In her New Jersey town house, Blossom was lying across the living-room couch keeping track of time. She called Dude's cell phones dozens of times and got no answer. She was way past pissed. At this point, she didn't know if she should be mad or worried. Dude had never pulled a stunt like this. She jumped up and ran upstairs when she heard the telephone ringing.

She answered, out of breath. "Hello!"

She only heard a dial tone. She looked at the caller ID and dialed back the number.

Dude answered. "Hey, what's up?"

"You tell me what's up. You didn't see me calling you all day?"

"No, I didn't, 'cause I don't have my phones and I haven't had them all day."

"And why is that . . . ? And since when you don't carry your phones on you?"

"Look, I can't explain right now. I got caught up in some shit. I just called to let you know everything was okay."

"That's all?"

"What?"

"That's all you have to say? You didn't have your phones on you and you're just calling to let me know you're okay?"

Dude sat up and popped a Demerol. He was in too much pain to go through the emotions with Blossom.

"Hello! Oh, you don't have nothing say now, huh! You know what, Dude—I've taken about as much as I can take. I'm packing my shit up and I'm going back to Brooklyn . . . Oh, yeah, the doctor said my pressure is up and that's not going to be a good thing for the baby!"

"Baby?" he questioned.

"Yeah, I'm pregnant! I'll set the alarm and leave the house keys on the kitchen counter. Good-bye!"

The phone went dead in his ear. He started redialing the house, but never made it to the last four numbers. The Demerol had his body numbed. His eyes got heavy. He fell into a deep and much needed sleep.

The nurse pushed Dude through the long hallway. Black walked a few steps ahead of them, looking out for anything unusual.

"Thank you, nurse, I can make it from here," Dude said, getting out of the wheelchair.

"Are you sure?"

"I can handle it from here," Black said.

Black helped him into the car, looking around.

"Somethin' 'bout this shit ain't right, son. I'm not feelin' dis shit at all. I think we better keep our eyes open and watch our backs," he said while looking around.

"Tell me something, man," Dude began. "I've been thinking about this Fernando situation. I feel like I should tell him what went down, but I don't want to scare him away. I mean, he's on the low with a capital *L*. But we've broke bread together. I've sat with him at his table and had dinner with his family. He's been family to me, and not once in my heart have I ever felt anything but love from him. When that gun was put to my head and I was given a choice to either roll over on him or die . . . I never gave takin' a bullet a second thought. 'Cause I know he's a man of loyalty and respect, like me, and he would have done the same for me. I rather die with honor and respect than live a rat. I chose to live the life I'm living; nobody helped me or forced me to make the decisions I've made. So if the things I've decided to do land me in hot water, I'm the only one responsible for being in the hot seat . . . Why pull somebody else down with me, when it was my choice to do what I do and be who I am?"

Blake listened but said nothing. The two sat motionless and silent for a few minutes, then Dude reached in the armrest and pulled his cell out. He dialed Fernando.

"Dude! My friend, what is happening with you?" Fernando asked right away. "You okay, yes? I waited for you hours yesterday. I call you phone over and over but no answer. I tell the boys this is not you, to not show up or call. What has happened?"

"I need to see you," Dude told him. "I'm on my way home to change my clothes, then I can meet you."

"Yes, this is no problem. Come into the city. I'll be at the penthouse waiting for you."

When they got home, Dude ran up to the bedroom. "I have to change my clothes real quick. It's only going to take a minute. Grab something to drink or something," he shouted to Black.

Black double-locked the door and went into the kitchen.

It didn't hit Dude, until he reached the bedroom, that Blossom was gone. He walked to her closet. The majority of her things were gone. He checked her vanity table in the bathroom; all of her perfumes and toiletries were gone as well. He stood still for a minute. He didn't have time to call and debate with her. He had more important things to deal with.

Black pulled in front of the fancy high-rise apartment building.

"You sure you straight?" Black asked. "I can come up with you if you want."

Dude shook his head from side to side as he pulled himself out of the passenger seat. "No, I'm straight. Just wait for me here and keep your walkie clear."

Fernando was waiting for Dude when the elevator doors to the penthouse opened.

Fernando stood in shock. "My friend, what has happen to you? Junior, come!"

Junior came rushing into the room. "What happened, Dude?"

Dude walked farther into the penthouse and sat on the antique couch.

"I ran into some problems yesterday—"

His words were cut short by Maria's voice.

"Papa, have you seen my Escada scarf—" She was thrown off track when she saw Dude sitting in the living room.

"My God, Mr. Dude, what has happened?" she asked with concern.

"Hey, Maria. It's nothing. I had a little accident."

"What is it you looking for?" Fernando asked Maria.

She answered, trying to keep her eyes off of Dude. "Oh, my green-and-white silk Escada scarf."

"Oh, my gosh! All of the scarfs you own, you expect me to keep up wit' one!" He laughed and kissed his daughter on the cheek.

Dude's attention was taken away from the conversation. His eyes beamed on the plasma TV in front of him. Two familiar faces appeared on the screen. As the camera panned out four uniformed men were carrying two plastic body bags away from a river. The two agents that picked him up yesterday were in the bags. Then a picture of Teddy appeared. The story said the two men were dirty FBI agents who got caught up in a bad drug deal with Teddy.

"Dude, my friend, what has you attention over here?" Fernando called to him, grabbing the remote off of the coffee table and turning the volume up.

"What is this . . . ? Oh, who fucking care about some stinking FBI?" Fernando asked Dude.

The picture of Teddy appeared again on the television. Fernando chuckled and leaned over to Dude. He whispered in his ear, "And look at dis fucking cocksucking rat! Rats like him should no get one second of airtime! All three of dem *bontas* is where they deserve to be! You see, Dude, man like those dead men on the news . . . They no built like you and me. You know respect and loyalty. Even with a gun to you head, you will still choose respect and loyalty. You are part of my family and any living human being even tink about bringing harm to you . . . will end up in a body bag."

Fernando gave him a friendly slap on the back and lit a cigar. Everything started to come into play for Dude. That's how the agents knew about him wiping off the doorknob. A person had to have been there to see him wipe off the doorknob. They knew he was there . . . 'cause they were there, too. They were the ones that murdered Teddy. However, he was not quite sure how Fernando fit into the picture. Then it all came to him. He thought about Fernando's words. *Even with a gun to you head, you will still choose loyalty and respect.* He read between the lines. Fernando had the agents on his payroll. He'd paid them to kill Teddy and he'd used them to test Dude's loyalty to him. The agents' splitting Dude's head had nothing to do with Fernando. In doing that, they'd acted on their own.

"So, my friend, you say you needed to see me. Is everything okay?"

There was no longer any need for Dude to share what happened the night before.

Maria left, and Junior muted the television and sat down across from Dude and his father.

"So, Dude, tings are moving very well back home, with the resort," Junior began. "I'm leaving in the morning to sign the transportation contracts. Papa has told me you want to come back down as soon as possible. So I'm going to make sure everyting is set up by the time you reach."

"Junior, I tell Dude he should bring his lady wit' him, make it like vacation. I'm sure Maria and her can find lots of tings to do!" Fernando added.

Dude smiled and thought to himself, Yeah, and fighting would be at the top of the list.

"Yeah, that might be a great idea. That might loosen up some of the tension between us and it might be good for the baby," he said.

"Baby! You mean you will be a papa soon?" Fernando jumped up, excited,

"Yes, Blossom is pregnant. We just found out."

"Oh, Dude, my friend, this is very fragile ting. There can't be no tension between you and she. Being pregnant is really . . . How you Americans say it? Very . . . um, important ting. Now, I insist you and you lady come down. The beginning stages are important."

"Yeah, I'm going to talk to her today about going."

"No! I will not take no for answer. You two will fly back with me on my jet and that's final."

Junior popped the champagne bottle. "Oh boy, Dude, you no know it's a losing battle wit' Papa when it comes to the baby ting!"

The three men drank for hours. Dude kept thinking about T Mac. His brother was gone; the person closest to Dude had been cremated the day before yesterday. Besides Black, he did not have any real homies. He'd always been a down-low cat who didn't fuck with people like that. His brother had always been not only his best friend but his only family. At this point, Fernando and his family were the closest thing to what he considered family. His only concern with Blossom going down to DR with him was her being in Maria's presence. But fuck, he thought, she was about to be the mother of his child and some things were going to have to change.

Dude took another sip of champagne and said good-bye to the men. He promised them he would bring Blossom to have dinner with them later that evening. His conversation with Fernando about Blossom's pregnancy had given him a whole different outlook on life.

When Dude got back into the car, he directed Black to drive straight to Brooklyn and called Blossom.

"Hello."

"Damn, you thirsty like that! What's up? I'm on my way to Brooklyn to get you."

"For what?"

"What do you mean, for what?"

"Just what I said, for what?"

"Yo, stop playing with me. I'll be there in twenty minutes."

"Look, Dude, I'm tired of the back-and-forth and whenever I get mad with you I'm running back to Brooklyn. Baby, I just think there are some things you need to work out within yourself. Don't get me wrong,

I understand you're going through a lot right now and I don't want you to think I'm not being understanding . . . But I'm not up for being hurt or ending up unhappy with the person that's made me so happy. You understand?"

There was silence between the two. Something in her voice led him to believe that she wasn't bluffing. He knew deep in his heart, though, that he wasn't ready to let her go.

"Look, just be dressed, baby."

He hung up without waiting for a response.

"Everything's aight?" Black asked with concern.

"Yeah . . . I think."

"Good, 'cause I like Blossom. You lucked up wit' dat one. Pure and untouched, hard to find one of those these days."

Dude thought about Black's words—Black, who was supposed to be the man with no "heart and no feelings."

"Yeah, you're right. I couldn't have picked a better person to be the mother of my child."

Black shot a look in Dude's direction. Dude smiled.

"Yeah, man, I'm going to be a father."

"That's what I'm talkin' 'bout! I'm tellin' you, man, ain't no feeling like the one you 'bout to experience. Ain't no amount of money could even come close to making you feel the way that baby's gon' make you feel, kid."

"I know, that's why I have to start making some changes in my life, son. For real, I want to have my freedom . . . I want to be around when my seed is growing up. I'm tired of this shit, man. The game changed, all across the board, the shit changed. It's not worth it no more."

"You right, man. Take it from me, and you know I know, it's not worth it. I never had no regrets about my life. Only thing I regret was not doing the right thing . . . So my wife and unborn child coulda had life."

As Dude imagined something happening to Blossom and his baby, he realized for the first time the source of Black's anger.

Black kept on. "Let me tell you somethin', kid. I been in these streets all my life, and when I say all my life, dat's what I mean. And you, Dude, you one of a kind. I'm older den you, so I seen street cats from back in da day. And you remind me of a few of those niggas from back den. They not built like dat no more. You a true businessman and I always dug you for dat. You not a punk-ass nigga. You just know how to avoid shit, you play straight. And dat's why you gon' always have good luck. My advice? You own your own business, and you got ya hand in mad investments. Live your life the right way. You too da good far as dough! If you gettin' dat gut feelin', go wit' it."

Black pulled up in front of Blossom's building. She was standing in front with her arms crossed.

"Now, what's all this junk you were poppin' on the horn?" Dude asked her.

"I'm not playing this time, Dude."

He grabbed her and held her tight in his arms. "I know you're not, baby. Why you think I'm here?"

He pulled her from him and looked her in the eyes.

"Be honest with me, Dude, no matter what," Blossom said, looking him in the eyes. "Even if you know the truth will hurt me?"

"Yes, baby."

"Tell me, did you sleep with that Maria chick?"

He took a deep breath, and before he knew it, the lie had already rolled off his tongue. "No, I didn't!"

13 *A week later*

Blossom was running frantically from her closet to the suitcase that was sitting on the bed. Dude sat nearby, looking astonished.

"You must have twelve bathing suits and a hundred and one outfits. We are only going to be there for one week, not the rest of our lives."

She kissed him softly on his lips. "I know, baby. I just don't want to get all the way out there and forget something."

"Well, they do have a mall out there, too. Believe it or not, they have all that designer stuff you like, too. Now hurry; we only got an hour."

The last week had felt like the beginning to Blossom. They had been spending the kind of quality time they used to spend together. She knew that Dude had his mind made up; he was fallin' back.

"Come on, the car's here!" Dude shouted from the top of the stairs.

Blossom had pictured Fernando to be this old Mafia-looking man from one of those gangster movies. But he didn't look like she'd thought he would. He turned out to be sharp and clean; she could tell he was a no-nonsense man. He had aged very well. Dude sat back and watched them converse. He would have never thought he would be sitting with Blossom on Fernando's jet, heading to DR.

"So Blossom, you like shopping?" Fernando asked.

Blossom smiled. "Yes, love it."

"Good! You and my daughter will get along very well. She can show you around to all of the spots. I can tell you girls have a lot in common."

"I'm glad I'll have somebody to hang with while Dude's working," Blossom said.

• • •

When they landed at the airport Maria was waiting next to Junior, looking even more beautiful than the last time Dude had seen her. Dude noticed the handsome Dominican man she was talking to outside of her salon also standing beside her. Maria made direct eye contact with Dude. He noticed that the man from the salon was well dressed and that he was holding Maria's hand.

"Rico, how you doing, my man?" Fernando hugged him

"I'm okay, sir. How was you trip?" Rico said with a deep accent.

"It was a good one, my friend. And how is my favorite girl doing?" Fernando gave Maria a kiss.

"I'm doing good, Papa."

Fernando introduced Dude and Blossom. "Rico, this Dude. Have you two met?"

Rico reached his hand out to Dude. "No, we haven't. But I hear not'ing but good tings about him. Please to meet you."

They all shook hands and off they went. Blossom and Dude rode in the back of a black Bentley with Fernando. Blossom took in the beautiful scenery as they rode up into the hills. Dude sat by her side, trying to figure out when Maria and Rico had become an item.

"So, Blossom, you like what you see so far, yes?" Fernando asked.

"Oh my God, it's beautiful!" was all she could answer.

"I tell Dude he should get a home built here so you all have somewhere nice to get away to."

Blossom looked at Dude with a warm smile. The line of cars pulled up slowly in front of the house. Blossom, trying to hold her composure, sat stiff. She had never seen anything like this anywhere but on television.

"Welcome to *mi casa!*" Fernando called out.

A man opened up the door for Blossom and held out his hand. Blossom got out of the Bentley and looked around in amazement.

"Dude, I will have you bags sent immediately," Fernando said. "You should be ready in a hour, for Maria and Rico's engagement party."

Dude almost lost his breath. "Okay.

Once they were in the quarters, alone, Blossom flipped out.

"Oh my fucking God, Dude! Is this shit all his property? This shit is bananas!"

She spotted the pool. "Yo, we have this pool to ourselves?"

The phone in the bedroom rang, killing the moment. Dude went into the bedroom and answered it.

"Hello."

"Hello, Mr. Dude. It's no good time to talk?" Maria whispered.

He peeped out to the pool and saw Blossom lying in a lounge chair. "Hey, what's up?"

"Look, I need to talk some tings to you. How could we make this happen?"

"Um . . . I don't know. You tell me?"

"Hold on for one minute."

He could hear her hand cover the mouthpiece of the phone. Then he heard a male voice, speaking Spanish in the background. After a few seconds, she returned to the phone.

"I'm sorry for that. Look, after the dinner I will try to make it to you side. You can meet me in the staff's kitchen. Let's say thirty minutes after we return from the dinner."

Blossom walked back into the room, choking him up. "Okay, I'll try to make that happen."

"No, you *must* make this happen. It's important! I must go now."

She hung up before he could reply. He placed the phone on the cradle and lay down across the bed.

"Who was that?" Blossom asked.

"Oh, it was Junior."

"What is it you're going to try to make happen?"

"Huh?"

"I heard you say you were going to try and make something happen. What is that?"

He played it off. "Oh! Us being ready in exactly a hour. He said he knows how you women can be."

She laughed and thought nothing of it. There was a knock at the door, and a man's voice spoke pleasantly on the other side, reminding them to be ready for dinner in thirty minutes.

Dude walked into the bathroom a few minutes later and stood staring at Blossom's naked body through the huge European-style shower doors. Her back was turned to him, showing off her perfectly built soapy body. The thought of him being the only man to have explored her body, inside and out, made his manhood hard and stiff. He started peeling off his clothes until he stood butt-ass naked. She felt a presence and spun around. A huge smile took over her face. She opened the shower door, silently inviting him. He stepped into the shower, too anxious for foreplay, and lifted her up by her waist. She wrapped her legs around him while he held her butt for support. He then slid slowly inside of her. They made love in three different positions. When they got out of the shower, they dried each other off.

"Baby, you didn't take anything out for me to wear?" Blossom said when they returned to the bedroom.

He walked over to her and hugged her tight. "Sorry, I had other things on my mind."

She kissed him. "Yeah, I must say you did. I love you, baby, so much."

He kissed her on the forehead. "I love you, too, baby. And I promise I'm going to get my shit together before the baby comes. I want to watch my child grow."

That meant so much to her, hearing him say that. It was like everything was back to normal.

"Dude, I can admit when I'm wrong. And I don't have too much pride to apologize when there's an apology due . . . I'm sorry for accusing you of sleeping with Maria."

He remained staring at her, trying not to show all the guilt he was feeling.

He kissed her on her forehead again. "Don't worry about it, boo, it's nothing. Now let's get a move on it. We don't have much time before we have to be ready."

The two quickly dressed and went outside to meet Fernando. When they reached the parking area, Dude immediately noticed Maria in the arms of Rico, laughing. He was so confused; he had no idea where this had come from. The impression Maria had given him was that she and Rico were nowhere near serious. He caught himself before his thoughts took over. His priority was Blossom and their unborn child. He just felt like Maria had played him like she was the man and he was the bitch. But he quickly let it go from his mind and pulled Blossom close to him. Shit, it wasn't like his girl wasn't a dime piece, too. As a matter of fact, she was just as hot as Maria. Maria just was more on the exotic side.

Everyone got into the cars, same seat assignment as earlier, and headed toward the restaurant.

There were a host of family members and friends waiting for them when they reached the restaurant. Inside, Fernando sat at the head of the long table, along with Dude, Blossom, and his family. Rico sat close to Maria. Every time Dude snuck a peek at her, she seemed to be very happy and content with Rico.

The guests drank, ate, and danced for hours. Then Fernando instructed that the music come to a stop. He stood up and called for everyone's attention.

"Hello, everyone," he said in Spanish. "I would like to thank everyone for coming out tonight to celebrate my baby girl's engagement. I guess there comes a time when every man has to face the fact that his children are grown. And I will tell you all that realizing my Maria is officially a big girl has been the hardest ting I have ever have to deal with. So, saying this, I would like to give a big toast to my Maria and her fiancé. May God watch over them and their unborn child with not'ing but blessings."

Dude's heart almost dropped to the floor! Unborn child? he thought to himself. What unborn child? He automatically clapped along with everyone in the room. He made eye contact with her, but she couldn't look at him.

Fernando hit his champagne glass with a fork. "Listen . . . Listen, everyone! I have another announcement to make. I would also like to congratulate my good, good friend Dude. He and he beautiful girlfriend Blossom, too, are expecting their first child."

Everyone started to clap again, even Maria. Though she actually was numb inside from head to toe. This was just as big a bomb for her as her surprise was to Dude. She looked at Dude and Blossom with a warm smile, but Dude saw right through it. It was an uncomfortable moment for the both of them, but it was something that could not be fixed or changed.

Fernando hit the glass again to regain the crowd's attention. "And I would like to say to Dude and Blossom, it would be such a good ting if one day soon we could celebrate the marriage of the two of them. Who knows—maybe even a wedding here in my country! Now let's make another toast and continue to party!"

The music started up and the crowd picked up where they had left off. Maria and Rico made their way around the room shaking their guests' hands and giving out hugs. When Maria got to Dude and Blossom, she put on a huge warm smile.

She and Blossom reached for each other at the same time.

The two hugged. "Congratulations, sweetie!" Maria said.

"Yes, and the same to you," Blossom replied.

"We have to go shopping tomorrow," Maria went on with forced enthusiasm. "Maybe someting nice for us. It's too soon to buy for baby; it's bad luck. But I know we can find someting nice and shiny for us. Someting that says 'welcome to motherhood.' What you say?"

Blossom smiled. "I say hell yeah! Just tell me where to meet you and what time. I never turn down a day of shopping."

At that moment, Rico walked over. "What's goin' on over here?" He gave Dude a friendly slap on the shoulder and continued. "Is dees ladies plotting over here, my friend?"

"Naw, they're talking about shopping. And it sounds like they're trying to put a little dent in our pockets!"

The two men laughed and suddenly Dude started to feel a little more comfortable. He was peeping out Rico and he thought he was a pretty cool cat. He figured he would dismiss any recollection of his and Maria's fling and continue as if it had never happened. And it appeared to him that she'd chosen to do the same thing.

14

Dude rolled over and pulled the covers over his head. He reached over to hug Blossom, but the other side of the bed was empty. He slowly lifted his head from under the covers. He peeped around the room with one eye open. His head was spinning; he didn't know if he wanted to throw up or sit on the toilet. He had drunk way too much last night. He and the guys had taken numerous shots on top of drinking champagne the whole night. He managed to pull himself from under the covers. He sat up in the huge bed and looked around the room. There was no sign of Blossom.

"Yo, Blossom!"

Her head peeped out from the large walk-in closet. "You up, drunky Smurf! Man, I ain't seen you like that since Hawaii, Dude."

She walked out of the closet, fully dressed.

"Where you going?" he asked.

"Out with Maria. You thought we were playing last night about going shopping?"

"Oh, that's right. You spoke to her?"

"Yup, she called this morning. She's sending someone for me. They should be here in a few minutes."

She kissed him on the lips, softly, and held her hand out.

He slowly climbed out of the bed and laughed. "I guess that's my cue to get up and get you some paper."

He went to look at a painting that was hanging on the wall inside the walk-in closet. Blossom stood watching him, with curiosity. He pulled the painting outward, as if it was a door hanging on the wall. Behind the painting there was a safe built into the wall. He turned right, then left, then right again. He opened the safe and turned to Blossom.

"Now, what kind of shopping are y'all doing?" he asked.

She glared at the many stacks of money in the safe and smiled. "You heard what she said last night . . . We're shopping for shiny things today."

He knew what they were shopping for. He reached in the safe. He handed her several stacks of money. "This should be enough. Take your big Gucci shoulder bag. You'll be straight, though. Security will be with y'all."

Blossom put the money in the Gucci bag and zipped it up. She didn't want to make herself look like a crab by counting it in his face. Dude closed and locked the safe back up. Blossom followed him back into the bedroom.

"You better put something in your stomach, Dude," she said as he climbed back into the huge bed.

He mumbled and placed the covers back over his head.

Blossom pulled the covers back. "I'm serious, and you're going to be sorry. You want me to make you something to eat real quick?"

He sat up and looked at her like she was crazy. "You don't have to cook when you're here. I told you, there's a full staff here."

Just then there was a knock at the door, followed by a male's voice. "Excuse me, Dude. I'm here to get Blossom."

Dude opened the door; the same man who'd come for them the day before was standing on the other side. Blossom gave Dude a kiss on the cheek and disappeared with the man. Dude lay back down in the bed. Suddenly he remembered he was supposed to meet Maria last night, after they returned from the engagement party. He tried calling her cell before Blossom got down to meet her, but it went to voice mail. He hung up and pulled the covers over his bed again.

Maria was standing next to a black-on-black, dark-tinted Yukon truck, waiting for Blossom. She was just ending a conversation on her cell phone when Blossom walked up.

"Hey, how are you dis morning?" Maria asked.

"Ready to shop things off of my mind."

The two laughed and climbed into the truck, with two security men. Blossom snuck a peep at Maria's ring finger, to check out what kind of rock Rico had hooked her up with. Little did she know Maria was doing the same to her.

"So, Blossom, what is it you want to shop for first? I called our jeweler and told him we was coming by."

"Sounds like a plan."

The truck pulled up in front of a very intimate, classy-looking jewelry store and the security walked the two women in. A very short man greeted them as soon as they entered. He had a bottle and glasses in his hands.

He hugged Maria. "Hey, Maria. You looking beautiful as usual."

She laughed. "Oh, Felipe, you just saying this 'cause you know I come to spend today."

"Come! Come! I have champagne, food, and some sweet chocolate-covered strawberries. You favorite, Maria!"

The words were barely out of his mouth when a beautiful female came from behind the counter, holding a silver tray full of chocolate-covered strawberries. Maria lifted one of the napkins and took one of the strawberries off the tray.

She handed the strawberry to Blossom. "Here, you have to try this. This is from the best shop out here."

Blossom took the strawberry and ate it. Maria didn't have to ask what she thought; Blossom's facial expression said it all.

The short man led them into his spacious office, in the back of the shop.

"Sit! Sit! Drink some champagne while I pull you out some tings I design for you two beautiful mothers-to-be." He paused for a second. "Oh, I'm sorry, I forgot you no can drink dis. Would you like some juice?"

Blossom was caught off guard. She wondered how he knew they were expecting. She knew there was a possibility of him knowing Maria was pregnant, but how could he have known about her?

The man continued. "Maria, I did the best I could in the time frame you give me. When you called me, six o'clock dis morning, I get up right away and started working."

Okay, maybe Maria mentioned it to him when she called earlier, Blossom told herself.

The man went into one of the desk drawers and pulled out several sketches of pieces of jewelry. "Here, you take a look at what I come up wit'. If you no like, I will create someting else for you."

Maria took the sketches and looked them over with Blossom. It appeared the two had a lot in common when it came to style. After a good thirty minutes, the two both decided on the same set. A platinum necklace and bracelet. Both the necklace and bracelet had diamond charms hanging from them. There was a baby rattle, a stroller, a Bible, a baby bootee, two diapers stacked on top of each other, and then, at the last link hung a cross, larger then the rest of the charms. The whole cross was nicely stacked with yellow diamonds, as clear as Caribbean waters. It was the most beautiful piece of jewelry Blossom had ever seen. The set looked so beautiful on paper that Blossom began to think Felipe wouldn't be able to make the actual pieces of jewelry look as exquisite.

"I love it, Felipe. It's so unique and says so much," Blossom stated.

Well, he had said enough for Blossom. She and Maria stayed for a while with Felipe, conversing, then they headed to an upscale department store. It took three trips to the truck to load all of the things they purchased. Once there was nothing left for them to buy, they went to lunch. It was like everywhere the two women went, everyone knew Maria. Not only did they know her, Blossom could tell people had a great deal of respect for her. Maria took her to a very classy restaurant. The two women were personally seated by the owner of the restaurant, a beautiful young Dominican woman.

"How's this, Maria?" the owner asked as she walked them to a private section of the restaurant.

Maria replied, "Oh, this is just fine. Tank you, sweetie."

The owner kissed Maria on the cheek. "No problem, anytime. If you would have called, I would have been more prepared. I'll send Gus over wit' a nice bottle of champagne for you and you friend. Enjoy, and if there is anything I can do or get for you, just send someone for me."

"Oh, that's okay," Maria told her. "We'll jus' take two glasses of sparkling grape juice."

The two security men sat at a table close to the entrance of the small intimate room.

"She's a sweetheart," Maria told Blossom. "Her papa and my papa grow up together. Her papa buy her dis place five years ago, and since then she's opened up two more. She is a very hardworking young woman. She's always been a go-getter, ever since we were schoolgirls."

"Oh, so that's your homie?"

Maria laughed. "Yeah, she is one of my very few homies. I do not mix too much with a lot of women. Women can be a lot of problems sometime."

"Girl, tell me about it. My sister and my friends are my only friends and have been every since I could remember."

"So you know what I mean. You are from Brooklyn, yes?"

"Born and raised all of my life."

"So, you are ready to be a mother?"

Blossom thought about the question and decided she felt comfortable with Maria. "I guess I am. And you?"

Maria thought for a second. "I guess it's the same with me. I really do not know what to expect. I've always been the baby in my family."

"Well, at least you are getting married, huh?"

"Yeah, I am."

"Rico seems like a nice guy."

"Yeah, he has no other choice. Papa would have his head on a platter!"

Blossom let Maria order for her. They drank and talked for hours, even after they ate their meal and dessert. Blossom liked Maria a lot. She felt bad about talking shit about her to Dude. She felt she had Maria totally mistaken.

"Look, what is it you have to do tomorrow?" Maria asked her.

"Shit, not much. I think Dude has to go with your pops to take care of some things."

"Good, then that's that! Me and you will go show off the bathing suits we bought today. We have to take advantage of our shapes while we still have them."

"Man! That's the only thing I'm worried about . . . besides Dude marrying me before the baby gets here."

"What, your shape?"

"Yeah, I see it and hear about it all the time. A female having a baby and her body being rearranged."

"I know. That has run through my mind a few times, too. But you know what, Blossom?" Maria got serious, before continuing. "I tink I'm going to be so wrapped up in my baby when it gets here, I don't tink I'm going to care too much about what my body look like."

Blossom thought about what she had said and decided she was right.

Maria broke her thought. "Now, back to the other ting you worry 'bout."

"Huh?"

"You say you worry if Dude will marry you before the baby come."

"Oh! Yeah, I always wanted to be married to the man I have children with. It's no big thing."

"Yes, it *is* a big ting! If dis is how you feel, it is not only big ting, but it is important. And Dude is a very good man, so I know he will do right by you. Plus, the rock on you finger . . . Marriage can only follow!"

When Blossom got back to the house, Dude had also just gotten back.

"Damn, girl! Did you leave anything in the store?" he said when he saw everything she'd bought.

"Shut up! I had a ball!"

"Yeah, I see. What happened to shopping for something nice and shiny?"

"Oh, I got that, too. It's off the hook, baby! It won't be ready for another two days or so. Oh, we're going to the beach tomorrow, so if you wake before me, make sure you get me up."

He held her in his arms, tight.

"I'm glad you're having a good time, baby."

She slowly pulled away. "I love you, Dude."

"I love you, too, baby. Me and Fernando was talking earlier today. He really digs you . . . Baby, I know how you feel about a big wedding and everything . . . But I just want to do it, and maybe when we get home, we can have a big reception or something."

She stood with her mouth dropped open. "Are you serious, Dude? Don't play with me, boo!"

He reached inside the nightstand drawer and pulled out a plush leather box.

He opened up the box and inside sat a wedding-band set, so huge it almost blinded her!

"Dude! Oh my God, baby!"

She hugged him as tight as her strength would allow.

"I love you, Blossom, and I want to spend the rest of my life with you . . . Fernando said he would get all of the documents and whatever paperwork we need. All he needs is our passports. He said we should be ready to go in about three days."

"Three days! Dude, where are we going to . . . I mean, what am I going to wear? And I have to get your band. You know the female is suppose to buy the man's ring?"

"Oh, baby, don't worry yourself—"

She cut him off. "I don't want to hear nothing! I'm going to Felipe tomorrow and get your ring. Something banging."

"Who the hell is Felipe?"

"Oh, he's the family jeweler."

"Well, I hope you got a piece of lingerie in one of those bags. You know, to celebrate and shit."

Blossom ran and picked up a fancy black and copper bag, with Spanish words written across it.

"Oh, you know I do, baby!"

He smiled and walked over to the intercom. He instructed one of the staff members to bring a bottle of champagne to their quarters and a bottle of sparkling grape juice, if they had it.

And the rest of the night was spent working up a sweat!

The next couple of days Blossom and Maria hung tough while Dude spent most of his time at the resort site. Fernando made arrangements for Blossom and Dude to have a small wedding ceremony on the beach. Dude arranged for Tamika and the girls to fly out. Blossom counted down the days until their arrival. Fernando made sure the girls were put up in the finest hotel, in the penthouse suite, of course. Maria shopped for a wedding gown and Blossom was right by her side.

The two had been inseparable for the last couple of days. Both anxious to get their jewelry, they arrived one morning at Felipe's shop as soon as it opened.

The necklace and bracelet were the most beautiful pieces of jewelry Blossom had ever seen. They were as amazing as the picture Felipe had shown her, almost too beautiful to wear, she thought. The diamonds were as clear as Caribbean waters.

Maria smiled so hard, it looked like her cheeks were stuck in her ears.

"Wow, Felipe! Dis is the most beautiful piece of work I ever see. Don't get me wrong, I love everyting you ever make for me. But dis . . . Dis is just simply amazing! I do not know if it is because it is such a personal piece, but my breath is taken away."

"Oh, my child, I'm so please you like! How about you, Blossom. You like?"

"Oh my God, I love it! I have never seen anything like it. Thank you, it is truly beautiful!"

He hugged both of the girls, happy that his work met with their approval.

"Oh, my Felipe," Maria said hastily. "I hate to run off on you, but Blossom's family is arriving from America in one hour. What is it we owe you?"

Felipe smiled. "You owe me not'ing. You papa took care of everyting for you girls yesterday."

Even Maria was surprised; Fernando had not mentioned anything about paying for the jewelry.

They rushed off to the airport. Tamika and the rest of the girls were scheduled to arrive only twenty minutes before her mom's plane was arriving. En route, Maria made several phone calls, to make sure all of the arrangements for Blossom's people were being carried out. She called and checked on the limo, which was supposed to pick them up at the airport. It turned out the driver was already parked and waiting at the airport, way ahead of the pickup time.

"Everyting is straight with hotel and limo driver, all you family have to do is get off the plane," Maria told Blossom after her last call.

"Thank you so much, Maria."

"Oh, no, this is not'ing," Maria assured her. "I am happy to help. I have closed down the shop today so we can have special attention. My staff is waiting for us to come. I figure two can get massage while others are getting their facials and nails done. If you friends want to get roller set, like the Dominicans do in America, I have my girls there to do this, too. I figure I'd have food delivered from the house. I didn't know what kind of drinks you friends and family liked, so I have champagne and a few bottles of some other tings. And of course, juice for us."

When they pulled up to the airport, Tamika and the girls were walking out of the doors. There were three men carrying their bags; Blossom recognized them from being around Fernando. The men loaded the bags in the trunk of the stretch Benz limo. There was another limo waiting for Blossom's mother and aunt to arrive from down south. As soon as Blossom saw the girls she jumped out and ran over to them.

"What's up!"

"What's up!" The girls shouted, all at the same time.

They hugged and jumped up and down like they hadn't seen one another in years.

Shareen walked over to the limo. "Girl! You sure doin' it up out here, huh?"

Tamika joked, "Oh, so you an' Maria is buddy-buddy now, huh?"

"Yeah, we pretty tight. I was wrong about that Dude shit. Not only is she engaged to be married, too, but she's pregnant. Come on and meet her."

The girls all walked back to the car, where Maria was waiting to meet them. There was a police officer standing outside of the car; he tapped on the back window.

"Excuse me, you must move this vehicle now!" he told them.

Maria rolled down the window. "I'm waiting for friends."

The police officer's attitude changed quickly when he realized who she was. "Oh, Miss Maria, I'm so sorry. I didn't know it was you sitting here. Please take as long as you need. Have a good day."

The girls looked on, impressed, while Blossom took charge of the introductions.

"Maria, this is my sister, Tamika. This is Shareen and Kim."

"How was you trip?" Maria asked.

"Shit, that open-bar jump-off made the flight tight!" Shareen blunted.

Tamika nudged her in her side and whispered under her breath, "Stop bein' so ghetto, like you never been in first class before."

Shareen whispered back, "Shit, I *ain't* never been in first class."

Tamika rolled her eyes at Shareen and joined the other girls' conversation.

"That sounds like a plan," Kim was saying.

"What sounds like a plan?" Tamika asked.

Kim answered, "Maria takin' us to her salon slash spa, for a whole day of pamperin', girl."

"Oh, Blossom, this is you mother, no?" Maria suddenly started, pointing toward the airport doors.

Blossom and the girls walked toward the doors. Blossom's mother and aunt were smiling from ear to ear. Blossom could tell they had enjoyed the "open-bar jump-off" in first class just as much as Shareen had.

"Ma!" Blossom shouted, hugging her mother tight.

Blossom instantly noticed the difference in her mother. She still reminded Blossom of how she looked in her earlier years. Her mother's hair was neatly pulled back into a tight bun and her skin was flawless. She was so full of life, Blossom could see how her mother had changed for the better.

Tamika and the rest of the girls hugged her and Blossom's mother and aunt before jumping into the limos. Maria and Blossom got in with the rest of the girls while Maria's driver and security followed behind. Maria had ordered a separate limo for Blossom's mother and aunt. Both vehicles were fully stocked with champagne, so by the time they got to the salon, everybody was well beyond tipsy. Everybody except Blossom and Maria, of course. When they arrived, the food was being delivered. The staff was ready and waiting when they walked through the doors. Maria began speaking in Spanish. The girls could tell she was giving the staff orders.

"If you all are hungry, there's food here and more champagne," Maria informed them.

Everyone separated; Tamika and Blossom went in for massages while the others went for facials, manicures, and pedicures.

"So, little sis, are you ready for tomorrow?" Tamika asked as she and Blossom lay facedown on tables getting side-by-side massages.

Blossom took a deep breath. "Yeah, I think so."

"A lot's happened in dis year. Who'd think you would be gettin' married and havin' a baby. I wish Trina was here . . ."

"Yeah, me, too. I was thinking about that earlier. I think Dude feels like that, too—you know, wishing T Mac could be here on his day."

The girls sat with their thoughts and silently enjoyed their massages.

"Blossom, I need to talk to you about somethin'," Tamika suddenly began.

Tamika turned Blossom's way when she didn't reply. She had fallen asleep. Tamika closed her eyes, too, promising herself she would talk to her little sister before the night was out.

Five, almost six hours later, the women were finished and on their way to the hotel. Everyone was feeling relaxed and at ease. When the elevator doors opened, the women's eyes almost popped out of their

sockets! They had never seen a place even close to what they were looking at. It was that type of shit where it's so sharp and clean, you're
scared to touch anything. You might have to pee like a motherfucker,
but the bathroom is so spotless and elegant you don't even want to sit on
the fucking toilet.

Blossom's mother walked in and looked around with a huge grin.
"Okay, this is some real 'movin'-on-up' Jefferson shit here! Shit, I'm not
gonna wanna leave out this muthar!"

"So you girls like, yeah?" Maria asked.

"What! Hell yeah!" they all replied together.

Maria walked them through the penthouse and showed them a
room that was especially designed for dressing. All of the women's
dresses for Blossom's wedding the next day were neatly hung up in the
room. Each dress was adorned with a platinum-and-diamond cross pin.
Pinned to each dress was a tag with each one of their names, letting
them know whose dress was whose.

"The pins on the dresses is my gift to Blossom's wedding party,"
Maria told them proudly.

Shareen, being the ghetto-head that she was, went straight to the
dress with her name and unpinned the cross.

"Oh, yeah, these is the good shit!" she stated.

"It's very pretty, thank you," Tamika said.

The rest of the women thanked Maria and proceeded to try on their
dresses. The fit was perfect for every one except Blossom's mother's.
Her dress was about two sizes too big.

"Oh, do not worry," Maria quickly told her. "I will call to the house
and have the tailor come over right away. She will fix in no time." She
hurried from the room.

"I'm sorry, Ma. I didn't know you lost so much weight," Blossom said.

"Yeah, girl, ya mama tryin' to get her groove back!"

Maria returned to the room two minutes later. "Okay, everyting is
straight. One of the drivers is bringing Ms. Lopez over now to fix you
dress. The car will be here to pick everyone up tonight at nine o'clock,
for the dinner. I will see you all at the dinner tonight."

• • •

Fernando arranged for Dude and Blossom to ride to the dinner in a car alone. He had the backyard of his favorite restaurant set up for the small group. He had a large white-and-black tent set up, with lights outlining it. There was a live band playing on a platform. An ice sculpture of two wedding bands, intertwined, stood in the middle of the room. The tables and chairs were covered in black and white silk. White and black silk bunting, outlined with lights, draped low from the ceiling of the tent. The tables were set with fine china trimmed in twenty-four-karat gold. Blossom's friends and family, along with the rest of the guests, were already at the dinner waiting when Dude and Blossom arrived.

Fernando stood and signaled for the band to stop playing the music. "Everyone, they are here," he announced.

Everyone rose to their feet and clapped as Dude and Blossom walked in. The band began to play again.

A man dressed in a tuxedo escorted them to their table.

Dude stayed standing while the rest of the group sat.

He looked down at Blossom, smiling, with stars in her eyes. It was confirmed: he was truly in love with her. Then he looked to the left of the room and saw Black. He hadn't known anything about Black coming down. Fernando had secretly set it up; he knew Black was about the closest he could get to T Mac being there. Dude smiled at his friend and lifted his glass. Black returned the smile and lifted his thumb up.

Dude cleared his throat and signaled for the band to stop playing. "Can I please have everyone's attention. First and foremost, I would like to thank everyone for being here. I love this woman so much and I'm happy to have all of you here to witness the beginning of our lives together. Blossom, a lot has happened in this past year we've been together. Some good, some bad, and some tragic. Nevertheless, with you there by my side, you have made it all copable. Baby, I love you and will never stop loving you. I am so proud and honored to have you as the mother of my child and my wife. And, Fernando, you've been like a pops to me. There's no amount of words to explain how I feel about you and your family except . . . I love you guys. Black, you already know what it is, son. We still standing and gon' be for a very long time. I love you, man. Now, let's get the party started! I'll save the rest of my speech for tomorrow, at the reception."

The band began to play again and the party started.

Tamika looked at her little sister and knew she was the happiest she'd been in her whole life. Tamika knew Blossom was madly in love with Dude, so what she had to tell her little sister probably wouldn't make a difference. She promised herself again that she would talk to Blossom before the wedding tomorrow.

Dude looked around the room, satisfied with not only his life but the people in it. His eyes stopped on Maria and Rico, who looked like they were having some sort of disagreement. His mind strayed back to his last episode with Maria, then he looked at Blossom laughing with her friends and family. He smiled to himself and got a warm feeling in his heart. He was truly in love with Blossom, but he felt guilty about the Maria situation. He figured since he had made up his mind not to betray Blossom like that again, everything was cool. What she didn't know wouldn't hurt her. He was well beyond content with his life at this point.

Blossom was standing in front of the mirror, staring at herself. Her thoughts were far away from her body, and she had drowned out the commotion in the background. Tamika and the girls were running around the room like chickens with their heads cut off! You would have thought it was them who were getting married. Tamika noticed her sister's distraction. She broke off from the rest of the women and walked over to Blossom.

"Blossom, you aight?"

Blossom snapped out of her daydream. "Huh? . . . Yeah, I'm straight. I just was thinking."

"This is what you want, right?"

"Yeah, why would you ask that?"

"No real reason. I just see you over here dazed out and I just wan' to make sure you okay with everything."

"Yeah, I'm okay with everything . . . It's just I can't believe I'm getting married and having a baby. Don't get me wrong—I'm the happiest I've ever been. It's just a lot going on at one time. I'm lucky to have a man that I truly love and who has my back to the fullest . . . And I'm blessed to have a big sister like you, who's always there for me no matter what."

Tamika hugged her sister tight. "You know I'm always here for you, and no matter what, I love you with all my heart . . . I wanted to talk to you about somethin', but I'm not sure if now is the right time."

Blossom looked at her big sister with her big brown eyes. "What's the matter, Mika?"

Tamika paused and took a deep breath. "Blossom . . . I—"

Her words were cut short when their mother walked over and hugged both of them.

"What's going on with my babies over here?"

Blossom returned the hug. "Nothing much. I think everything's finally hitting me."

Their mother grabbed her younger daughter's hand. "Baby, you'll be just fine. And trust me, ain't shit hit you until labor hit ya ass!"

The three women laughed. "Ma, you always talkin' 'bout labor and how it's worst than goin' on a vacation to hell. You gon' scare Blossom half to death, Ma."

"Well, shit, labor is something to be scared of. You ripped me from front to back. Twenty-two stitches I had to get wit' your ass! Hopefully Blossom'll have one of those quick, slip-right-out labors."

"Well, I'm going to walk until I can't walk no more and I'm planning on taking some of those yoga classes for pregnant women."

Tamika and her mother looked at each other and busted out laughing.

"What's so funny?" Blossom asked.

Her mother rubbed her back in a motherly way. "Nothing, baby, you'll be aight. Me and ya sister will be there for you every step of the way. Now come on, it's almost that time."

The three women hugged once more, this time tighter and longer. Then Tamika and their mother adjusted the train on Blossom's wedding gown. She looked like a princess out of a fairy tale.

Her gown was made of silk satin. Its top hung off her shoulders, hugging her petite arms. Tiny pearls and clear crystals covered the entire gown, even the long silk trail that dragged ten feet long. The bottom of her gown sat out like Cinderella's gown. The pearls and stones, stitched perfectly one at a time by hand, sat on the entire bottom of the gown. Blossom had made sure she found an extra-full slip to go under her gown. She wore a pearl-and-diamond tiara on her head, with a sheer veil covering her face.

Maria walked into the room with a huge smile. "Oh my God, you look beautiful, sweetie! Just like a princess. Are you ready?"

Blossom took a deep breath. "Yes, I'm ready; a little nervous."

Kim hugged her. "Oh, sweetie, don't be nervous. You look beautiful and you got a good man out there waitin' to spend his whole life wit' you."

The girls hugged Blossom and followed her out of the room.

Blossom's heart pounded as she got closer to the walkway that led to the aisle. Under a large arch covered in white blooming roses, Dude was waiting for her, dressed in all white. The band gave the cue, playing Anita Baker's "Angel" at Dude's request. The small crowd stood and turned around, waiting for the guest of honor to walk down the aisle. After Tamika and the girls walked down the aisle, Blossom and her mother followed.

Dude's breath was taken away by her beauty. It was like they were falling in love all over again.

Blossom was numb with happiness when she reached the arch. She was saying "I do" in no time. Before she knew it, they were husband and wife.

After having some pictures taken, Blossom and Dude joined their guests in a small ballroom of the hotel. Before they walked through the ballroom doors, Dude stopped and grabbed Blossom's hand.

"Baby, I love you."

They walked through the doors and were greeted with everyone clapping. After a brief toast by the bride and groom, it was party time! Blossom and the girls started a soul-train line while Dude sat at Fernando's table talking. Dude looked over Fernando's shoulder and saw Maria standing with Rico. It looked like the two were having another disagreement. Rico grabbed Maria by her arm, and she snatched it away and rushed out of the ballroom. Dude watched as Rico followed. Dude looked at Fernando, who was in the middle of a deep conversation. He excused himself from the table and walked out of the ballroom. He heard voices coming from the far right of the hallway. The voices got louder the closer he got.

Maria spoke firmly. "Look, Rico I just need some time and space!"

"What is this mean? Time and space! We are engaged to be marry and you are having my child. Where do time and space fit in? Maria, what is going on wit' you?"

"I'm going through someting that you would not understand. I need you to just leave me alone!"

Her eyes were red and swollen and tears rolled down her face. Rico's frustration overwhelmed him; he exploded.

"Leave you alone, you say! You know what, Maria? I tink dees is a good idea—leaving you alone is long overdue! I have allowed you to drag me along for years. I have stepped to the back while you spread you wings and 'get to know youself,' as you would say.

"I have loved you unconditionally and it has never been enough for you. You are a spoiled, coldhearted bitch! With no consideration for no one but you'self! You always were and always will be! Trust me, the only person you have fooled is you father! I don't even know why I even bothered wit' you after the last time you were 'going through something.' You fucking little slut, you went off and started fucking the help and I still took you back! Numerous times you have disrespected me, as a man, I still loved you the same! Now dis stunt here you pull to embarrass me once again! Right before we are to be married, you wait until you are pregnant to need space! I swear if it wasn't for you papa, I would slap you down where you stand."

Dude felt that was his cue to intervene. "Hey, everything okay?" he asked.

Rico had a look of hurt on his face. "Yeah, everyting is good, my man."

Maria stood with a blank look on her face. She was wondering how much of what Rico had said had been heard. She suddenly felt embarrassed, knowing Dude could have heard the hurtful things Rico had said.

"I'm going to get me a drink," Rico said, walking away.

Dude stood watching the tears run down Maria's face.

Rico walked slowly down the hall, leaving his heart behind. He saw Blossom coming out of the ballroom doors as he was going through them.

"Hey, Rico. You okay?" she asked.

"Hey, Blossom . . . Yeah, I'm okay. My allergy is acting up."

"Have you seen Dude?"

"Yeah, he just go that way." He pointed to where he had left Maria standing.

"Thanks."

She held her gown and walked slowly down the hall. She followed the sound of voices.

"Dude, I fucked up this time," Maria said tearfully.

"What happened, Maria?"

She was crying hysterically. "I tried to talk to you, but then all of that shit happened wit' you and those feds, and then it was like everyting else just started happening so fast . . . I thought I was doing the right ting. And Blossom is such a nice girl. I feel so bad!"

Dude moved closer to her. "What are you talking about, Maria?" He was confused; she was talking in riddles.

"I can't marry Rico. I love Rico, but I can't marry him . . ."

He didn't know what to say. "Why? Rico is a good guy and he seems like he would be a good father—"

"Yeah, but not for my child!" She began to cry even harder. "This is you baby I'm carrying, Dude! This is what I wanted to tell you back in

America, Dude. I don't know how I was going to pull it off. I just didn't want anyone to be hurt."

Dude stood in shock; he was speechless. Maria felt like her heart was dropping to the ground as her confession rolled off her tongue.

Dude swung around when he heard a thump. He saw Blossom fall to the floor, the air seemingly sucked right out of her. She looked up at Dude and Maria with hate in her eyes. Dude knew she had heard everything. He felt like the sky had fallen down on him. This was too much for him.

He looked down at Blossom, sitting almost lifeless on the floor, and tried to plead his case. "Baby . . . I didn't know . . . this is the first I heard of this shit. Baby, please . . . believe me . . ."

Suddenly Blossom was on her feet again and looking sharply at Dude and Maria. "You motherfucker! You lying son of a bitch!" Her body shook as she yelled at the top of her lungs. "How dare you betray me like this . . . I gave you a chance to come clean, to tell the truth about this bitch! And I would have forgiven you and moved on! How could I have been so stupid! You are that monster Kandi described you as! What type of sick shit you on, Dude! What, you get turned on by seeing your girl and your slut hanging with each other!"

Maria tried to interrupt. "Blossom—"

Blossom jumped on her. "Bitch, don't say shit to me!"

Dude grabbed Blossom off Maria and held her tight, but she broke loose and kicked off her stilettos.

"Oh, now you protecting this bitch! I'll kick both of y'all asses!" She grabbed one of her stilettos off the floor and banged Dude in his head. Blood started trickling down his temple. Within seconds, the hotel manager, accompanied by security, appeared. When they saw it was Maria, they reframed from using any type of force. Instead, the manager ordered one of the security officers to inform Fernando that there was a problem. Minutes later, Fernando and half of the guests were on the scene.

Blossom had somehow gotten her hands on Maria again. She held her in a tight headlock, punching her in the face.

"And you bitch, playing me close like we buddies and you fucking my man!"

"What is this! What is going on here!" Fernando shouted.

It took Dude and Maria's two brothers to get Blossom off of Maria. Fernando's eyes were wide with shock.

"Maria what is she saying, is this true?"

Maria just stood there, with a bruised face and blood running out of her nose.

Fernando spoke louder. "Answer your papa!"

Blossom shouted, "Yeah, tell ya papa how you've been fucking Dude all this time! Oh, yeah, please don't forget to tell your papa how his precious baby girl is knocked up, not by Rico but by—" She threw her shoe at Dude and started to cry. "Pregnant by my husband! By the man I thought was worthy enough to be the father of my child! The only man I ever fucked in my whole life!"

Dude grabbed Blossom and tried to embrace her, but she snatched herself away from him.

"Don't you touch me!" She turned to Fernando. "I want out of here, now! Please, I need one of those cars to take me from here before I lose my mind!"

Tamika, their mother, and the girls walked up.

"Yo, what the fuck is up out here?" Tamika asked.

Blossom explained. "Dude's been fucking this ho bitch Maria all this time she up in my face playing me close. Oh, and the bitch is pregnant by him, too! Look, I gotta get the fuck out of here! If nobody's going to get me a car, fuck it, I'll walk!"

She pushed by everyone and stomped up the hallway.

"Junior, go make sure she gets a driver and tell him to take her wherever she asks. Leave my personal cell number with her also," Fernando instructed his son.

Dude followed her, pleading, "Blossom, wait a minute, please!"

She stopped in her tracks and swung around. "For what, so you can tell me more lies! I asked you if you slept with that girl! You looked me in my eyes and swore you didn't fuck her! Now I see why Kandi wanted to kill you! I never want to see you again in my life! From this moment on, you can consider me dead and I'll do the same for you!"

She turned and walked away. Tamika and their mother ran behind her, but lost her when she jumped into the limo and rode off.

Blossom was sitting in the back of the limo with tears running down her face. She didn't know where to go, just that she wanted to be far away from Dude.

"Driver, please take me to the house."

She quickly came up with a plan. When they reached Fernando's estate, she told the driver to wait for her. She raced to the room and gathered her things. She went into the closet and moved the painting that was hiding the safe. She'd managed to keep the combination in her head. She opened the safe and took out the stacks of money. She stuffed the money inside her Gucci bag. She took out the piece of paper with Fernando's cell number on it, then picked up the phone and dialed.

He answered, talking loud over the commotion in the background. Blossom could hear sister and friends shouting in the background.

"Fernando, it's Blossom . . . Um, I need to leave now. Can you work something out?"

He paused, looking at Dude with disappointment. "Yes, I understand. Where are you now?"

"I'm at the house. I came to get my things."

"You driver still there, yes?"

"Yeah, he's out front."

"Okay, good. In fifteen minutes, go out to the car and he'll take you to my private jet. Let me make a phone call and get everyting set up. I probably can get you clearance to fly to New York. Do you need anyting? Do you have enough money on you?"

She looked over at the Gucci bag, knowing she had more than enough. That wasn't the problem; she had to get past the checkpoint with the money.

She replied, "Yes, I have more than enough money. That's what might be a problem. You know with customs and the checkpoints. I don't want to have problems because I have a large amount of money on me."

"Oh, no, you do not have to worry about any of that. All you have to do is get on the plane. So you go down in fifteen minutes, yes?"

"Okay, and thanks a lot Fernando."

"Don't worry, it's not'ing. And I'm sorry, Blossom. You're a good girl."

"Thank you."

She hung up, and fifteen minutes later she was back in the limo, on her way to the airport.

Blossom's whole world had crashed around her within minutes. One minute she was happily married and the next she was dying inside.

Fernando's pilot and jet were waiting when the limo arrived at the airport. The limo pulled up mere feet away from the jet. The driver loaded her bags onto the jet for her and she boarded. She looked around the luxury, twelve-passenger jet. There was a stewardess waiting to tend to whatever need she had. She was so stressed, all she wanted to do was drink. She still had her wedding gown on—she'd ripped the train off it back at the house. She hadn't realized she was still barefoot until she sat down on the plane. She began to map out a plan of what she'd do once she landed in New York. She drank a whole bottle of champagne and two shots of Rémy before falling into a deep sleep.

She woke up when the jet hit the ground. She jumped out of her seat as the pilot announced their landing.

Once the plane had came to a total stop, the stewardess helped Blossom with her carry-on bags and off of the plane. Blossom held on to her large Gucci bag, as she had done the whole flight.

"Listen, I will walk you through so you do not have a problem," the stewardess told her. "Just follow me. Fernando tell me who to make sure sees you. He also wanted me to let you know a car will be waiting for you to carry you to you final destination. Follow me." This was the most the woman had said to Blossom the entire flight, besides asking her if she needed anything.

Blossom walked through customs with no problem and there was a man standing outside of the terminal holding a sign with her name on it, just like the stewardess said.

She climbed into the back of the limo and gave the driver the address to her town house. Once they arrived, she ran inside while the driver waited for her to return. She went straight to her bedroom and took all of the money that Dude had in the town-house safe and stuffed it into the Gucci bag along with the money from the Dominican Republic. She dug out an old shoe box and took out all of her personal papers, her checkbook, and ATM card. She looked around the room, knowing it was going to be the last time she would be standing there. Then she turned around and walked out without looking back. She got back into the limo and instructed the driver to go to the next and last stop—Dude's place. When they pulled up, she had the driver sit her bags outside of her car.

"You can leave them right here. I'm going to load them into my trunk." She reached into her bag and pulled out a crisp hundred-dollar bill and handed it to the driver. "Here you go, this is for you. Thank you for being so patient."

The driver smiled and shook his head. "No, miz. I cannot take this. Mr. Fernando would never approve."

She insisted. "Oh, come on. Look, you know what I just learned? What somebody don't know won't hurt. It could only do damage if they were to find out. And trust me, I won't tell if you won't."

The driver was still hesitant, but Blossom wouldn't give up. "Come on, I'm sure you have a family, right?"

He nodded. "*Sí.*"

"Then here, please take it."

He finally gave in and placed the hundred-dollar bill in his jacket pocket. "Thank you so much. Are you sure you do not want me to stay and help you put you bags into the car?"

"No, I'm okay. I'm going in and out."

The man drove off and Blossom ran inside, going straight upstairs to the bedroom she'd frequently shared with her husband. She went directly to the safe in this house as well. The Gucci bag could not hold any more money, so she got her large alligator bag from the top of her closet. Dude had shared the combination with her, in case of an emergency. And as far as she was concerned, this was definitely an emergency. She opened the safe and cleaned it out! She didn't bother to take any of her clothes or shoes. She snatched her cell phone from the dresser and put it inside the bag with the money. She threw the gator bag on her shoulders and ran down the stairs. She set the bag on the floor in front of the door, along with the money-filled Gucci bag. She peeped outside to make sure her other bags were safe. Her heart broke down on her again and she began to cry out loud. Still in her wedding gown and barefoot, she flopped onto the couch. She had to figure out her next move. She jumped to her feet and ran back upstairs, to her closet. She ripped her wedding gown off and changed into a pair of jeans. She threw a sweatshirt and a pair of sneakers on. Her heart was racing as she thought about everything that had gone down on her wedding day. Rage took over and she honestly felt like she could kill Dude. She had a feeling running through her she had never felt before. She grabbed a pair of scissors out of the nightstand drawer and started cutting her wedding gown to pieces. She left the shredded wedding gown in the middle of the bedroom floor. Needing another drink, she went down to the liquor cabinet in the kitchen, took out a new bottle of Rémy, and threw the bottle in the gator bag and walked out of the house, again without looking back. Once she'd loaded her bags into the car, she sped off and went straight to the highway. Too tired and frustrated to drive all the way to her crib in Brooklyn, she went and checked into a hotel suite.

She ran herself a bath as soon as she got settled in. She soaked in the hot bath, suffering from a broken heart. The more she thought, the more she turned the bottle of Rémy up to her mouth. When the bottle was empty, she called down and ordered a bottle of champagne, as if the cognac wasn't enough. Then she stretched out across the plush king-size bed, butt-ass naked and drunk. The thought of Dude betraying her sent her heart racing again. For Maria to claim she was carrying Dude's child, he had to have slept with her unprotected. Blossom felt totally disrespected, giving her body to him pure and untouched and in return he slept with another woman without wearing a condom. He didn't even know how many men Maria had slept with or what kind of diseases she could have infected him with, diseases he'd then have passed on to Blossom. The more she thought about everything, the more violated she felt.

Finally, she closed her eyes. Warm tears squeezed out and ran down her face. She lay on the bed with her thoughts until she couldn't think anymore; all she could do was sleep.

Dude and Black ran to the long-term parking lot and jumped into Black's car. There wasn't any room left on the flight Tamika and the rest of the women were on, so they grabbed the last flight that had space. The others landed in New York several hours before the guys did.

Not only during the flight but after they landed in New York and were in Black's car, Dude continuously tried reaching Blossom on her cell, but it just rang out.

"That's how I know she's back, man. Her cell keeps ringing to her voice mail. She must have the phone and just not answering me. She left the phone in the crib when we left the country. She had to go to the crib and get it."

Black just listened quietly as Dude spoke. Truth be known, he was a little disappointed in his old friend. He'd thought that Dude had matured enough to realize that he had a winner, that he had hit the jackpot with Blossom.

Dude was feeling Black's vibe. "I fucked up big-time now, huh?" he said.

Black just shook his head. "Yeah, you did."

"I know. I got to fix this. Take me by her town house. Maybe she's there and I can reason with her."

Black hit the highway and followed Dude's request.

• • •

Blossom turned over, her head spinning. She lifted herself off the bed, staggering as soon as her feet hit the floor. She looked at the clock on the wall and whispered to herself, "What! Shit, I know I didn't sleep *that* long."

She walked over to the window and pulled the curtains back. It was pitch-black outside. She had slept all the way through the wee hours of the night, or rather the wee hours of the morning and afternoon. She couldn't understand how she could have gone to sleep at 1 A.M. and the clock was saying it was a little after midnight! She stumbled to the bathroom and took a long overdue piss. She tried to make herself feel better by throwing cold water on her face. She looked at herself in the mirror and then pinched herself. She took a deep breath and walked back into the bedroom. It wasn't a dream; her life was really in an uproar! Still naked, she lay back down in the bed and grabbed the TV remote. She figured she'd rest for a few minutes and get her thoughts together. She jumped up when she heard the message tone on her cell. She grabbed the cell out of the gator bag. She had several missed calls from Dude's cell.

"Shit! He's back, probably looking all over for me." She spoke aloud to herself as she ran around the room getting dressed and gathering her things. She didn't want to see his face! She knew he would be going crazy looking for her. She wanted to go home to Brooklyn without bumping into him and she knew he would definitely go there at some point. Especially when he saw that she'd taken all of the money out of the cribs. She grabbed her bags and jetted out of the hotel and into her car. Her cell phone began to ring off the hook again. It was Dude and she didn't want to talk to him. As far as she was concerned, he didn't even exist. She finally got frustrated with the phone and snatched it from the passenger seat, ready to power it off. But she noticed this call was from a North Carolina number. She contemplated answering it, thinking it might be her mother.

Finally, she answered.

"Baby, you all right?" her mother asked.

Blossom could not help breaking down when she heard her mother's voice. Crying, she replied, "Ma, I'm so fucked up right now, Ma. I'm so hurt and angry . . ."

Her mother started to cry, too. "I know, baby. Where are you?"

"I'm in my car, driving. Where you at, Ma? You went back home?"

"Go home and not know what's goin' on wit' my child? You must be crazy! I'm here in the city. Your aunt wanted to sight fuckin' see! You know I hate fuckin' crowds and she wanna come stay in the city! Talkin' 'bout she ain't been in New York in over thirteen years! I asked her who fault that was! But anyway, baby, are you gon' be okay?"

Blossom answered honestly. "I don't know, Ma. I just—"

Her mother cut her off. "Listen to me; you have to be strong, sweetie. If you lose grip of yourself, it's gon' be much harder to snap back. And snappin' back from a broken heart ain't nothing to fuck with. I'm your mother and I'm only gon' tell you the truth. It's not gon' be easy to fix yourself after this. Trust me, I know about broken hearts and I know about being betrayed and disrespected by the one person you love endlessly. I'm going to tell you this, though: you follow your heart. However you feel most comfortable getting over this, that's how you do it. If you feel staying without a man in your life will aid you in fixing your heart, then, baby, that's what you do. Shit, if jumping right into another relationship'll help you get through this shit, do it! But only do it the way you really want to do it in your heart. You hear me?"

Blossom replied with snot and tears running down her face. "Yes, I hear you, Ma."

"Now, where you goin'?"

"I was going home, to Brooklyn."

"Good, you do that. I'm gon' be there first thing in the morning to see you. I figure you probably gon' want to be alone for a while. So just in case you decide to go off for a minute, I want to see you."

Blossom smiled and felt better than she had felt since everything had happened. "Yes. And I love you, Ma."

"I love you, too, baby."

Blossom hung up the phone and headed to Brooklyn, where she knew she would find some peace. Especially once she saw her big sister. Tamika always knew what to say or do to make Blossom feel better.

The lights were out in Blossom's town house when Dude and Black arrived. Dude had his own set of keys. He told Black to stay in the car while he checked to see if she was there. Black thought about how crazy Kandi had gone and insisted he'd go in with him. Dude assured him he'd be okay and went inside. He turned on the light as soon as he walked in.

"Blossom, baby, are you here?" he called out.

He walked upstairs to the bedroom when he didn't get a reply. He walked into the room and turned the lights on, but there was no sign of her. He walked over to her closet to see if she had taken her clothes. He looked around and noticed the safe was open. He looked inside; it was bare. He jumped up and ran back to the car.

"Yo, she's gone, man! I'm telling you, she broke the fuck out!"

"What happened?" Black asked.

"She left all her clothes and took all the money out of the safe! I knew I was going to get here too late. Ain't no telling where she at now! I knew I should of let two of the girls get on the last flight and we get on the early flight."

"Maybe she went to your crib."

"Yeah, maybe. Let's shoot by there."

Black raced down the highway toward Dude's crib. Dude tried calling Blossom's cell, but it rang out again.

He whispered to himself, "Damn, baby, where you at?"

Blossom grabbed the two bags with the money in them and walked to her building, leaving the rest of her bags in the trunk. She looked over her shoulder, making sure Dude wasn't lurking around somewhere. Then she rushed inside of the building, her keys in her hand. She walked slowly to her door, just in case Dude was waiting for her. She stuck her key in the door as quietly as she could. She walked in and double-locked the door behind her. There was loud music playing in Tamika's room, so Blossom slipped straight into her room and closed the door. She dropped the bags of money on her bed and kicked off her sneakers. She wanted to talk to her sister, but she didn't want to disturb her and Rob's groove. She picked up the cell phone and dialed the house phone. She could hear the phone ringing over the loud music.

In her bedroom down the hall, Tamika looked at the caller ID and saw Blossom's cell number. She jumped out of bed and turned the music down.

"Blossom, where you at, are you okay?" she asked with concern.

"Hey, sis. Did I wake you up?"

"Shit no, girl! Where you been?"

"I been fucked up, Mika. You got company?"

Tamika looked to the other side of the bed before answering. "No . . . No, you straight."

"Okay, I'm going to call you right back."

Blossom hung up before Tamika could reply. She took her clothes off and slipped on a pair of sweatpants and a wife beater. She stuffed the two bags in the back of the closet before going into her sister's room. Tamika had turned the music back up, so she couldn't hear Blossom knocking at the door.

Tamika was in another world, enjoying the head job she was getting. Blossom opened the door and walked in the room.

"Girl, why you got the music blasting—"

Blossom words were cut off by what she had walked in on. She saw the silhouettes of two bodies and got stuck.

Tamika opened her eyes and saw Blossom standing at the foot of her bed. She jumped, pushing the man from between her legs.

"Oh shit, Blossom!"

The man looked at Tamika with confusion and turned around. "What . . ."

He turned again and this time he saw Blossom standing in the room. He jumped and snatched the sheet over himself.

Blossom dropped the bowl of ice cream she had stopped in the kitchen to get before going to Tamika's room.

"Wow, Mika! Motherfucking wow! I mean, goddamn, give me a chance to pull the other knife out my back, before you stick yours in, bitch!"

Tamika jumped out of the bed and tried to plead. "Blossom . . . We . . . I mean, I didn't know you were coming. I . . . tried to tell you in DR, but every time I started to tell you, something—"

Blossom cut her off. With no more tears left to cry, she spoke with one hundred percent hurt in her voice. "*Tell* me? Fuck telling me, how the fuck it happened in the first place! I mean what made y'all want to even do some shit like this! Why would y'all even want to—"

She was interrupted by the man in the bed, speaking in a nervous tone. "Blossom . . . It just happened . . . I mean, it's not one of those situations where I've always had something for Tamika. I was going through something and I came here to talk to you . . . And you wasn't around . . . and Tamika listened . . . We just clicked."

She could practically feel the steam shooting out of her head. She picked up the bowl of ice cream and threw it at Lil' Richie, busting him in the head.

"And you motherfucker! You shut the fuck up, you fucking idiot-ass clown!"

She lost her mind! She ran in the kitchen and grabbed a butcher knife. She yelled from the kitchen, "I'm going to kill y'all motherfuckers up in here tonight! Hell no, I'm not getting played back-to-back! Some-body's gotta pay!"

Just then, the house phone rang. Tamika began nervously looking on the bed and floor for the cordless phone. She found it and answered it without looking at the caller ID.

"Hello!"

At the other end, Dude was standing in his closet, staring at his empty safe. "Tamika?"

Blossom came back into the bedroom with the butcher knife pointed at Tamika and Lil' Richie.

Dude could hear the commotion in the background. "Tamika, what's going on over there! Is that Blossom I hear in the back?"

"Yeah, she's in here going crazy!" She held the phone down and yelled at Blossom, "Put that knife away!"

Blossom charged at her and Lil' Richie screaming, "Oh, bitch, you ain't see crazy!"

Dude yelled on the other end, "Yo, what the fuck is going on over there! Tamika!"

Dude hung up the phone. He and Black jumped back into the car and headed to Brooklyn.

Meanwhile, Tamika and Lil' Richie were ducking as Blossom charged wildly at them. Lil' Richie didn't move quick enough and Blossom caught him in his right side.

"Blossom!" Tamika shouted.

Blossom looked at her with no concern or remorse. "Fuck you, bitch! I got some for you, too!"

Blossom charged at her sister and almost caught her neck. Tamika got hold of Blossom's wrist and tried to make her drop the knife, but Blossom's strength was too much for her. It was like she had turned into some sort of monster. Blossom snatched away from Tamika, still holding the knife. She went for Tamika's face, but Tamika quickly threw her hands up to block the blow, and Blossom caught her in the middle of her hand. Blood instantly began pouring out of her hand. It felt like the knife had broken a bone. Tamika dropped to the floor in pain. On the other side of the room, Lil' Richie was crouched over, holding his side. Blossom dropped the knife and ran out of the room. She stepped into a pair of sneakers, grabbed the two bags of money from the closet, and left the apartment.

She walked to the corner and jumped into a cab.

"Thirty-fourth Street, Penn Station," she told the cabbie.

He smiled. "Sure, no problem. That's going to be thirty dollars."

She reached into her bag and handed the man a fifty-dollar bill.

"Here. And you can keep the change. Just get me there as fast as you can."

The cabbie took the money and sped off. "Oh, no problem, pretty lady. I'll have you there in no time."

Within minutes, they were going over the Brooklyn Bridge, and soon the cab was pulling up in front of Penn Station. Blossom grabbed the two bags and disappeared down the steps.

She walked up to a ticket window. "Can I have a one-way ticket, please?"

The ticket agent stood on the other side of the glass, waiting for her to finish.

After a second or two, the agent asked, "You would like a one-way ticket to where?"

Blossom paused. "Give me a ticket for whatever train is leaving next. It doesn't matter where it's going. Destination is not the issue. I'm more concerned with time."

The agent smiled. "Well, what are you running from, young lady?" she asked.

Blossom thought about the bags of money she was traveling with and got paranoid. She didn't want to seem suspicious to the ticket agent.

She leaned closer to the window and whispered, "It's not *what,* it's *who.* An abusive boyfriend is who I'm running from. I can't take it no more and it's time for me to move on and start a new life."

The ticket agent gave her a warm smile. "I understand . . . Let's see. If you hurry, you can catch the train to Florida and there just happens to be one sleeper car left. Would you like it?"

"Yes, please. Florida is a long way."

Blossom paid for the ticket and went toward the escalator.

The agent called her back on the microphone. "Excuse me, Ms. . . ."

Blossom turned and rushed back to the window. "Yes."

The agent moved up close to the window and whispered, "There are a lot of nice little towns on your way to Florida. You don't have to get off in Florida." She then winked. "If you know what I mean."

And Blossom did know what the agent meant. She smiled and ran toward the track her train was leaving from.

She sat in her sleeper car and looked out the window as the train pulled out of Penn Station, going to wherever she decided to get off. She'd made up her mind to take her mother's advice and get through her heartache the way she felt best. And this was the way for her. To just turn around, move forward, and not look back. Until she was good and ready. She placed her hand on her belly and apologized to her unborn child. She said sorry for the reckless drinking she had done the night before and for putting it through so much stress in the last twenty-four hours. She prayed to God that He would forgive her for putting her seed in harm's way. She begged God not to let her drinking the night before physically harm her child.

She closed her eyes, as the train moved farther away from New York. And the farther the train got, the more she forgot her past and everyone in it.

To be continued . . .